D1377040

SIDEWINDERS

**Center Point
Large Print**

**This Large Print Book carries the
Seal of Approval of N.A.V.H.**

SIDEWINDERS

William W. Johnstone
with J. A. Johnstone

CENTER POINT PUBLISHING
THORNDIKE, MAINE

This Center Point Large Print edition
is published in the year 2008 by arrangement with
Kensington Publishing Corp.

The text of this Large Print edition is unabridged. In other
aspects, this book may vary from the original edition.
Printed in the United States of America.
Set in 16-point Times New Roman type.

ISBN: 978-1-60285-296-9

Library of Congress Cataloging-in-Publication Data

Johnstone, William W.
    Sidewinders / William W. Johnstone, with J.A. Johnstone.--Center Point large print ed.
    p. cm.
    ISBN: 978-1-60285-296-9 (lib. bdg. : alk. paper)
    1. Drifters--Fiction. 2. Cowboys--Fiction. 3. Large type books. I. Johnstone, J. A. II. Title.

PS3560.O415S57 2008
813'.54--dc22

2008027847

*Man that is born of woman
is of few days and full of trouble.*
—Job 14:1

We're peaceable men, I tell you.
—Scratch Morton

CHAPTER 1

"All I'm sayin' is that a man who ain't prepared to lose hadn't ought to sit down at the table in the first place," Scratch Morton argued as he and his trail partner Bo Creel rode along a draw in a rugged stretch of Arizona Territory.

"You didn't have to rub his nose in it like that," Bo pointed out. "That cowboy probably wouldn't have gotten mad enough to reach for his gun if you'd just stayed out of it."

"Stay out of it, hell! He practically accused you of cheatin'. I couldn't let him get away with that, old-timer."

There was a certain irony in Scratch referring to Bo as "old-timer." The two men were of an age. Their birthdays were less than a month apart. It was true, though, that Bo *was* a few weeks older. And neither Bo nor Scratch was within shouting distance of youth anymore. Their deeply tanned, weathered faces, Scratch's thatch of silver hair, and the strands of gray in Bo's thick, dark brown hair testified to that.

The Arizona sun had prompted both men to remove their jackets as they rode. Scratch normally sported a fringed buckskin jacket that went well with his tan whipcord trousers and creamy Stetson. He liked dressing well.

Bo, on the other hand, usually wore a long black coat that, along with his black trousers and dusty, flat-crowned black hat, made him look like a circuit-riding preacher. He didn't have a preacher's hands, though. His long, nimble fingers were made for playing cards—or handling a gun.

He had been engaged in the former at a saloon up in Prescott when the trouble broke out. One of the other players, a gangling cowboy with fiery red hair, had gotten upset at losing his stake to Bo. Scratch, who hadn't been in the game but had been nursing a beer at the bar instead, hadn't helped matters by wandering over to the felt-covered table and hoorawing the angry waddy. Accusations flew, and the cowboy had wound up making a grab for the gun on his hip.

"Anyway, it ain't like you had to kill him or anything like that," Scratch went on now. "He probably had a headache when he woke up from you bendin' your gun over his skull like that, but he could'a woke up dead just as easy."

"And what if that saloon had been full of other fellas who rode for the same brand?" Bo asked. "Then we'd have had a riot on our hands. We might have had to shoot our way out."

Scratch grinned. "Wouldn't be the first time, now would it?"

That was true enough. Bo sighed. Trouble had a long-standing habit of following them around, despite their best intentions.

Friends ever since they had met as boys in Texas, during the Runaway Scrape when it looked like ol' General Santa Anna would wipe the place clean of the

Texicans who were rebelling against his dictatorship, Bo and Scratch had been together through times of triumph and tragedy. They had been on the drift for nigh on to forty years, riding from one end of the frontier to the other and back again, always searching for an elusive something.

For Scratch it was sheer restlessness, a natural urge to see what was on the other side of the next hill, to cross the next river, to kiss the next good-lookin' woman and have the next adventure. With Bo it was a more melancholy quest, an attempt to escape the memories of the wife and children taken from him by a killer fever, many years earlier. All the fiddle-footed years had dulled that pain, but Bo had come to realize that nothing could ever take it away completely.

After the ruckus with the redheaded cowboy, they had drifted northward from Prescott toward the Verde River, the low but rugged range of the Santa Marias to their left. Some taller, snowcapped mountains were visible in the far, far distance to the northeast. Flagstaff lay in that direction. Maybe they would circle around and go there next.

It didn't really matter. They had no plans except to keep riding and see where the trails took them.

Changing the subject from the earlier fracas, Scratch went on. "I think we ought to find us some shade and wait out the rest of the afternoon. It's gettin' on toward hot-as-hell o'clock."

Bo laughed and said, "You're right. Where do you suggest we find that shade?"

He waved a hand at the barren hills surrounding the sandy-bottomed draw where they rode. The only colors in sight were brown and tan and red. Not a bit of green. Not even a cactus.

Scratch rasped a thumbnail along his jawline and shrugged. "Yeah, that might be a little hard to do. Could be a cave or somethin' up in those hills, though. Even a little overhang would give us some shade."

Bo nodded and turned his horse to the left. "I guess it would be worth taking a look."

They had just reached the slope of a nearby hill when both men heard a familiar sound. A series of shots ripped through the hot, still air. The popping of revolvers was interspersed with the dull boom of a shotgun. Bo and Scratch reined in sharply and looked at each other.

"Sounds like trouble," Scratch said. "We gonna turn around and go the other way?"

"What do you think?" Bo asked, and for a second his sober demeanor was offset by the reckless gleam that appeared in his eyes.

The two drifters from Texas yelled to their horses, dug their boot heels into the animals' sides, and galloped up the hill. The shots were coming from somewhere on the other side.

Bo was riding a mouse-colored dun with a darker stripe down its back, an ugly horse with more speed and sand than was evident from its appearance. Scratch was mounted on a big, handsome bay that was somewhat dandified like its rider. Both horses were strong and took the slope without much trouble. Within moments, as the shots continued to ring out, Bo and Scratch crested the top of the hill and saw what was on the other side.

The rocky slope led down to a broad flat crossed in the distance to the west by a meandering line of washed-out green that marked the course of a stream. A dusty road ran from the east toward that creek, and along that road, bouncing and careening from its excessive speed, rolled a stagecoach.

The driver had whipped his six-horse hitch to a hard gallop, and for good reason. Thundering along about fifty yards behind the stagecoach were eight or ten men on horseback, throwing lead at the coach. Even in the bright sunlight, Bo and Scratch could see spurts of flame from the gun muzzles. A cloud of powder smoke trailed after the pursuing riders.

As if the circumstances of the chase weren't enough to convince Bo and Scratch that the men on horseback were up to no good, the fact that they had bandannas tied across the lower halves of their faces to serve as crude masks confirmed that they were outlaws bent on holding up the stage. The two drifters brought their mounts to a halt at the top of the hill as their eyes instantly took in the scene.

Scratch reached for his Winchester, which stuck up from a sheath strapped to his saddle. "We takin' cards in this game?" he called to Bo.

"I reckon," Bo replied as he pulled his own rifle from its saddle boot. He levered a round into the Winchester's firing chamber and smoothly brought the weapon to his shoulder. As he nestled his cheek against the smooth wood of the stock, he added, "Since we don't know the details, might be better if we tried not to kill anybody."

"I figured you'd say that," Scratch grumbled as he lined up his own shot.

The two of them opened fire, cranking off several shots as fast as they could work the levers on the rifles. The bullets slammed into the road in front of the masked riders, kicking up gouts of dust. The men were moving so fast it was hard to keep the shots in front of them, and in fact one of the bullets fired by the Texans burned the shoulder of a man's mount and made the horse jump.

That got the attention of the outlaws. They reined in briefly as Bo and Scratch stopped shooting. It was their hope that the masked men would turn around and go the other way, but that wasn't what happened.

Instead, the gang of desperadoes split up. Three of them dismounted, dragging rifles from their horses as they did so, and bellied down behind some rocks. The other seven took off again after the stagecoach.

"Well, hell!" Scratch said. "That didn't work. We should'a killed a couple of 'em."

"Come on," Bo cried as he wheeled his horse. "They're going to try to pin us down here!"

Sure enough, the three men who had been left behind by the rest of the gang opened fire then. Bullets whined around the heads of the Texans like angry bees, one of them coming close enough so that Bo heard the wind-rip of its passage beside his ear.

They heeled their horses into a run again, following the crest of the hill as it curved to the west. The outlaws continued firing at them, but none of the bullets came close now.

The hill petered out after about three hundred yards. Bo and Scratch started downslope again, angling toward the wide flats and the road that ran through them. They glanced over their shoulders and saw that the three men who had tried to neutralize the threat from them had mounted up again and were now fogging it after the rest of the gang, which had carried on with its pursuit of the stagecoach.

In fact, the outlaws had cut the gap to about twenty yards, and from the way one of the men on the driver's box was swaying back and forth and clutching his shoulder, he looked like he was wounded. The other man, who was handling the reins, looked back and appeared to be slowing the team.

"He's gonna stop and give up!" Scratch shouted over the pounding of hooves. "Those owlhoots got their blood up! They're liable to kill everybody on that coach!"

"They might at that!" Bo called in agreement. He had rammed his Winchester back in the saddle boot. Now he unleathered the walnut-butted Colt on his hip and said, "We won't hold back this time!"

Scratch whooped. "Now you're talkin'!" He drew

one of the long-barreled, ivory-handled, .36-caliber Remington revolvers that he carried.

Both men opened fire as they veered toward the road. The hurricane deck of a galloping horse wasn't the best platform for accurate marksmanship, but Bo and Scratch had had plenty of experience in running gun battles like this. Their flank attack was effective. A couple of the outlaws were jolted by the impact of the drifters' slugs and had to grab for the horn to keep from tumbling out of the saddle.

Despite having a heavy advantage in numbers, the masked outlaws began to peel sharply away from the road. They threw a few shots at Bo and Scratch, but didn't put much effort into it. The Texans slowed their horses as the would-be robbers abandoned the chase, picked up the three stragglers, and galloped off to the east.

"We goin' after 'em?" Scratch asked.

Bo's forehead was creased in a frown. "Have you gone loco? With five-to-one odds against us, I plan on thanking my lucky stars that they decided it wasn't worth it to rob that stagecoach after all!"

"We winged at least a couple of 'em. I saw the varmints jump."

Bo nodded. "Yeah, I did, too." He inclined his head toward the coach, which had rocked to a halt by now, with thinning swirls of road dust rising around it. "Let's go see how bad that fella on the stage is hurt."

The wounded man was still conscious. They could tell that from the furious cussing they heard as they approached. The driver had climbed down and was helping the other man to the ground. As the hoofbeats of the Texans' horses rattled up, the driver turned and pulled a gun.

"Hold on there, son!" Bo called as he reined in. "We're friends."

Scratch brought his bay to a halt alongside Bo's dun. "Yeah," he said. "In case you didn't notice, we're the hombres who got those owlhoots off your tail." He jerked a thumb over his shoulder in the direction that the gang had fled.

The driver nodded and holstered his gun. "Yeah, I know that," he said. "Sorry. I'm just a little proddy right now."

"You've got reason to be," Bo said as he swung down from his saddle. "How bad is your friend hurt?"

The driver was a young man, probably in his mid-twenties. He wore a brown hat and a long tan duster over denim trousers and a blue bib-front shirt. A red bandanna was tied around his neck. His wounded companion was considerably older and sported a brush of bristly gray whiskers. He had lost his hat somewhere during the chase, revealing a mostly bald head.

He answered Bo's question by saying, "How bad does it look like I'm hurt, damn it? Them no-good buzzard-spawn busted my shoulder!"

The right shoulder of his flannel shirt was bloody, all right, and the stain had leaked down onto his cowhide vest. Crimson still oozed through the fingers of the left hand he used to clutch the injured shoulder.

"Take it easy, Ponderosa," the younger man told him. "Sit down here beside the wheel, and we'll take a look at it. It might not be as bad as you think it is."

"Oh, it's bad, all right," the old-timer said. "I been shot before. Reckon I'll bleed to death in another few minutes."

"I don't think it's quite that serious," Bo said with a faint smile as he tied his dun's reins to the back of the coach. Scratch had dismounted, too, and tied his horse likewise. Bo went on. "My partner and I have had some experience with gunshot wounds. We'd be glad to help."

"Much obliged," the young man said. "If you'll give me a hand with him . . ."

Bo helped the driver lower the old man called Ponderosa to the ground. Ponderosa leaned back against the front wheel while Bo pulled his vest and shirt to the side to expose the wound. Under Ponderosa's tan, the bearded, leathery face was pale from shock and loss of blood.

While Bo was tending to the injured man, Scratch glanced inside the coach and said to the driver, "No passengers, eh?"

"Not on this run," the young man said with a shake of his head. "And not much in the mail pouch either. If those outlaws *had* caught up to us, they would have been mighty disappointed." He held out his hand. "My name's Gil Sutherland, by the way."

16

"Scratch Morton." As Scratch shook Gil Sutherland's hand, he nodded toward Bo and added, "My pard there is Bo Creel."

"And I'm Ponderosa Pine," the old-timer introduced himself through gritted teeth as Bo probed the wound. "Given name's Clarence, but nobody calls me that 'less'n they want'a tangle with a wildcat."

"We wouldn't want that," Bo said with a dry chuckle.

"Good news, Ponderosa. That bullet didn't break your shoulder. I think it missed the bone and just knocked out a chunk of meat on its way through."

"You sure? It hurts like blazes, and I can't lift my arm."

"That's just from the shock of being wounded. We'll plug the holes to stop the bleeding, and I think you'll be all right." Bo looked up at Gil Sutherland. "How far is the nearest town?"

"Red Butte's about five miles west of here," Gil replied. "That's where we were headed when they jumped us. This is the regular run between Red Butte and Chino Valley."

"Let's get Ponderosa here on into town then. He needs to have a real doctor look at that wound, just to be on the safe side."

"That's assumin' there's a sawbones in this Red Butte place," Scratch added.

Gil nodded. "Yes, there's a doctor. Don't worry, Ponderosa. We'll take care of you."

"Ain't worried," Ponderosa muttered. "Just mad.

Mad as hell. I'd like to see Judson and all o' his bunch strung up."

"Who's Judson?" Bo asked as he used a folding knife he took from his pocket to cut several strips of cloth from the bottom of Ponderosa's shirt. He wadded up some of the flannel into thick pads and used the other strips to bind them tightly into place over the entrance and exit wounds.

"Rance Judson is the leader of the gang that was chasing us," Gil explained.

"Him and those varmints who ride with him been raisin' hell in these parts for six months now," Ponderosa added.

Scratch asked, "If folks know who he is and that he's responsible for such deviltry, why don't the law come in and arrest him?"

Gil Sutherland shook his head. "We're a long way from any real law out here, Mr. Morton. There's a marshal in Red Butte who does a pretty good job of keeping the peace there, but he's not going to go chasing off into the badlands after Judson's gang. That would be suicide, and he knows it. We all do."

Bo finished tying the makeshift bandages into place. He straightened from his crouch, grunting a little as he did so. "Old bones are stiffer than they used to be."

"Tell me about it," Ponderosa grumbled. "And I'm quite a bit older'n you, mister."

"Let's get you in the coach," Gil suggested. "It won't be all that comfortable, but it should be better than riding up on the box."

"Wait just a doggone minute! I signed on to be the shotgun guard, not a danged passenger!"

"I'll ride shotgun the rest of the way," Bo said. "Where's your Greener?"

"On the floorboard where I dropped it when them polecats ventilated me, I reckon."

Gil said, "I don't think Judson and his men will make another try for us. You don't have to come with us into town."

"We don't mind," Bo said.

"Truth to tell, all this dust has got me thirsty," Scratch added with a grin. "You got at least one saloon there, don't you?"

"Several," Gil admitted.

"Then what are we waitin' for? Let's go to Red Butte!"

CHAPTER 2

Once they had loaded the still-complaining Ponderosa Pine into the stagecoach, Bo climbed onto the driver's box next to Gil Sutherland, leaving his horse tied at the back of the coach. Scratch mounted up and rode alongside as Gil got the vehicle moving.

"Used to be a Butterfield coach, didn't it?" Bo asked as he swayed slightly on the seat from the rocking motion. He had Ponderosa's double-barreled scattergun across his knees.

"How did you know?" Gil said.

"You can still see some of the red and yellow paint on it in places."

Gil grunted. "We didn't strip the paint off on purpose. The sun and the dust and the wind in this godforsaken country took care of that for us."

"We?" Bo repeated.

"My father was the one who started the stage line. It runs from Cottonwood to Chino Valley and on over to Red Butte, where the headquarters are. There's another line that runs from Flagstaff down to Cottonwood and then on south, but there was no transportation from Cottonwood west to the Santa Marias until my father came along. Chino Valley and Red Butte were growing fast because of all the ranching and mining in the area, so he thought it would be a good gamble that they'd need a stage line. He figured some other settlements might spring up along the way, too."

"Sounds like a worthwhile gamble," Bo said with a nod. "How's it working out?"

Gil scowled and shook his head. "Not so good."

"Because of those outlaws? Folks are too scared of being held up to ride the stage?"

"Well, it didn't help when Judson and his bunch started raising hell, but that's not all of it. Those other settlements never sprang up. There's just Chino Valley and Red Butte. And the mines played out, for the most part. There's only one still operating at a good level."

"So there's not as much business as your pa thought there would be."

"That's right. It's been a struggle to make ends meet." Gil's voice caught a little. "It didn't help matters when my father got sick and died."

Bo looked over at the young man with a frown. "You're running the stage line now?"

Gil shook his head again. "My mother's in charge. I do what I can to help, just like when my father was still alive. I've got a younger brother, too, but he—" Gil stopped and drew in a breath. "Let's just say that he's not much for hard work and leave it at that."

Bo didn't say anything in response to that. Clearly, there were some hard feelings between Gil Sutherland and his little brother, and they might well be justified. But Bo knew it usually didn't pay for a fella to stick his nose into family squabbles.

Gil drove on in silence for a few minutes, then said, "Thanks for pitching in back there. Judson's bunch would have caught us in another minute or two, and there's no telling what they might have done, especially when they found out they weren't going to get much in the way of loot."

"It looked like you were about to stop and let them catch up," Bo said.

"That's right, I was. I knew we couldn't outrun them, and the way Ponderosa was only half conscious and bouncing around on the seat, I was afraid he might get pitched off and break his neck. I was hoping they'd just take the mail pouch and let us go."

"Is Judson in the habit of doing things like that?"

Gil shrugged. "They've killed a few men during their holdups, but only when somebody tried to fight back. Like when they hit the bank over in Chino Valley last month."

"They're not just stagecoach robbers then."

"No, they've rustled cattle and run them south across the border into Mexico, they robbed the bank like I said, and they raided the Pitchfork Mine and stole an ore shipment that was about to go out. They've stopped the stage half a dozen times, I guess, even though they've never made a very big haul at it. Killed a driver and a guard, though, so nobody wants to work for us anymore. Ponderosa and I have been taking all the runs ourselves lately. Now he's going to be laid up for a while, more than likely." Gil sighed. "I don't know what we'll do. Shut down, I guess."

Bo didn't say anything to that either. He had some thoughts on the matter, but he kept them to himself for the time being.

The creek that Bo and Scratch had seen from the top of the hill turned out to be a narrow, shallow stream, not much more than a twisting thread of water in a gravelly bed. As Gil drove across it at a ford, he said, "This is Hell Creek. Not much to look at, but it's the only water this side of the Santa Marias and it never dries up, no matter how hot the weather gets."

"Spring-fed, I reckon," Bo said.

Gil nodded. "That's right. North of here, in the ranching country, it's bigger."

Bo sniffed the air. "Sulfur springs, too, unless I miss my guess."

"That's how it got its name," Gil said. "From the smell of brimstone. Not very pleasant, but the water

22

doesn't taste too bad. You get used to it after a while, I suppose."

The terrain began to rise a little once they were on the other side of Hell Creek. The slope was very gradual at first, but became more pronounced. More tufts of grass appeared, and even some small bushes. Bo saw trees up ahead, where the foothills of the Santa Maria Mountains began.

A little over an hour after they left the site of the attempted holdup, the stagecoach arrived at Red Butte. Bo and Scratch saw why the settlement had gotten its name. A copper-colored sandstone mesa jutted up from the ground about half a mile north of the town, which had a main street, half a dozen cross streets, and a couple of streets paralleling the main drag. The buildings were a mixture of adobe, lumber from the trees growing in the foothills, and brick that must have been freighted in from Flagstaff or some other big town.

"Not a bad-lookin' place," Scratch commented. "Wouldn't exactly say that it's boomin', but it don't look like it's about to dry up and blow away either."

"There are enough ranches along the Santa Marias, both north and south of town, to support quite a few businesses," Gil said. "Throw in the Pitchfork, too, and folks do all right. They just don't have much need of a stage line except to deliver the mail." His mouth twisted. "And we probably won't have that contract much longer."

"What do you mean by that, son?" Bo asked, but Gil

didn't answer. The young man was busy bringing the stagecoach to a halt at the edge of the settlement, in front of a neatly kept adobe building with a wooden barn and some corrals behind it. Someone had planted cactus roses on either side of the three steps that led up to the shaded porch attached to the front of the adobe building. The bright yellow roses were blooming, providing a welcome splash of color in an otherwise drab setting.

The front door of the building opened while the coach was still rocking back and forth on the broad leather thoroughbraces that supported it, after coming to a stop. A dark-haired woman wearing a long, blue dress with tiny yellow flowers on it came onto the porch. She pushed back her hair from her face, and relief showed in her eyes as she looked at Gil.

That relief was fleeting, lasting only a second before it was replaced by worry. She looked at Bo, a sober, almost grim stranger riding with Gil, and at Scratch, another stranger who had reined his horse to a halt alongside the team. Then she asked anxiously, "Where's Ponderosa?"

The old-timer swung the door of the coach open before Gil could answer, saying, "I'm right here, Miz Abigail—what's left of me anyway!"

The woman cried out in surprise and lifted a hand to her mouth. Then she hurried forward. "For God's sake, Ponderosa!" she exclaimed. "What happened to you?"

"Judson's men again, Mother," Gil said from the

box. "They hit us about a mile the other side of Hell Creek."

The woman, who was obviously Abigail Sutherland, turned her head to look up at her son as she was helping the wounded man from the coach. "Did they get the mail pouch?" she asked, and the slight quaver in her voice was evidence of just how important that question was to her.

Gil shook his head. "Not this time. These two strangers came along and lit into Judson's bunch. They wounded a couple of the outlaws and ran them off."

"Not in time to keep me from gettin' plugged, though," Ponderosa grumbled.

Scratch had dismounted. He came around the back of the coach, leading his bay with the reins in one hand. He used the other hand to sweep the cream-colored Stetson off his head and gave Abigail Sutherland a big, toothy smile.

"Scratch Morton, at your service, ma'am," he introduced himself.

Abigail turned to him. "Thank you for your help, Mr. Morton," she said. "And your friend is . . . ?"

Scratch waved the hand holding the Stetson in Bo's general direction. "That's Bo Creel. Don't let that look on his face fool you, ma'am. He ain't as sour in disposition as he appears. Not quite."

Bo grunted and said from the driver's box, "I'm pleased to make your acquaintance, Mrs. Sutherland. Just wish it was under better circumstances."

"So do I," said Ponderosa. "In case anybody's forgotten, I got a dang bullet hole in my carcass!"

"Yes, and I'll take you down to Dr. Chambers' house right now," Abigail told him. "Can you walk all right?"

Ponderosa sniffed. "I reckon. Got hit in the shoulder, not the leg. I was a mite dizzy earlier, but I'm feelin' better now."

Abigail got an arm around his waist to help support him, and they started along the street toward the rest of the settlement. She glanced up at her son as they passed the front of the coach and asked, "Can you take care of the team, Gil?"

"Sure. But where's Dave?"

"I don't know," Abigail said, and that worried look was back on her face, as well as the concern that could be heard in her voice.

"We'll give you a hand with those horses, son," Scratch said as he put his hat back on. "Won't we, Bo?"

"Yeah." Bo placed the shotgun on the floorboard where he had found it.

Gil got the team moving again and drove the stagecoach around the adobe office to the barn in the rear. He took the coach all the way into the barn before stopping. Scratch followed, leading his horse.

Bo and Gil climbed down from the box. Along with Scratch, they went to work unhitching the horses. Watching the sure, practiced actions of the older men,

Gil commented, "You fellas have worked around stagecoaches before, haven't you?"

"We ran a way station in Kansas for a while," Bo replied.

"And we hired on as jehus and shotgun guards in other places," Scratch added. "Fact is, you won't find many jobs on the frontier that we ain't done at one time or another. Ain't that right, Bo?"

"Except for donning aprons and clerking in a store," Bo said. "I don't think we've ever done that."

A shudder went through Scratch. "And we ain't gonna," he declared.

When the team had been unhitched and the horses turned out into the corral, Gil reached into the compartment under the driver's seat on the coach and pulled out a canvas pouch. "I'll take the mail down to the post office," he said. "If you're going to be staying around Red Butte for a while, feel free to unsaddle your horses, give them some grain, and put them in the corral with the others if you want to."

Scratch looked at Bo and asked, "What do you think? We gonna be stayin' in these parts for a while?"

"We don't have anywhere else we have to be," Bo replied. "And Red Butte looks like a pretty nice little town."

Scratch grinned. "That's what I was thinkin'." To Gil, he added, "Much obliged for the hospitality, son."

Gil lifted a hand in farewell and left the barn while Bo was untying his dun from the back of the stagecoach. Bo commented, "I notice you started calling that boy 'son' as soon as you got a look at his mother. Thinking about settling down with the Widow Sutherland, are you?"

"Me?" Scratch held his hand over his heart for a moment, then grinned. "You got to admit, Bo, she's a fine figure of a woman."

"It *was* a pretty picture," Bo mused, "her standing there on that porch with the wind in her hair and those cactus roses blooming at her feet. But we don't know a blasted thing about her, other than the fact that she's got a couple of sons and a stage line started by her late husband. We don't even know how long he's been gone. She may still be in mourning."

"Wasn't wearin' black," Scratch pointed out.

"No, she wasn't, that's true," Bo admitted as he undid one of his saddle cinches.

"And she's got a whole heap o' problems on her plate, from the sound of it. Might be we could give her a hand with 'em."

"Nobody's asked us for our help."

"Give it time. Anyway, ain't you curious about what's goin' on around here? You always did like to get to the bottom of any trouble we ran into."

"That's true," Bo said with a shrug. "I guess we could hang around for a while and see what happens. Like I said, it seems like a pretty nice little town."

Scratch grinned. "And a pretty nice little woman, too."

Bo just rolled his eyes and shook his head.

CHAPTER 3

There were a couple of rocking chairs on the porch of the adobe office. Bo and Scratch walked around the building after tending to their horses and sat down in those chairs to wait. They weren't sure what they were waiting for, but that was a pretty common situation. Years of drifting had taught them to be patient.

They didn't have to wait long for something to happen. Three men came down the street and stopped in front of the headquarters of the Sutherland Stage Line. One of them was young, twenty or twenty-one, more than likely, and his brown hair and the cast of his features resembled those of Gil Sutherland. Bo figured he and Scratch were looking at the heretofore-missing Dave Sutherland, Gil's younger brother.

The other two men were older but still in their twenties. One was tall and scrawny, with a shock of straw-colored hair under a battered, pushed-back hat. The other was short and broad, built like a bull, with an animal-like dullness in his eyes and on his face. He wore a derby over dark hair that grew down low on his forehead.

"You hombres looking for somebody?" asked the young man Bo and Scratch took to be Dave Sutherland. He swayed back and forth, and his speech was slurred enough to indicate that he'd been drinking.

The afternoon was well advanced, so it wasn't like he was drunk first thing in the morning or anything

29

like that. Still, he was a mite young to be putting away enough liquor to get him in such a condition. His companions might have been drinking, too, but they didn't appear to be as snockered as young Dave.

"We're waiting for Mrs. Sutherland to get back," Bo said.

"If you wanna buy tickets on the st-stage, you might as well wait until in the morning. There's one due in this afternoon any time now, and there won't be another one leaving until tomorrow."

Dave was making a visible effort to stand up straight, and he was being more careful and precise when he talked now, two more signs that he'd guzzled too much rotgut.

"Today's stage is already in," Scratch said. "We came in with it."

"Then why are you hanging around here? Go on about your business!"

Bo frowned. "What did you say, mister?"

"You heard me! You look like saddle tramps to me. Probably want a handout or something. Well, you won't get it here!"

"You're makin' a mistake, son," Scratch said.

"You're the one who made the mistake, old-timer. I'm Dave Sutherland. My ma owns this stage line, and I'm telling you to rattle your hocks!"

Dave had confirmed what Bo and Scratch already suspected, that he was Abigail's younger son, but his belligerence took them by surprise. Some people got proddy like that when they'd had too much to drink, though, and evidently Dave was one of them.

The tall, straw-haired man stepped forward. "You heard Dave. Vamoose, you two old pelicans!"

Scratch frowned, too, and looked over at Bo. "You hear what he called us?"

"Yeah," Bo said. "Looks like this town isn't as friendly as we thought it was."

"Hey! We're talkin' to you!" the straw-haired man said.

Scratch nodded. "Oh, we heard you. Either that or there's a donkey brayin' somewhere close by."

The man's hands closed into bony fists. "Why, you—"

"We'll just wait here for Mrs. Sutherland," Bo cut in. "We're not looking for trouble."

"You got it whether you're lookin' for it or not. Now drift, or—"

"Or what?" Scratch said.

"Or Culley and me will make you wish you had!"

Scratch nodded toward the short, broad man and said to Bo, "You figure the baby bull there's Culley?"

"I reckon," Bo said.

"He looks strong enough to bend a railroad tie."

The straw-haired man sneered. "He is, and you're about to find out for yourself, old man."

"But dumb as dirt," Scratch went on as if the other man hadn't spoken.

Bo heaved a sigh. If a fight hadn't been inevitable to start with, it sure as blazes was now. Culley's face darkened with slow anger, and he started toward the porch steps. He was so muscular that his walk had a peculiar rolling gait to it.

Bo made one final attempt to stave off a ruckus. He stood up, held out a hand, and said, "You boys don't want to do this." He looked at Dave. "I'm betting your mother won't like it if there's a brawl on her front porch."

"My mother doesn't tell me what to do," Dave shot back. "And you shouldn't have mouthed off to Angus and Culley."

"Hey!" Scratch said indignantly as he got to his feet. "I'm the one who mouthed off, and don't you forget it!"

Culley spoke for the first time, rumbling, "Gonna rip you apart, old man!" He charged up the steps, followed closely by the straw-haired man, whose name was Angus evidently.

Scratch lifted his right leg, planted his boot heel in Culley's chest, and shoved. Culley went backward into Angus, knocking him over like a ball in a game of ninepins. Both men sprawled in the dirt in front of the porch, looking surprised. Scratch hadn't seemed like he was moving very fast. His movements had appeared almost casual.

Dave gaped. "You gonna let that old varmint do that?" he demanded, the slur slipping back into his voice.

"Not hardly," Angus vowed as he scrambled to his feet. He had to help Culley up, because the muscle-bound man was flailing his arms and legs like a turtle that's been flipped over onto its back.

Once they were both up, Angus said to his companion, "All right, we're gonna go at this different. I'll take the preacher, you handle the Fancy Dan in the buckskin jacket."

Culley nodded. He didn't have much of a neck, just a thick column of muscle. "Yeah. Gonna bust him to pieces."

Scratch grinned and said, "Come on, baby bull. You try it."

Angus and Culley advanced up the steps side by side this time, moving slower and more carefully. The Texans split up, Bo going down the porch to the right, Scratch to the left.

"Try not to bust up those rockers," Bo called to his trail partner. "They're pretty comfortable. Be a shame if they got broken."

"Yeah," Scratch agreed. "Might upset Mrs. Sutherland, too."

Dave yelled, "You leave my mother out of this, saddle tramp!"

Angus charged, swinging a malletlike fist at Bo's head. At the same time, Culley barreled toward Scratch.

Bo blocked Angus's punch with the same sort of effortless ease that Scratch had demonstrated in kicking the two ruffians down the porch steps a few minutes earlier. In a continuation of the same movement, Bo's right fist shot forward in a short, sharp blow that landed flush on Angus's nose. Blood spurted under the impact. Angus staggered back with a howl of pain.

He retreated only a couple of steps, though, before he caught himself and attacked again, this time wind-milling punches at the black-clad stranger. Bo blocked the first few blows, but then one of Angus's knobby fists clipped him on the jaw. Angus might be scrawny, but his punches packed plenty of power. Bo was knocked against the railing that ran along the front of the porch. With a shout of triumph, Angus crowded in on him, trying to seize and hold the advantage.

Meanwhile, at the other end of the porch, Scratch had his hands full with Culley. The pocket-sized titan was slow, but even though Scratch was able to land several sizzling punches, Culley just shrugged them off. He appeared to be able to absorb as much punish-ment as Scratch wanted to deal out.

At the same time he swung his tree-trunk-like arms in lumbering roundhouse blows that Scratch was able to avoid without much trouble. If one of those big fists ever landed, though, it would be like being hit with a piledriver. Scratch would go down hard.

He didn't intend to let that happen. He darted in and out, peppering Culley's face with punches in hopes that sooner or later the fella's brain would realize how badly it was being pummeled.

To his horror, Scratch suddenly felt Culley's arms snap closed around his torso like bands of steel, and he knew that he had made the mistake of getting too close. Scratch's arms were still loose, but Culley just ignored the blows and squeezed. As those brawny arms tightened more and more, Scratch grunted and felt his ribs begin to creak.

While Scratch was trying to deal with that bone-crushing threat, Bo thrust a foot between Angus's ankles as the straw-haired man tried to crowd him into the railing. Angus lost his balance long enough for Bo to hook a left to his jaw and stagger him. Bo reached out, grabbed the front of Angus's shirt, and heaved him around in a turn that sent Angus hard into the railing.

The wooden rail was sturdy enough so that it didn't break under the impact of Angus's body. Instead, Angus's momentum caused him to flip over the railing. With a startled cry at this unexpected turn of events, he fell to the ground in front of the porch.

And landed right in those cactus roses.

Bo winced at the sudden screeches of agony that came from Angus as his flesh was pierced by hundreds of the razor-sharp cactus needles. Angus tried to jump up, slipped and fell again, and just made his situation that much worse as he landed in the cactus again. He finally rolled clear of the spiny plants but continued shrieking in pain.

Some of the roses had been crushed. Bo shook his head in regret at that. The blooms had been mighty pretty.

He turned to see how Scratch was doing and was alarmed to see that Culley had Scratch trapped in a bear hug. Bo could see Scratch's face over Culley's shoulder. It was almost purple from the lack of air, and Scratch's eyes were open wide in pain and desperation.

Bo palmed out his Colt as his long legs carried him quickly to the other end of the porch. He raised the gun, reversing it as he did so, and brought the butt crashing down on Culley's skull. Bo didn't hold back, figuring that Culley was one hardheaded son of a gun. The blow landed with a heavy *thunk!*

Culley just shook his head and kept squeezing.

Bo hit him again, and this time Culley's grip relaxed a little. It took a third wallop, though, before the baby bull finally let go. Scratch slipped out of the bone-crushing, suffocating embrace and slumped against the adobe wall of the building, his chest rising and falling violently as he tried to drag air back into lungs that were starved for it.

Culley swung around ponderously toward Bo. His little piglike eyes still glittered with fury, but they glazed over as he took a step forward. The damage he had taken finally soaked all the way into his brain, and he pitched forward to land at Bo's feet, out cold.

Bo stepped over to Scratch and put a steadying hand on his friend's arm. "You all right?" he asked.

Scratch managed a shaky nod. "I . . . I will be . . . once I . . . catch my breath."

"Hey!" That was Dave Sutherland again. "You can't do that!"

Bo turned toward the young man, and saw that Dave

seemed more sober now. Seeing his two friends being defeated like that must have gotten to him. Culley was unconscious, and Angus was curled up in a ball on the ground. He had stopped screaming, but was still whimpering pathetically.

Furious, Dave reached for the gun holstered on his hip. Before he could even touch it, Bo's Colt had flipped around again so that his hand was curled around the walnut grips and he had a finger on the trigger. The barrel was centered on the young man's chest.

"Don't do it, Dave," Bo said in a quiet, solemn tone. "I don't want to hurt you, but I won't stand here and let you shoot me or Scratch either."

Dave stared at him, taken by surprise yet again. Clearly, he hadn't expected Bo to react so swiftly. His hand hovered over the butt of his gun as he visibly struggled with the decision of what to do next.

He was saved from having to make it by the sharp, angry voice that cut through the air. "Mr. Creel! What are you doing threatening my son?"

CHAPTER 4

Bo glanced to the right and saw Abigail Sutherland striding quickly along the street toward the stage line office. The old-timer, Ponderosa Pine, trailed several yards behind her, his right arm now in a sling and bandages swathing his wounded shoulder.

Bo's eyes flicked back to Dave, and saw that the

youngster was trying to take advantage of the distraction. He had gripped the revolver on his hip and was hauling it out as fast as he could.

The Colt in Bo's hand roared. Dave let out a startled yelp, and clumsily dropped his gun as his hat went flying off his head. The weapon thudded to the ground at his feet.

Abigail stopped short and gave a frightened cry before rushing forward again to get between her son and Bo. "Dave! Are you hurt?"

Numbly, Dave shook his head. "No, I . . . I don't think so."

Abigail spun around to glare at Bo, who had lowered his Colt but hadn't holstered it yet. "What's wrong with you?" she demanded. "Why would you try to kill my son?"

"No offense, ma'am," Bo said, "but if I'd wanted to kill him, he'd be dead now. I was just trying to shock a little sense into him."

"By shooting at him?"

"Didn't shoot at *him*," Bo said. "I shot at his hat."

Abigail didn't look like she thought there was much of a distinction there, but of course there was. She was just too mad to see it. She waved a hand at the still-whimpering Angus and said, "What happened here? What's wrong with Angus?"

Ponderosa had caught up by now. With a sour grin, he said, "Looks to me like that bullyin', no-account varmint your boy calls a friend finally got his needin's handed to him. He's liable to be pickin' cactus needles outta his mangy hide for a week, he's got so many stuck in him."

Scratch had gotten his breath back. He said, "Beggin' your pardon, Miz Sutherland, but Bo and me sure didn't mean to cause any trouble. These two seemed bound and determined to start a ruckus, and we were just defendin' ourselves."

"Is that Culley Blake up there on the porch?" Abigail asked. "What happened to him? Is he still alive?"

"He's breathin'," Scratch said. "That was almost more'n I could say. He got me in a bear hug and likely would've busted all my ribs if Bo hadn't buffaloed him with a gun butt."

Abigail gave Bo a withering look. "So you assaulted poor, slow-witted Culley, too?"

"You're not listening," Bo snapped. "They attacked us."

Abigail turned to her son. "What happened, Dave? Maybe I can get a straight answer from you."

He had retrieved his hat by now but hadn't put it back on yet. Instead, he stood there looking at the neat hole in the crown that Bo's bullet had drilled on its way through. He swallowed and turned pale for a second, as if realizing just how close he had come to having his brains splattered all over the street.

"Dave, I asked a question."

He looked up. "Sorry, Ma. I came along and found these two old saddle tramps sitting on the porch. They said they weren't looking to buy tickets on the stage,

39

so I told them to move along. That's when they started mouthing off and causing trouble."

Bo started to say that that wasn't quite the way things had happened, but then he decided to remain silent instead. Abigail Sutherland was either going to believe her son or she wasn't, and there didn't seem to be anything Bo could say that would make a whole lot of difference one way or the other.

"So you sicced Angus and Culley on them."

"They're my friends," Dave said in a sullen voice. "Sure, they stuck up for me."

Ponderosa slapped his thigh with his good hand. "And got whipped good an' proper, from the looks of it!" He cackled with laughter, ignoring the glare that Dave sent in his direction.

Dave turned back to his mother and said, "I didn't figure you'd want worthless trash like these two hanging around the place. If I hadn't come along, they might have gone inside and tried to steal something."

"What do we have that's worth stealing, little brother?"

Gil Sutherland's question made Abigail, Dave, and Ponderosa turn around. Bo and Scratch had seen Gil coming along the street, returning from the post office, where he had delivered the mail pouch, but the others hadn't noticed his approach.

"What do you mean, Gil?" Dave demanded. "There's money in there—"

"Not much," Gil said. "We'd have to be turning a profit for there to be much cash on hand." He nodded toward Bo and Scratch. "Anyway, these two men aren't thieves. They helped fight off Rance Judson and his men when those outlaws tried to hold up the stage this afternoon."

Dave looked surprised. "Judson hit us again?"

"Tried to. He didn't get away with it this time, thanks to Mr. Creel and Mr. Morton."

"Yeah," Ponderosa put in. "Blasted owlhoots might've murdered us both if those two fellas hadn't come along when they did."

Dave looked down at the ground. "I reckon I was wrong," he said grudgingly.

"You mean you were drunk and looking for trouble," Gil snapped.

"That's enough," Abigail said. "Regardless of who started the trouble, Angus is in pain. Dave, get him up and help him down to the doctor's house."

"We're givin' Doc Chambers plenty o' business today," Ponderosa said.

Abigail ignored him. "Gil, see if you can wake up Culley."

"He's Dave's friend, not mine," Gil said. "Let him tend to him."

"Dave's going to be busy with Angus, and I don't want someone lying unconscious on our front porch. It doesn't look good."

Ponderosa put his good hand on Gil's arm. "Come on, fella. I'll help you. We'll get a bucket o' water from the well and dump it on him. That oughta wake up even a rock-headed rascal like Culley."

Abigail looked up at Bo and Scratch and went on. "I'd like to talk to the two of you inside, if that's all right."

Bo wanted to ask her if she planned to yell at them some more, but since she seemed to have calmed down a mite, he supposed they could give her the benefit of the doubt and listen to whatever she wanted to say.

Scratch felt the same way and said without hesitation, "Why, sure thing, ma'am. We'd be honored to visit with you for a while."

Abigail came up the steps and went between them to the door. She opened it and went inside. Bo and Scratch followed.

The thick adobe walls of the building meant that the air inside the office was considerably cooler. Scratch still had his hat in his hand. Bo took off his black Stetson as well and looked around the room.

It was comfortably furnished with a heavy sofa and a couple of armchairs that sported embroidered slipcovers. A colorful Indian rug was spread out on the floor. More subdued curtains hung over the windows. Those were the feminine touches. The more masculine items included a large rolltop desk, a gun rack with several rifles and shotguns resting in it against one wall, a squat, sturdy-looking safe, and a big fireplace with a cow's skull mounted on the wall above it.

A door led into the rear of the building. That was probably where the family's living quarters were located.

Abigail went to the desk and stood beside it rather than pulling out the swivel chair from the kneehole and sitting down. She gestured toward the sofa and told the two drifters, "Please, gentlemen, have a seat."

Scratch shook his head and said, "That sort of goes against the grain for us, ma'am, while you're still standin'."

"This is *my* office, sir. I'll stand if it pleases me."

"Yes, ma'am, but—"

Bo tugged on Scratch's sleeve and said, "Sit down and shut up. The lady has something she wants to say."

Abigail smiled thinly as Bo and Scratch sat down. "Thank you, Mr. Creel. And I suppose I should thank you as well for not blowing out what passes for my son Dave's brains."

"I never meant to hurt him, Mrs. Sutherland. But I wasn't going to stand there and let him start shooting at us for no good reason either."

Abigail shook her head. "No, of course not." She sighed as she leaned a hip against the desk. "I owe you an apology for the way I acted out there. It's just that I came up and saw you pointing a gun at my son, and Angus and Culley were hurt and there had obviously been a fight of some sort . . ."

Her voice trailed away into an uncomfortable silence. Bo broke it after a moment by saying, "I imagine those two get into fights pretty often."

"They're no-account bullies, just like Ponderosa said. I wish Dave had never started spending time with them. But what can I do? He's a grown man."

Bo and Scratch exchanged a glance. As far as they were concerned, Dave Sutherland might be a grown man, as his mother said, but he sure as blazes wasn't acting like one. Hanging around saloons, getting drunk, partnering up with violent trash like Angus and Culley . . . They had seen youngsters act like that in the past, hombres from good families who strayed into bad company.

Of course, neither of them wanted to climb up on a high horse either. They had spent more than their share of time in saloons, dance halls, and gambling halls over the years. They didn't have much room to talk when it came to behavior that proper folks would consider disreputable.

"Anyway," Abigail went on, "the reason I wanted to talk to the two of you wasn't just to apologize for how I acted outside. I was thinking about something while I was down at the doctor's with Ponderosa. I discussed it with him, too, and he agrees that it's a good idea."

"If you came up with it, ma'am, I'm sure it's a good idea," Scratch said.

She smiled. "Maybe you'd better wait until you've heard what I have to say, Mr. Morton."

"Scratch, ma'am. I mean, you can call me Scratch. I wasn't sayin' that you had an itch . . . I mean . . ."

She held up a hand to stop him before he dug himself a deeper hole. "Please. What I want to ask you gentlemen is if you'd consider going to work for me."

"I sort of saw that coming," Bo said. "Gil told us about how Rance Judson and his gang have been running roughshod over this part of the territory for a while. He said that you're having trouble finding men who are willing to work for you anymore."

"I reckon most of 'em are worried that they might get shot right off the driver's seat the next time those owlhoots try to hold up one of your stages," Scratch put in.

Abigail nodded. "That's exactly the case. I can't say as I blame them either. Judson and his men are blood-thirsty bandits who don't hesitate to gun down anyone who gets in their way."

"Talk like that's not really likely to make us want to take the job, ma'am," Bo said with a smile.

"I'm not going to lie to anybody," Abigail said. "If you're going to help me, I want you to know exactly what you're getting into."

"The danger didn't seem to bother Ponderosa."

Abigail laughed softly. "Ponderosa came west with us, and even before that he and my husband worked together on the Butterfield line. We're all the family he has, even if we're not really related."

"With him laid up, you're going to be more short-handed than ever."

"That's right. I don't have a shotgun guard, so I suppose Gil's going to have to keep on driving every run by himself."

"You have *two* sons," Bo pointed out.

Abigail grimaced. "Dave helps out some here around the Red Butte station, but he won't take any of the runs."

"And he's too big to take a switch to his behind, ain't he?" Scratch said.

For a second, Abigail looked utterly weary and despairing. "That's right," she said. "I can't force him to help me."

Bo and Scratch glanced at each other again, both men thinking that a good, sound butt-kicking might make Dave Sutherland more inclined to be helpful. But it wasn't their place to interfere in family matters.

Lending a hand to Abigail Sutherland, though, that was a different story entirely. Scratch said, "It just so happens we've worked on stage lines before. We can both handle a team, and we're handy with scatterguns, too."

"If you could find one more good man who's willing to help out," Bo said, "you could switch out the runs and give Gil a break. But even if it's just me and Scratch signing on, we should be able to help out quite a bit."

Abigail smiled. "You'll do it then? I warn you, I can't pay much in the way of wages right now. Business has been slow because of those outlaws . . ."

"So what you're askin' us," Scratch said with a chuckle, "is to take on a mighty dangerous job for not much money?"

"In a nutshell, yes."

Scratch didn't hesitate in his reply. "We'll do it." Beside him, Bo nodded gravely.

"There is one more thing you need to know about," Abigail said. "A little matter of a war . . ."

CHAPTER 5

In the grim silence that followed Abigail's words, Bo said, "The last real war we were mixed up in was the one between the Blue and the Gray . . . and that one's been over for fifteen years."

"O' course," Scratch added, "we've gotten tangled up in a range war or two since then."

Abigail smiled, but there was no real humor in the expression. "What I'm talking about is more along the order of a range war. There's a man here in Red Butte who'd like to see the Sutherland Stagecoach Line out of business, and I think he'd go to just about any lengths to make sure that happens."

"I doubt if it's going to make any difference—" Bo began.

"Yeah, we've already said we're gonna work for you, and we don't go back on our word," said Scratch.

"But you'd better tell us what you're talking about," Bo concluded, even as he nodded in agreement with what Scratch said.

"All right. There's a man named Jared Rutledge who has a freight line that runs between Red Butte, Chino Valley, and Cottonwood. He established it not long before Will and the boys and I moved here to start the stage line. As it turns out, Mr. Rutledge planned to begin running stagecoaches in addition to his freight wagons, but our arrival ruined that for him."

Bo nodded and said, "I can see where there wouldn't

be enough business in these parts to support two stage lines."

"Sometimes, it seems like there's not enough to support *one*," Abigail went on with a faint smile. "But that didn't stop Mr. Rutledge from buying a coach and trying to compete with us anyway. In fact, he tried to buy us out after we got the mail contract from the government. That brings in more money for us than the passengers we carry."

"Rutledge probably wanted it, too," Scratch said.

"That's right. My husband Will was still alive then, and he turned down Mr. Rutledge's offer, of course. That just made Mr. Rutledge more angry with us. He swore that his stagecoach would be running long after we were out of business." She paused. "He made it sound like a threat."

Neither Bo nor Scratch said anything for a moment as they mulled over what Abigail had told them. Then Bo said, "Gil mentioned that his father took sick and passed on. Was there anything suspicious about what happened to your husband, ma'am?"

"You mean, did Jared Rutledge poison him somehow?" Abigail shook her head. "I trust Dr. Chambers, and he said Will died from the same fever that took the lives of several other people here in Red Butte about the same time. The doctor was worried that it might develop into a full-blown epidemic, but then the sickness seemed to pass. It does that way sometimes, Dr. Chambers said."

Bo nodded. "That it does."

"Anyway, I don't believe that Jared Rutledge would ever resort to something like poison. I wouldn't put it past him to shoot someone he considers an enemy, but he's too full of bluster to act in such an underhanded manner."

"So why do you say he's wagin' war against you?" Scratch asked.

"We've had some incidents of sabotage. There was a fire in the barn that could have gotten out of hand and burned it to the ground if Ponderosa hadn't happened to discover it in time. Both of our coaches were parked in the barn at the time. They would have been destroyed, too. I was suspicious about that right away and went to the marshal."

"Let me guess," Bo said. "Rutledge claimed he didn't have anything to do with the fire and had an alibi for the time it was set."

"Of course. Without any proof, there was nothing Marshal Harding could do."

"Anything else?" Scratch asked.

"Some other minor incidents, harnesses cut and things like that. Enough to cause delays and annoyances, but nothing that would put us out of business." Abigail's lips tightened. "Then Rance Judson and his crew of killers showed up. *That's* what's going to cause the stage line to fail, if things keep up like they're going now."

"Wait a minute," Bo said. "Are you saying that there's some connection between Rutledge and Judson?"

"I think it's possible."

Scratch rubbed at his jaw in thought. "Your boy told us Judson's bunch has been raisin' . . . heck around here for six months or so. It was longer ago than that that your husband passed away?"

"Will died a little more than a year ago."

Bo knew what Scratch was thinking—Abigail Sutherland was no longer officially in mourning. But there were more important things to discuss at the moment, so he said, "Have Judson and his gang held up Rutledge's stagecoach?"

"They've stopped it a couple of times." Abigail made a dismissive motion with her hand. "But that doesn't mean anything. That could be just a cover-up to make sure that suspicion doesn't fall on Mr. Rutledge. The outlaws didn't get much in any of those robberies."

"But the same thing would have been true today if they'd succeeded in stopping *your* coach," Bo pointed out.

"Yes, that's true. But they would have gotten the mail pouch, and that's important."

Bo nodded. "Because if you lose it often enough, the government will cancel its contract with you and award it to Rutledge's line."

"Exactly. Without that contract, this business can't survive. We'd have to give up . . . and Mr. Rutledge would win, just as he swore he would."

"Sounds to me like somebody ought to go pay this Rutledge fella a visit and read him the riot act," Scratch declared.

An expression of concern appeared on Abigail's face. "No, that's not what I want," she said quickly. "Mr. Rutledge has half a dozen men working for him, and they're all dangerous. I suspect some of them are gunfighters. It's bad enough that I'm asking the two of you to risk your lives by working for me. I don't want you confronting those killers in their lair."

"Sounds to me like what you really need around here is a better lawman," Bo commented.

"Tom Harding does the best job he can. He keeps the peace here in town, and that's the only jurisdiction he has. The county sheriff and his deputies never get over this way, or at least so seldom it might as well be never. The sheriff took a posse into the badlands once to look for Judson's hideout, but never found it."

Bo put his hands on his knees and said, "Well, ma'am, you've told us a lot, but none of it changes anything. You asked us for help, and we agreed to give it to you. We'll stick by our word."

"Darned right we will," Scratch said.

"Thank you both. I'll pay you what I can—"

Scratch waved a hand. "Don't worry about that. We'll work for room and board until you get the stage line back on its feet. Ain't that right, Bo?"

"That'll be fine," he said with a nod.

Abigail looked a little flustered. "You're sure—"

"Yes, ma'am," Scratch broke in. "Certain sure."

"Well . . . all right. Ponderosa bunks in the barn . . ."

"That's good enough for us," Scratch said. He pretended not to hear the faint sigh that came from Bo.

Boot heels sounded on the porch outside, and Gil Sutherland came into the office. "Ponderosa and I finally got Culley woke up and sent him packing," he reported.

"Is Dave back yet?"

Gil grimaced. "No, and I can still hear the yells coming from down at the doc's house. I figure Angus is still getting cactus needles plucked out. Dave will probably stay with him until Doc Chambers is finished, and then they'll go off to Sharkey's so Angus can numb the pain with a couple of bottles of whiskey."

The disapproval was evident in Gil's face and voice. Bo said, "Sharkey's is one of the local saloons, I reckon?"

"My little brother's home away from home."

"Gil!" his mother scolded. "There's no reason to talk like that."

"Why not?" he asked as he turned toward her. "It's true, isn't it? Dave spends more time down there guzzling who-hit-John than he does here working. If he'd pitch in more, maybe you and I wouldn't be running ourselves ragged."

"I've done something about that," Abigail said. She nodded toward Bo and Scratch. "I've hired Mr. Creel and Mr. Morton."

Gil's eyes widened in surprise. "Hired them? With what? We don't have any money!"

"We still have some," Abigail insisted. "Anyway, they've agreed to work for room and board right now, until things improve."

That explanation didn't make Gil any happier. He shook his head and said, "I don't think it's a good idea. Sure, they helped Ponderosa and me this afternoon, but we don't really know these men. Why, they could be outlaws just like Judson and his gang!"

"You said 'could be,'" Scratch drawled, "so I don't reckon we'll take offense, son . . . this time."

"For the record," Bo added, "we're not outlaws. You can go down to the marshal's office and check the reward dodgers he has on file if you want to. You won't find us."

"That doesn't mean anything, just because there are no wanted posters on you."

"Gil, I don't know why you're being so rude," Abigail said. "Even if they weren't going to be working with us, Mr. Creel and Mr. Morton are our guests. We owe them a little courtesy to go along with our thanks for helping you and Ponderosa."

"But Creel shot Dave's hat off his head!" Gil protested. "Lord knows, I've felt like doing that and worse to him myself, but—"

"You've said enough," Abigail cut in. "The arrangements have already been made. You should be grateful that you won't have to work quite as hard."

Gil didn't look grateful. He was still fuming, in fact, although he held his tongue.

Bo stood up, and Scratch did likewise. Abigail

turned to them and said, "Supper will be in about an hour, gentlemen. The dining room is right through that door."

"We'll be back," Bo promised. "That'll give us time to take a look around town and get familiar with the settlement."

"Have a drink, you mean," Gil said, ignoring the angry glance his mother sent his way. "If you run into my brother at Sharkey's, maybe you can bring him back with you."

Bo and Scratch didn't say anything to that. Hats in hands, they nodded to Abigail. Bo said, "Ma'am," and Scratch said, "We're obliged to you for your hospitality, Miz Sutherland. See you later."

They left the office, and as they paused on the porch to put their hats on, they heard Gil through the door as he complained to his mother about her hiring a couple of saddle tramps.

Scratch grinned and tapped the brim of his Stetson. "Boy's got us pegged pretty good, don't he?"

"He'd likely be even more upset if he knew that you're planning on romancing his mother," Bo said as they went down the steps to the ground.

"You heard what Miz Abigail said. It's been over a year since her husband passed on, rest his soul. She ain't in mournin' anymore."

"That doesn't mean she's looking for another husband," Bo said. He snorted. "As if you were in the market for a wife anyway!"

"It's true I never been the marryin' kind," Scratch

admitted as they started along the street. "I might change, though, for a fine-lookin' woman like that. And one with her own business, to boot! I tell you, Bo, it'd be just a pure-dee shame for a gal like Abigail Sutherland to waste away, pinin' for the touch of a man."

"I think she's probably got more important things to worry about, like that younger son of hers. He's liable to get himself killed one of these days, hanging around with varmints like Angus and Culley. Not to mention the trouble with Rutledge wanting to run her out of business, and those owlhoots lurking out there the other side of Hell Creek, waiting to hold up another stagecoach."

Scratch laughed. "Yeah, I reckon we've waltzed right into a heap o' trouble again. Outlaws on one side, Rutledge's hired guns on the other . . . You know what we need?"

"Some sense pounded into our heads?"

"No, what we need is for those two young fellas we ran into over in Colorado to come ridin' into town so they could give us a hand."

"You mean Bodine and Two Wolves?" Bo shook his head. "I don't think that's likely to happen. Those two are probably off somewhere getting into some devilment of their own."

"Yeah, they kinda reminded me o' somebody—you an' me about thirty years ago."

There was some truth to that, although Bo and Scratch had never developed the same sort of reputation as gunfighters and troubleshooters as Matt Bodine and Sam Two Wolves had. All four of them shared the same restless nature, though, and the tendency to have trouble follow them around.

"We'll have to handle this chore ourselves," Bo went on as they neared a good-sized building marked by its batwing doors and the tinny music coming from inside it as a saloon. In the fading light of dusk, a sign hanging from the awning over the boardwalk identified it as Sharkey's, the place Gil Sutherland had mentioned.

"What say we take a look?" Scratch suggested. "I could use a beer."

Dave and Angus and Culley might be in there; probably were, if what Gil had said was correct. That could lead to another confrontation and even more trouble.

But there was a fine line between being prudent and running away from a fight, and Bo didn't intend to cross that line. He nodded and said, "I'm a mite thirsty myself."

CHAPTER 6

The Texans pushed through the batwings and entered a saloon much like scores of others they had visited during their long years of wandering the frontier. A long bar of polished hardwood ran down the right-hand wall of the place. Behind it were shelves filled with liquor bottles, and above the bottles, displayed prominently, was a long, somewhat amateurishly executed painting of a nude woman whose endowments went beyond generous. She wore a coy smile on her face as she artfully concealed the most vital areas of her anatomy with her arms.

Scratch did some studying on the painting for a few moments. He'd always had a great appreciation for art, as he would be glad to tell you. Bo turned his attention to the rest of the room, which included a dozen or so tables where the customers could sit and drink, a couple of felt-covered tables for poker and other card games, a faro layout, and a roulette wheel. Stairs on the left led up to a balcony and several rooms where the girls who worked here delivering drinks could ply the other part of their trade, and below the balcony was a tiny raised stage with a piano on it and an open area where folks could dance if they were of a mind to. Potbellied stoves stood in three corners of the room, but at this time of year no fires burned in their bellies. In fact, the air in the big room was already hot and still and laden with tobacco smoke and a mixture of unwholesome smells.

"Ah," Scratch said, "always feels like comin' home again when you walk into a place like this."

"Your home maybe," Bo said. "Not mine."

Scratch grinned. "You ain't foolin' me, Bo Creel. You miss the night life just as much as I do when we been out on the trail for a while."

Bo didn't argue the point. He was busy looking for Dave Sutherland and the two bullies, Angus and Culley.

He spotted them sitting at one of the tables. Angus's face was dotted with red, puffy places where cactus needles had stuck him. Culley wore a dull frown, probably not that much different from his usual expression. Both of them glared at Bo and Scratch. Dave just glanced at the drifters, then tossed off the drink he had in front of him.

None of the three at the table seemed to be in any mood to resume hostilities. They just passed around a bottle and refilled their glasses.

Bo and Scratch angled toward the bar. They didn't much like turning their backs to the trio they'd clashed with earlier, but they were relying on their battle-honed instincts to warn them if any trouble cropped up. It would have been handy if there'd been a mirror above the backbar instead of that painting of a naked woman, but you couldn't have everything.

"Couple of beers," Scratch said to the aproned, slick-haired drink juggler behind the hardwood. He dropped a coin on the bar to pay for the drinks. He and Bo were running a mite low on funds, and since they wouldn't be drawing any wages from Abigail Sutherland, at least not right away, they would have to be careful with their drinking money and make it last as long as possible.

The bartender drew the beers, filling a couple of mugs and placing them in front of Bo and Scratch. The coin disappeared into a cash box. "You gents are new in town, ain't you?" the man asked.

Bo nodded. "That's right." He took a sip of the beer. It was barely cool, but at least it was wet.

Bo would have left his answer to the bartender's question at that, but Scratch was more talkative. "We're gonna be workin' for Miz Sutherland over at the stage line," he said.

The bartender's bushy eyebrows went up. "Is that so? I heard that the stage got held up between here and Chino Valley again. Say, are you boys the fellas who came along and ran off Rance Judson and his gang?"

"That's right," Scratch replied, and he didn't bother trying to keep the pride out of his voice. "Those owlhoots took off with their tails betwixt their legs when they saw us comin' with all guns blazin'."

"It wasn't quite that dramatic," Bo said, but Scratch was getting wound up and just talked right over his words.

"Yes, sir, the air was plumb filled with bullets for a while, but we didn't get even a nick! When them bandits saw what they was up against, they thought better o' tryin' to stop that stage."

"I hear that ol' Ponderosa Pine got himself shot during the robbery. Is that old pelican gonna live?"

"He's just got a flesh wound in his shoulder," Bo said. "He'll be all right."

"But he won't be able to work as no shotgun guard for a while," Scratch added. "That's why Miz Sutherland asked us to give her a hand. We said yes, o' course. We got us a downright hate for owlhoots, don't we, Bo? That's why we're gonna clean up that Judson hombre and his gang."

Bo just sipped his beer and didn't say anything. Scratch didn't need any help spouting off.

The boisterous discussion was drawing some attention from the other men in the room. Several of them turned to listen to Scratch talk. Bo glanced over his shoulder, saw that Dave, Angus, and Culley were still seated at the table. They were watching the scene at the bar, too, but not making any move to get up.

One of the drinkers took a step away from the bar and then sidled along it toward Bo and Scratch. He wore a dark red shirt, a black vest, and a black hat pushed back on his head. A grin was on what appeared to be a freshly shaven face. The faint smell of bay rum confirmed that he had come from the barbershop not long before.

"Say," he said, interrupting Scratch's boasts about what was going to happen to any outlaws foolish enough to try to hold up a Sutherland stagecoach, "you fellas are from Texas, ain't you?"

Scratch turned toward him. "That's right. You recognize the accent, friend? Or maybe you hail from the great Lone Star State, too?"

"Hell, no!" the man said. "If I was from that shithole, I wouldn't go around braggin' about it. I just know that Texas turns out more old windbags than anything else, even longhorned cattle."

Scratch blinked as if he couldn't believe what his

ears told him he'd just heard. "Sorry, mister," he growled. "I must'a misunderstood you—"

"No, I know Texans are dumb as rocks, but you understood me all right, you blowhard. You may dress fancy, but I know me a saddle tramp when I see one!"

From across the hardwood, the bartender said, "Take it easy, Langdon. Nobody wants any trouble in here."

The man's grin widened. "Won't be any trouble, not from these two. You see, as well as bein' dumb and smellin' like cowshit, Texans are gutless, too."

Bo had already taken note of the tied-down holster on the stranger's hip and the fancy nickel-plated revolver that rode in it. This man was a gunslinger, or at least believed himself to be one. And it was certainly possible that he was fast and slick on the draw. Plenty of men on the frontier were.

He wasn't alone either. A couple of other men had also stepped out from the bar and were watching what was going on with keen interest. They had the hard-eyed look and low-slung guns of killers, too, just like their friend.

The man called Langdon was grinning at Scratch. "Well, saddle tramp," he prodded. "You got anything to say for yourself?"

Scratch's eyes blazed with anger, but he was making a visible effort to control himself. "You got no call to talk about Texas or Texans that way, mister," he said, "but I reckon you've never been there, so I'll just chalk it up to ignorance."

"Oh, I been there, all right. And I was about sick at my stomach the whole time just from the stink o' the place. I tell you what really made me want to puke, though—the ugly women! I never saw an uglier bunch o' females in all my borned days!"

"That does it!" Scratch said. His muscles tensed as he readied himself to draw.

Bo was watching the other two men, and saw them reaching for their guns before Scratch had even made a move. He knew exactly what they figured was going to happen. Langdon would get out of the way, and his two partners would fill Scratch full of lead. Then they would claim they'd just been protecting their friend from an unprovoked attack by a stranger in town. It was an old trick.

Bo wasn't going to let it happen.

He still had a mostly full mug of beer in his hand. He let fly with it, flinging it mug and all into the face of one of the other gunmen as hard as he could. The man never saw it coming and went over backward as the heavy mug smashed into his nose. The beer from the mug splashed over the other man, distracting him long enough for Bo to lunge at him with surprising swiftness. The long black parson's coat swirled out as Bo pivoted and slashed down with the gun that had appeared almost as if by magic in his right hand. The barrel slammed against the skull of the second gunnie, right above the ear. The man went down hard, just like his companion.

Scratch's common sense and battle savvy won out

over the fury caused by the insults Langdon had leveled at Texas—and its women. At the same time as Bo was making his move against the other two men, Scratch's left hand moved with flashing speed, not toward the gun he wore on that side but toward Langdon's gun hand. Scratch's fingers clamped around the man's wrist and kept him from drawing his gun. Scratch's right hand came up in a sizzling punch that crashed flush against Langdon's jaw. The impact of the cleanly delivered blow drove Langdon to the side, against the bar. Scratch grabbed the back of his head, getting a good hold on the hair, and bounced Langdon's face off the hardwood. The gunman's knees unhinged. Scratch let go of him and allowed him to fall to the floor. He landed in the sawdust about the same time as his two partners.

Scratch looked across the bar and saw the bartender gaping at him and Bo. "Just because a couple of fellas are gettin' a mite long in the tooth don't mean they can't handle themselves in a ruckus anymore," he said with a smile. "That's worth rememberin'."

The bartender swallowed and then nodded, saying, "Yes, sir, I sure will."

Langdon and the man Bo had buffaloed with his gun were both out cold. The hombre who had caught the thrown beer mug in the face was still conscious but not interested in fighting. His nose was leaking blood and not exactly the right shape anymore. He groaned as he cupped his hands over his face.

Bo still had his gun drawn. He wasn't just watching

the man with the broken nose. He had an eye on the rest of the men in the saloon as well, especially Dave, Angus, and Culley. Those three hadn't moved during the brief fight, which surprised Bo a little. He had thought that they might try to take advantage of the situation and attack him and Scratch again.

The batwings were slapped open and a beefy, middle-aged man with gray hair and a mustache came into Sharkey's carrying a shotgun. A tin star was pinned to his leather vest. His eyes spotted the gun in Bo's hand right away. As the Greener swung in that direction, the star packer said, "All right, mister, just put that gun on the bar easy-like and step away from it."

"Sure, Marshal," Bo replied in a calm voice, although he didn't make a move to comply with the order just yet. "Since you're here, I reckon you'll make sure nobody else in this place tries to ventilate my partner and me."

"Nobody's gonna ventilate anybody," the lawman snapped. "Unless it's me doin' the ventilating. Now put that gun down."

Bo shrugged and placed the Colt on the bar. He moved away from it a little . . . but stayed within arm's reach.

That seemed to be enough to mollify the marshal. He said, "Claremont, what the hell's goin' on here? Somebody came runnin' down to my office sayin' that a war was about to break out in here!"

Claremont turned out to be the bartender. He said,

"There was, uh, a disagreement between Langdon and this fella here in the buckskin jacket. I told both of 'em that I didn't want any trouble in here, but they were bound and determined to start something."

Scratch glared at the drink juggler, who wasn't telling things exactly the way they had happened. Chances were, the man was a little worried about making enemies out of Langdon and the other two gunnies. That was understandable, but Scratch didn't have to like it.

"Who are you?" the marshal demanded of Bo and Scratch. "I don't think I've seen the two of you in Red Butte before."

"That's because we just rode in earlier this afternoon," Bo said, keeping his voice calm and level. "We'd never been here before."

"What're you doin' here now?"

"We came in with the stagecoach," Scratch said. "It was us who kept it from bein' robbed."

The marshal's frown deepened. "Yeah, I heard about that. You two are the fellas who had that shoot-out with Rance Judson's gang?"

"That's right," Bo said. "We're working for Mrs. Sutherland now, so I guess she can vouch for us—"

The batwings were shoved aside violently again, and the man who strode in, followed by several more gunhung hombres, heard Bo's statement and thrust out an arm, pointing accusingly at Bo and Scratch.

"I should have known when I heard that some of my men were in trouble down here!" this man said.

"Those two are hardcases hired by that woman. And look what they've done to Langdon, Simms, and Bartlett. Marshal, I demand that you throw them in jail, where their kind belong!"

CHAPTER 7

The man blustering just inside the saloon entrance was tall and broad-shouldered, with a ruggedly powerful face that showed he had spent a lot of time outdoors. He wore a brown tweed suit and a dark brown Stetson, and the butt of a gun carried in a cross-draw rig stuck out from under the suit coat on the left side.

The four men with him were cut from the same cloth as Langdon and the other two, which led Bo to make a guess based on what Abigail Sutherland had told him earlier. That guess was confirmed when the marshal said, "Take it easy, Mr. Rutledge, I'm lookin' into this."

"Damn it, Harding," Jared Rutledge shot back, "I don't want you 'looking into it.' I want you to arrest those troublemakers! Abigail Sutherland probably put them up to attacking my men!"

"You'd better rein in your hoss, mister," Scratch said in a low, dangerous voice. "Miz Sutherland didn't have anything to do with this fracas. Fact of the matter is, it was *your* men who started it by insultin' the great state o' Texas—and its ladies!"

"That's not the story the way Claremont told it," Marshal Tom Harding pointed out. He gave the bartender a hard look. "You stickin' to what you said earlier?"

Claremont opened and closed his mouth a couple of times without saying anything, and before he could manage to get any words out, another voice spoke up. "That old-timer's telling you the truth, Marshal. Langdon started it, and Bartlett and Simms were ready to bushwhack him when the other old gent stopped them."

Everyone looked around to see that Dave Sutherland was on his feet at last, moving toward the bar from the table where Angus and Culley still sat. The young man's eyes were still a little bleary, but by and large he seemed to be sober.

"Old-timer, is it?" muttered Scratch, but no one paid any attention to his indignant question.

Marshal Harding said, "No offense, Dave, but of course you'd stick up for these two if they're really workin' for your ma."

"That doesn't have anything to do with it, Marshal," Dave insisted. "You know me and my mother don't always get along. I wouldn't lie to the law just to help out a couple of strangers who haven't even been working for her an hour yet!"

Harding rubbed his jaw in thought. "Yeah, I reckon that makes sense—"

"Don't listen to him, Marshal," Rutledge said. "You've got Claremont's statement, and I'm sure when my men are in shape to talk to you, they'll tell you the same thing. Maybe they got a little proddy. I won't argue that with you. Men sometimes have to blow off some steam. But these two could have seriously injured them. My God, Bartlett's nose is broken! I'll swear out a complaint, and you arrest those saddle tramps."

Rutledge's arrogant tone put a burr under the lawman's saddle. Harding's back stiffened. He said, "Don't go tellin' me what to do, Mr. Rutledge. I'm the marshal of this town, and I know how to do my job."

Rutledge backed off some immediately. "Of course you do, Marshal," he said. "I didn't mean to suggest otherwise. But it's hard to stand by and watch that woman and her people deliberately cause trouble. Good Lord, I'm not convinced that there's not some sort of connection between the Sutherland Stage Line and those outlaws of Judson's!"

That bold-faced statement made both Bo and Scratch stare at Rutledge. Earlier, Abigail Sutherland had made exactly the same sort of accusation against Jared Rutledge.

Harding gave the freight line owner a dubious frown. "I dunno, Mr. Rutledge," he said. "That sounds mighty far-fetched to me."

"It's loco, that's what it is," Scratch burst out. "Why, it's only been a few hours since Bo and me was tradin' shots with those owlhoots while they tried to hold up one of Miz Sutherland's coaches!"

Rutledge sneered at him. "We've got only your word for that, don't we?"

"What about that bullet hole in Ponderosa Pine's

shoulder?" Bo asked quietly. "I'd say that's proof."

"Proof that the old fool got shot, that's all," snapped Rutledge. "It might have been an accident, or maybe one of you shot him just to make your story look good. For all we know you're part of Judson's gang!"

Scratch's eyes narrowed. "Mister, I'm gettin' mighty tired o' that line o' bull you're puttin' out."

Bo moved between Scratch and Rutledge. He said, "Marshal, you can ask Gil Sutherland and Ponderosa about the robbery. They'll tell the same story we do."

"Of course they will," Rutledge said.

Bo ignored him and went on. "And there have been other times when Judson's gang held up Mrs. Sutherland's stagecoaches. I'm sure there were witnesses to those crimes."

Harding nodded. "Yeah, that's true. I talked to the passengers who were on the coaches that got stopped, and their stories pretty well matched up."

"And I believe Mrs. Sutherland said that a driver and a guard who worked for her were killed during one of the holdups." Bo looked at Rutledge. "I know I just met Mrs. Sutherland, but I don't think she'd have anything to do with murdering innocent men just to keep suspicion from falling on her."

Rutledge at least looked a little uncomfortable now. "Maybe those men were killed accidentally. Things could have gotten out of hand . . . Anyway, I never said I thought there *is* a connection between Mrs. Sutherland and Rance Judson, just that there *could* be."

Scratch snorted. "You *could* be able to flap your arms and fly to the moon, too, mister, but I ain't gonna wait for it to happen."

"I think we all need to just settle down," Harding said. He had lowered the shotgun, and now held it in one hand at his side. With the other hand, he gestured toward Bartlett, whose groans had subsided to the occasional pathetic whimper. "Mr. Rutledge, why don't you have a couple of your boys take Bartlett down to Doc Chambers' place and see if the doc can do anything for him? And the rest of 'em can haul Langdon and Simms back to their rooms and let 'em sleep it off."

"They're not drunk," Rutledge said. "They were knocked out. Assaulted."

"This wouldn't be the first time those three have got mixed up in a shootin' and somebody else wound up dead," the marshal said. "I don't like killin's in my town. So I don't feel much like givin' 'em the benefit of the doubt this time, no offense."

Judging from the glare on Rutledge's face, though, he took offense, and plenty of it. But he didn't argue any more with the lawman. He just jerked a hand at his men and barked a couple of orders. Two of the hardcases helped Bartlett to his feet and assisted him out of the saloon. The others picked up the still-unconscious forms of Langdon and Simms and carried them out.

Rutledge took a cigar from his vest pocket, clamped one end of it between his teeth, and left it unlit as he said, "If I was you, Marshal, I'd keep a close eye on these saddle tramps. If you do, you'll see that it's *them* who are the real troublemakers."

With that, he turned and stalked out of Sharkey's, slapping the batwings aside with such force that they swung back and forth several times after he was gone.

Marshal Harding shook his head. "That's a stiff-necked man," he said, and the comment seemed directed as much to himself as to anyone else. "Lots of mad in him, and not much back-up." He turned to Bo and Scratch. "I'd keep an eye out behind me if I was you boys. Those three don't take kindly to anybody gettin' the best of 'em, especially Cal Langdon. When he wakes up he's gonna be touchy as an old grizzly."

"Are you saying he might try to shoot us from a dark alley or something like that, Marshal?" Bo asked.

"Well, no, I don't think he would . . . I'm just sayin' you ought to be careful, that's all."

Scratch grunted. "If we wasn't careful, we wouldn't have lived as long as we have."

"That's for sure," Bo agreed with a faint smile.

Harding turned to the bartender. "Claremont, when I ask you a question, I expect a straight answer, savvy?"

"I told you the way I saw it, Marshal," Claremont answered stiffly. "I'm working here. It's a busy night. Can't expect a man to see every little thing that goes on."

"Uh-huh." The dry sarcasm in Harding's curt answer made Claremont flush angrily, but the bartender didn't say anything else.

Harding turned back to Dave Sutherland, glanced past the young man to the table where his two friends still sat, and went on. "I'm a little surprised you'd stick up for these two, Dave. I heard you and Angus and Culley had a run-in with them yourselves a while ago."

"That was mostly Angus and Culley, Marshal. And we'd all had too much to drink."

"That don't surprise me none." Harding sighed. "Try to keep your nose clean, kid. Keepin' the peace around here is hard enough without you three young hellions goin' around stirrin' things up."

Dave didn't respond to that scolding. He just asked in a surly voice, "You done with me, Marshal?"

"Yeah, go back to your friends." Harding looked at Bo and Scratch. "You two . . . come with me."

"Are you arresting us, Marshal?" Bo asked. He and Scratch had a rule about not tangling with lawmen—at least not with the honest ones. As a result, they had found themselves in more than one hoosegow, usually without any just cause. Things always got straightened out in the end, though.

"No, I'm not arrestin' you," Harding said. "I just want to talk to you, but not here."

"That's all right with me," Scratch said. He threw a hard glance toward Claremont. "Ain't the friendliest place I ever been anyway."

The two drifters followed the marshal outside. The sun had set and night was settling down over Red Butte now. Stars had begun to flicker into life in the deep blue sky that arched above the settlement and the butte that gave it its name.

"You say you're working for Abigail Sutherland?" Harding asked as they began strolling down the street.

"That's right," Bo said. "We signed on as drivers, guards, or whatever else she needs us to be."

"Hired guns?"

"We're not gunslingers, Marshal," Scratch said. "That don't mean we can't handle these smokepoles when we need to, but we don't hire out to go gunnin' for folks."

Harding grunted. "I'm glad to hear it. Rutledge claims those hombres who work for him are just teamsters, but you saw 'em for yourselves. They haven't done a whole lot of honest work in their lives."

"And you thought we were more of the same, hired by Mrs. Sutherland to take her side in this little war that's brewing between her and Rutledge."

"I ain't sure how little it's gonna be," Harding said with a sigh. "But if it breaks out, it's gonna be pretty one-sided, that's for sure. Miz Sutherland's got one boy who means well but is green, one that's not worth much of anything, to be blunt about it, and a crippled-up old-timer."

"And us," Scratch said.

"Two more old-timers," Bo added.

That brought a laugh from the marshal. "You boys may have some years on you, but based on how you handled those three gunslicks, I wouldn't want to tangle with you. What are your names anyway? I may have heard 'em, but I disremember."

"I'm Bo Creel. This is Scratch Morton."

"Creel . . . Morton . . ." Harding mused. "I don't recall seeing any wanted posters on either of you."

"That's because there aren't any," Bo said.

"We're peaceable men," Scratch said.

"Yeah, I could tell that when I came into the saloon and found you standin' over a fella with a busted nose and two more who were out colder'n mackerels."

"That wasn't our fault—"

Harding held up his free hand palm out to forestall Scratch's protestations of innocence. "I know that. But you strike me as the sort of gents who just naturally find trouble, whether you want to be peaceable or not."

Neither Bo nor Scratch could deny that.

So instead, Bo said, "Rutledge was quick to hint that Mrs. Sutherland might be tied up with Judson's outlaws."

"Foolishness," Harding snorted.

"What about the other way around?"

The marshal shook his head. "I don't get your meanin'."

"What are the chances that there's some connection between *Rutledge* and Judson?"

Harding stopped and stared at Bo in the light that came through a window in one of the buildings they were passing. "That don't make any sense either," he said after a moment. "Rutledge's freight wagons have been held up, and so has that one stagecoach he runs back and forth between here and Cottonwood every week."

"Did he lose much of value?"

"Well . . . I don't know about that. And I can only go by what Rutledge tells me."

"Exactly," Bo said. "Has anybody been hurt in any of those holdups?"

Harding thumbed his hat back and scratched at his thinning hair. "Now that I come to think of it, I don't believe there has been."

"Then maybe they were the same sort of phony robberies Rutledge accused Mrs. Sutherland of being part of."

Harding closed his eyes and shook his head for a moment before opening them again and saying, "Sorry, Creel, but this is gettin' too mixed up for me. I think both sides need to quit flingin' accusations back and forth and just learn to get along." He paused. "I don't reckon that's gonna happen, though—the gettin'-along part, I mean—as long as Jared Rutledge wants to have the only stage line in these parts and the government mail contract, to boot. He's a fella who doesn't like it when he don't get what he wants."

"He'll just have to learn to live with," Bo said.

"Or die with it, if it comes to that," Scratch added.

CHAPTER 8

The marshal left them at his office with another warning to be careful. "And try to stay out of trouble," he added.

"We always do," Bo said.

"It's everybody else who don't cooperate," Scratch said.

The Texans continued walking along the street toward the headquarters of the Sutherland Stagecoach Line. As they drew near the adobe building that housed the office and the Sutherland family's living quarters, Ponderosa Pine came out onto the front porch and spotted them.

"There you fellas are," the old-timer greeted them. "Come on in. Grub's on the table. Feedin' you's part o' your wages, remember?"

Scratch took a deep whiff of the delicious aromas filling the air and grinned. "The best part, smells like!"

They left their hats on nails just inside the door. Ponderosa led them through the office and into the dining room that was part of the living quarters in the rear of the building. Like the office, it was comfortably furnished. A thick-legged table big enough for a dozen people dominated the room. Heavy chairs were arranged around it.

No one was sitting at the table, though. In a low voice, Ponderosa said, "Back when Will Sutherland was still alive, this place was always full at meal-times. There was the four o' them, plus enough drivers and guards and hostlers to fill up the rest o' the chairs. Now, with Will dead and Dave gone off who knows where doin' who knows what and ever'body else up and quit on us, it sure ain't like it used to be."

"Well, maybe we can help out a little in that respect, too," Scratch said.

"And Dave is down at Sharkey's," Bo added. "At least, he was a few minutes ago."

Ponderosa nodded. "That don't surprise me one blasted bit. Sittin' down there gettin' drunk with those two shiftless friends o' his, I reckon."

"They were together, all right," Bo said. "Dave didn't seem to be drunk, though. In fact, he stood up for us with the marshal when there was some trouble."

"Trouble?" Ponderosa repeated, his bushy eyebrows rising. "Tell me about it quick, before Miz Abigail comes in from the kitchen."

Bo and Scratch complied with that request, summarizing in a few short sentences the run-in they'd had with Jared Rutledge's men, then telling the old-timer about how Rutledge himself had shown up at Sharkey's after the fight.

Ponderosa gave a grim snort as the drifters concluded the tale. "Yeah, that's just like Rutledge," he said. "Shows up after the dirty work's over and done with. That fella Langdon's one o' his top gunnies, and Simms and Bartlett are the other two. They must'a been listenin' to you talkin', and when they heard that you're workin' for Miz Abigail, they knew their boss would want them to run you off."

"They had more in mind than running us off," Bo said. "They would have killed us if we'd given them the chance."

"Well . . . ain't much better way to make sure a fella don't interfere with your plans than to put him in the ground, now is there?"

Bo and Scratch couldn't argue with that.

Before they could discuss anything else with Ponderosa, Abigail Sutherland came into the room through a swinging door. The platter of roast beef she carried was evidence that the kitchen was on the other side of that door. Steam rose from the meat, along with an appealing aroma.

"I'm glad to see you, gentlemen," she said to Bo and Scratch. "I thought I might have to send Ponderosa to look for you. Where are the boys?"

"Gil's out in the barn tendin' to the horses," Ponderosa answered. "As for Dave . . ." He glanced at the two Texans.

Abigail stopped, still holding the heavy platter. Scratch sprang forward and said, "Let me take that, ma'am. I'd be happy to give you a hand."

"I'd rather you'd tell me where my younger son is, Mr. Morton," Abigail said, "since judging from Ponderosa's reaction, you might know something about that."

"Well . . ."

"He's was at Sharkey's Saloon a little while ago," Bo said. "I don't know if he still is or not."

Abigail sighed. "I'd say it's very likely he is." She let Scratch take the platter of roast beef now. "Just put it in the center of the table, Mr. Morton."

"Yes, ma'am."

Ponderosa said, "I'll go fetch Gil."

Abigail nodded. "Thank you. There's no point in waiting for Dave. We'll go ahead and eat."

Scratch was right beside her as she started into the kitchen again. "I'll help you with the rest of the food," he volunteered.

"Thank you, Mr. Morton."

"Why, you should call me Scratch . . ." he was saying as the door swung shut behind them.

Everyone was rather subdued during supper, except for Scratch. Plenty of good food and the company of an attractive woman made him ebullient, no matter what the rest of the circumstances might be.

And the food was good, no denying that. The roast beef was tender and savory, the potatoes that went with it were cooked just right, and the greens made a nice addition to the meal. The apple pie that finished off the meal was some of the best the Texans had ever had, as Scratch pointed out with his usual considerable enthusiasm.

But still, the shadow of two missing family members seemed to hang over the table—Will Sutherland, the patriarch who was dead and gone, and Dave, the younger son who was estranged from the rest of the family. That didn't even take into account the attempted holdup that afternoon and the injury to Ponderosa that had resulted from it, or the two violent clashes Bo and Scratch had had with other hombres just since arriving in Red Butte.

Of course, Abigail didn't know about the trouble with Rutledge's men yet, but she was bound to hear about it sooner or later.

That turned out to be sooner, as the pounding of a fist on the office door sounded while Bo and Scratch were clearing the table after supper was over. Scratch had been quick to volunteer for the task, and he had volunteered Bo at the same time.

"Who in the world can that be?" Abigail murmured.

"Can't be anybody looking to buy a ticket," Gil said, "since we don't ever have any passengers anymore."

Ponderosa snorted. "You're exaggeratin', boy. Just because the coach was empty on today's run don't mean we won't never have no more passengers."

The three of them went into the office while Bo and Scratch were carrying the dirty dishes into the kitchen. As they came back into the dining room a moment later, they heard angry voices from the front of the building. They exchanged a look, then hitched their gunbelts up and ambled into the office.

Jared Rutledge stood just inside the open front door, his face flushed with anger. When he saw Bo and Scratch, he snapped, "There they are now. I knew

Marshal Harding wouldn't arrest them, even though it was clearly his duty to do so."

Scratch hooked his thumbs in his gunbelt. "Been talkin' about us, have you, Rutledge?"

"I thought Mrs. Sutherland ought to know what kind of men she's hired. A couple of violent saddle tramps who are on the prod."

Abigail turned to look at the Texans. "Mr. Rutledge claims that you picked a fight with some of his men in Sharkey's Saloon. Is that true?"

Scratch glared at Rutledge and said, "Not hardly!"

"Rutledge's men started the fight," Bo said. "He knows it. There were plenty of witnesses. Some of them were too scared to speak up, and the bartender sort of shaded the truth a mite when the marshal asked him about it, but everybody who was there knows what really happened—including your son Dave, ma'am."

Abigail looked at the two of them for a long moment and then finally nodded. "All right. I believe you."

"That doesn't change the fact that I have a man with a broken nose and a couple who are lucky their heads aren't busted," Rutledge said. "According to Dr. Chambers, all three of them will be laid up for a few days. That's liable to leave me short-handed."

Abigail smiled. "What would you have me do about that, Mr. Rutledge? Loan you the services of Mr. Morton and Mr. Creel?"

"Hold on a minute," Scratch began. "I ain't gonna work for that—"

Abigail stopped him with an upraised hand. "Don't worry, Mr. Morton," she said. "I wouldn't ask you to do that." She turned back to the visitor. "What I would ask, Mr. Rutledge, is that you leave. Your men provoked the trouble, and I don't owe you any explanations or apologies."

Rutledge's face got even redder than it already was. "You'll regret hiring those two, Mrs. Sutherland. Mark my words, you'll regret it."

He left the stage line headquarters as abruptly and as angrily as he had left Sharkey's earlier. Abigail watched him go and shook her head. "What did he hope to accomplish by coming down here and trying to browbeat me?" she asked as she turned toward Bo, Scratch, and Ponderosa.

"I don't reckon he was tryin' to accomplish anything except to keep on bein' an arrogant jackass, just like always," Ponderosa said. "Pardon my French, ma'am."

"Yeah, a fella like that's just in love with the sound of his own voice," Scratch added. "He just likes to carry on for the sake o' carryin' on."

Abigail nodded. "You're probably right." She hesitated, then went on. "And please don't take this the wrong way, gentlemen. I know that tonight you were just defending yourselves, and that's exactly what I want you to do. But in the future, if such situations can be avoided . . ."

"We'll do our best to avoid them, ma'am," Bo promised.

"It's just that a lot of people in Red Butte see Mr. Rutledge's freight company as being more important to the survival of the town than our stagecoach line." She sighed. "And I suppose it is. His wagons bring in most of the goods that are sold in the stores. Red Butte could get by without our stagecoaches easier than it could without Mr. Rutledge. So naturally, people tend to support him."

"What about the mail?" Ponderosa asked. "Folks wouldn't like it if they couldn't get their mail no more."

"But they *would* get their mail, and they know it. If the stage line goes under, Mr. Rutledge will take over the mail contract, too."

"That's not going to happen," Gil said. The young man had been quiet until now, staying out of the discussion. He was pale and his mouth was tight with anger as he went on. "Rutledge has run roughshod over everybody else around here for too long. It's time he was taken down a notch or two."

Abigail's face wore an expression of concern as she went over to her older son. "We want to avoid trouble if at all possible, Gil, not go looking for it," she said. "I don't know what you have in mind—"

"Nothing," he said with a quick shake of his head. "I'm not going to do anything. I was just talking."

Abigail didn't look completely convinced, but she nodded and said, "Good." She put a hand on his arm. "I don't care nearly as much about the stage line as I do for my family. I couldn't stand to lose you or Dave—"

"You've already lost Dave," Gil snapped. He pulled away from her. "You lost him when Pa died."

"Gil! You shouldn't say such things. Your brother will straighten himself out—"

Gil's disgusted snort revealed just how much he believed that.

He reached for his hat and said, "I'm going back out to the barn. One of the horses has a problem with a shoe."

"I'll come with you, boy," Ponderosa said. From the look on his face, it seemed that conversations like the one between Gil and Abigail made him uncomfortable.

Bo and Scratch weren't all that fond of emotional turmoil either. They excused themselves and drifted out onto the front porch, where they sat down in the rocking chairs. Scratch took out the makin's and began to roll a quirly. Bo slipped his pipe and tobacco pouch from a pocket and started packing the bowl of the old briar.

The night was warm and quiet. Music drifted up the street from the saloons, several different tunes blending together into a melody that should have been discordant, but had a certain catchiness to it instead. A wagon wheel squeaked somewhere, and hooves plodded in the dusty street. From inside the building, a faint clinking could be heard as Abigail washed the dishes from supper.

"We should'a done that for her," Scratch said as his fingers deftly formed the cigarette.

"She probably wouldn't have let us." Bo thumbed tobacco into his pipe. "Most women don't like anybody else messing around in their kitchen."

"They don't want another woman in there," Scratch said with a grin. "They don't mind near as much when a man rolls up his sleeves and gets soapsuds on his arms. That's your trouble, Bo. You just don't understand women."

"And you do."

"Damn right I do. Better'n you anyway. When was the last time you——"

"There's more to it than that, you know," Bo said, interrupting.

Scratch chuckled. "Yeah, but without that, the rest of it don't add up to near as much."

"Think what you want, old-timer," Bo said as he started searching his pockets for a match.

"I gen'rally do." Scratch licked the paper and sealed the quirly, twisting the ends. "You think she's right? You think there's any chance that boy Dave'll ever straighten up and behave?"

"I don't know." Bo grinned over at Scratch. "I've been acquainted with some pretty disreputable characters who finally grew up . . . sort of."

"I ain't got the foggiest notion who you're talkin' about." Scratch grinned, too, and snapped a lucifer to life with his thumbnail. He held the flame to the end of his cigarette.

"I can't seem to find a match," Bo said. "Reckon I could light my pipe off that one of yours?"

"Sure." Scratch held out the burning match, and Bo leaned over to take it from him.

That was when the whipcrack of a rifle split the peaceful night.

CHAPTER 9

Bo felt as much as heard the slug as it sizzled through the air next to his ear before smacking into the back of the rocking chair. Splinters stung the back of his neck. Instinct and reflexes took over. He dropped the pipe and flung himself forward, diving out of the chair.

Scratch hit the floor of the porch at the same time Bo did, having reacted to the shot the same way. His left hand came down on the still-burning match, which he had dropped as he left the rocking chair, and smothered the flame.

The Texans put some distance between themselves. Bo rolled to the left as Scratch rolled to the right. They had both filled their hands already. That reaction was instinctive and instantaneous, too.

Bo had seen the gout of orange flame from the rifle muzzle when the first shot rang out. It came from a clump of scrubby trees across the road. The stage station was on the edge of town, so there were vacant lots between most of the buildings around here. As Bo came to a stop on his belly at the end of the porch, three more shots ripped out from the trees. The bullets hit the adobe walls of the building, which were thick enough to stop them.

The Colt in Bo's hand roared as he returned the fire. A few yards away, past the steps, both of Scratch's pearl-handled Remingtons began blazing, too.

The drifters sent seven or eight shots into the trees, then held their fire for a second. At that moment, the front door was jerked open and Abigail called in a frightened voice, "What's going on out here?"

"Get back inside, ma'am!" Bo told her.

"And keep your head down!" Scratch added.

The door slammed shut, thankfully. Bo and Scratch had enough to worry about without the possibility of Abigail getting hit by a stray bullet. That bushwhacker across the road could open fire again at any moment.

Or he might be lying dead over there with Texan lead in him. That was certainly a possibility. He could have fled, too, taking off for the tall and uncut. There was also the chance that he was just biding his time, waiting for Bo or Scratch to show themselves.

Neither of the drifters budged, though, sticking to the thick shadows on the porch. Bo heard swift footsteps hurrying from the rear of the place, along the wall of the building, and turned his head to call softly, "Gil! Ponderosa! Stay back, men!"

The running footsteps stopped, and Gil asked, "Are you all right, Mr. Creel?"

"Yeah. You hit, Scratch?"

"Nope," Scratch replied. "You reckon that varmint's still over there, Bo?"

"No telling."

"Why don't I circle around and try to find out?"

"All right, but don't dawdle along the way."

Scratch chuckled. "Didn't intend to."

Bo heard the faint sounds of movement as Scratch rolled off the far end of the porch. He caught a glimpse of his trail partner darting behind a wagon that was parked farther down the street. Scratch's actions didn't draw any fire. Bo had his Colt leveled and ready in case more muzzle flame spurted from the darkness among the trees.

Scratch worked his way along the street for several more yards, utilizing every bit of cover he could find, then finally sprinted across the open ground when he thought he had gone far enough. He expected a rifle bullet to come fanging out of the night, searching for him with deadly ruthlessness, but no shots sounded. When he reached the other side of the street, he dropped into a crouch in front of a saddlemaker's shop that was closed for the night and began moving back toward the vacant lot where the bushwhacker had lurked—and might still be lurking, for all Scratch knew.

On the porch of the stage line building, Bo heard Abigail Sutherland ask softly through a window, "What's happening now?"

"Scratch is circling around to get closer to whoever fired those shots," Bo told her.

"I hope he's being careful."

"Scratch *does* have a pretty reckless nature some-times," Bo said, "but not when it comes to gun-fights. He'll be all right . . . You might want to blow out the lamps in there, ma'am, if you haven't already."

"I thought of that and took care of it already, Mr. Creel."

"Good job, ma'am." For a second he thought about telling her to call him Bo, but this was hardly the time or place and he didn't know where that thought came from anyway.

He saw motion down the street from the corner of his eye and turned his head to take a better look. A figure was trotting along toward the stage line headquarters, and as the man came closer Bo recognized him as Marshal Tom Harding. All the shooting had drawn the attention of the law.

Bo lifted his voice and called, "Marshal! Stay back!"

Harding ducked behind the wagon where Scratch had taken cover a few moments earlier. "Creel?" he said. "Is that you?"

"Yeah."

"What in blazes is goin' on now?"

"Somebody over in those trees started taking potshots at Scratch and me."

"Anybody hurt?"

"Not on our side. Don't know yet about the bushwhacker. Scratch has gone to take a look."

As if he had been waiting for that cue, Scratch shouted from across the street, "All clear! Whoever the varmint was, he's gone!"

Bo pushed himself to his feet. Keeping the gun in his hand, he stepped down from the porch and met

Marshal Harding in front of the building. Gil and Ponderosa came around from the side, and Abigail opened the door and stepped out onto the porch.

Bo half turned and motioned her back in with his free hand. "Maybe you better stay inside, ma'am," he told her. "Just because the bushwhacker's not where he was a few minutes ago doesn't mean he's not still around."

"I suppose so. Gil, Ponderosa, be careful."

"Let's go take a look over there," Harding said. "Might find something to tell us who he was."

Bo doubted that, but anything was possible. The four men trooped across the street to join Scratch, who had emerged from the shadows under the trees.

"I got back yonder and then worked my way to the street," Scratch said, nodding toward the rear of the little grove. He still held both Remingtons. "There's nobody here anymore."

"Gil, you reckon you could fetch a lantern?" Harding asked.

"Sure, Marshal," the young man replied. "I'll be right back."

He returned a few minutes later with a lit lantern, which Harding took and held up so that the yellow glow from it washed over the ground under the trees. Some other townspeople had come up by now, and the marshal snapped at them, "You folks stay back until I've had a look around. If there's any sign up in here, I don't want it messed up."

It didn't take long to determine, though, that the

bushwhacker hadn't left any clues to his identity. There were bootprints on the sandy ground underneath the trees, but evidently this vacant lot sometimes served as a shortcut for the citizens of Red Butte, because there were too many prints to be able to pick out any one particular set as belonging to the rifleman.

Bo found several empty rifle cartridges, too, when the brass reflected the lantern light, but that didn't tell them anything except that the weapon used .44-40 ammunition. There were probably dozens of such rifles in the settlement.

Marshal Harding glared at Bo and Scratch. "What is it about you fellas?" he asked. "You've only been in town a few hours, and already you've been mixed up in two separate brawls and a shooting."

"None of which we started," Bo pointed out.

"And don't forget that attempted stage holdup," Scratch said.

"I'm not forgettin' anything," Harding said. "Is this sort o' ruction what we've got to look forward to as long as you're in Red Butte?"

"It's not our fault somebody started shooting at us," Bo said.

"And we weren't gonna just sit there and let him do it without shootin' back," Scratch said.

"No, I don't reckon anybody could blame you for doing that," the marshal admitted. "Still, it'd be just fine with me if the two of you decided to ride on in the mornin', instead of goin' to work for Miz Sutherland."

"That's not going to happen," Bo said. "We gave the lady our word."

Scratch just nodded this time.

"All right," Harding said with a sigh. "I'm gonna stop and have a talk with Clayt Addison on my way back to the office, though."

"Who's that?" Scratch asked.

"The local undertaker. I want to tell him he's liable to be a mite busier than usual for a while, as long as you boys are in town."

"Now, that ain't fair!" Scratch protested. "We ain't killed nobody in this town."

"Yet," Bo put in.

Harding just shook his head and walked away.

Ponderosa slapped his thigh and laughed. "I got to tell you, it looks like things are gonna be poppin' while you fellas are around. Life'll be more entertainin' anyway."

"Entertaining?" Gil asked in a gloomy voice. "Or just more dangerous?"

Scratch holstered his twin Remingtons. "Come on," he said. "We'd best go tell Miz Sutherland that everybody's all right and there's nothin' to worry about."

Bo wasn't sure that was the case. From what he had seen of the situation in Red Butte, there was plenty to worry about.

The formation that had given the settlement its name rose some one hundred feet from the mostly flat ground surrounding it. To anyone approaching it at night on horseback, it loomed high enough to blot out some of the stars, and its dark bulk was menacing. The shadows at its base were so thick that not even the keenest eyesight could penetrate them.

That was why the rider heading for Red Butte tonight reined to a halt just before he reached those stygian shadows. He gave a low whistle, and a few moments later, in response to the signal, he heard hoofbeats nearby. Another rider emerged from the shrouding darkness.

"That you, Judson?" the rider who had come from the settlement asked.

The other man gave a harsh chuckle. "You'd have a mighty big problem if it wasn't, wouldn't you? You would have just admitted that you're on speakin' terms with the leader of the outlaw gang that's got everybody in this part of the territory stirred up."

"That doesn't matter," the first man snapped. "What's important is that the man you sent to take care of Creel and Morton missed!"

Rance Judson's voice lost its amused tone. He sounded angry, too, as he said, "You didn't tell me those two old buzzards were so fast on the draw and such good shots. You said they were a couple of mostly harmless drifters, but you didn't want 'em meddlin' in your plans anyway. Isn't that what you said when you asked me to get rid of 'em for you? They came damn close to partin' Hollister's hair with some lead!"

"I didn't know they could handle themselves that

well. I'm more convinced than ever now that we can't have them poking around in our business."

Judson shrugged, the movement indistinct in the starlight. "Next time we stop one of the Sutherland coaches, we'll make sure Creel and Morton are on it. They won't live through that holdup, you can count on it."

"I hope you're right," the man from the settlement said. "We've got too much riding on this to let a couple of old coots ruin everything."

"You know yet when the big payoff's gonna be?" Judson asked.

The other man shook his head. "No. I'm working on it, though. It's just a matter of time until it happens. And when it does, we'll be rich men, Rance."

"Rich men," Judson repeated. "I like the sound of that. Yes, sir, I surely do."

"Then just be patient and don't lose sight of the real objective. It would ruin everything if you and your men got yourselves killed or caught pulling a little job somewhere."

"I got to throw the boys a bone now and then," Judson protested. "They don't know what we're really after, so holdin' up a stage or hittin' the bank in Chino Valley keeps 'em happy."

"You know what I'm saying. Just be careful, is all, because I need you for the big payoff."

"Damn right you need us," Judson said. "That's why you wouldn't even think about double-crossin' us, now would you, pard?"

"I haven't steered you wrong yet, have I?" the other man snapped. He lifted the reins and pulled his horse's head around. "I've got to get back. Just remember what I said, and as soon as you get the chance . . . *get rid of Creel and Morton!*"

Judson nodded, and the two men wheeled their horses and rode away, heading in different directions, the outlaw leader circling the butte and riding north for the badlands, his partner trotting back toward the lights of the settlement where he made his home.

CHAPTER 10

The rest of the night passed quietly, for which Bo and Scratch were grateful. They made themselves comfortable in the barn. The accommodations weren't fancy, of course, but they had slept in lots worse places in their lives.

The next morning, everyone gathered in the dining room for breakfast. Even Dave Sutherland was there, although from the bleary look in his eyes and the way he winced at the slightest noise, he was plenty hungover. He didn't have much to say. Instead, he wore a surly frown and concentrated on his food.

"When's your next run over to Chino Valley and Cottonwood scheduled?" Bo asked.

"Day after tomorrow," Abigail replied. "The driver and guard spend the night in Cottonwood, then make the return trip the next day with the mail pouch and any passengers that need a ride."

"Not many of those lately," Gil added.

Scratch said, "Business ought to pick up once word gets around that you got Bo and me ridin' shotgun."

"Why? You two aren't famous gunfighters or anything like that."

"And we don't want to be," Bo said. "I reckon we can handle those outlaws, though."

Gil looked like he had some doubts about that, but he didn't say anything.

Bo looked at Abigail, who sat at the head of the table in the dining room, and went on. "Scratch and I can take the next run and give Gil a break. What would you like for us to do in the meantime?"

"I wouldn't feel right about asking you to do anything," she said. "After all, I'm not paying you, remember?"

"You're feedin' us," Scratch said. "And doin' a mighty good job of it, too. I don't think I've ever had any flapjacks better'n these."

"Thank you, Mr. Morton." She smiled and added, "I mean, Scratch," before he could tell her to do so.

"We don't mind doing whatever we need to in order to help out," Bo said.

Ponderosa spoke up. "I got a heap o' harness that needs some mendin'. Been puttin' it off for a while, and now with just one arm, I reckon I'd have some trouble doin' it."

"And if you're sure you don't mind, I could use a hand with some repairs here in the house," Abigail said.

"I'll take care o' that, whatever you need," Scratch responded. "And ol' Bo there is a good hand at mendin' harness. Ain't that right, Bo?"

"I suppose. I've done plenty of it in my life, that's for sure."

Bo didn't have to think about it for very long before he realized what Scratch had done. Scratch had arranged things so that he'd be working inside the adobe building with Abigail, while Bo was out in the barn with Ponderosa. Scratch had made no secret of how attractive he found the middle-aged widow, and if he stayed true to his nature, he would be working on more than odd jobs and chores. He would be flirting shamelessly with Abigail, too.

That was all right, Bo told himself. It wasn't like *he* was interested in Abigail or anything. And she was a grown woman who ought to be able to take care of herself and fend off Scratch's advances—if she wanted to.

Abigail turned to her younger son and asked, "What are your plans for today, Dave?"

Before Dave could answer, Gil gave a disgusted snort. "I'm sure he plans to do what he always does—hang around one of the saloons and get drunk with those worthless friends of his."

Dave's head snapped up and he glared across the table at his brother. He looked so angry that for a second Bo thought the young man might launch himself right over the breakfast dishes at Gil.

"There's no call for talk like that, Gil," Abigail told him with an angry frown of her own.

"Why not? It's the truth. Dave doesn't contribute anything around here. You ought to just throw him out."

"There won't be any talk about throwing anybody out. And you're not helping the situation, you know."

Gil grunted. "At least I pull my share of the weight around here—and his, too!"

"I'm not gonna sit here and listen to this," Dave muttered as he pushed his chair back and got to his feet.

"No, you're going to run off like you always do."

"Gil!" Abigail said. "Stop it!" She turned her head to glance at Bo and Scratch. "I'm sorry about this—"

"No need to apologize, ma'am," Bo said.

"Ain't like we never saw a little family squabble before," Scratch said.

Dave had already turned and stalked out of the room, leaving his breakfast half-eaten on the table. He went through the office part of the building, slamming the front door on his way out.

"Better check the petty cash, Ma," Gil said in a scathing voice. "He probably helped himself to some whiskey money as he was leaving."

She glared at him. "You just have to make things worse, don't you?"

"How can they get any worse than they already are? The stage line's barely afloat, Ponderosa's got a bullet hole in his shoulder, and we've been reduced to hiring saddle tramps for help! Maybe you ought to just go ahead and give up and sell out to Rutledge. He probably doesn't want to buy the line anymore, though. Why should he when all he has to do is wait for it to collapse on its own?"

Abigail leaped to her feet and hurried out to the kitchen, letting the door swing back and forth behind her. Gil didn't say anything else. After a moment, he gave a dour shake of his head, got up, and went out into the office without looking at Bo, Scratch, or Ponderosa.

Ponderosa hadn't stopped eating during the argument. His movements were a little awkward since he had to use his left hand, but he was managing to put away quite a bit of food without much trouble.

Now, as Ponderosa swallowed a bite and then reached for his coffee cup, Bo asked, "Do they go at it like that very often?"

"All the time," Ponderosa replied, "especially whenever Dave's around. That boy just plumb provokes his brother, just by bein' here."

"Looks like he'd be glad to have Dave around," Scratch commented. "You'd think he'd want the boy to take some o'the load off'a him."

"Yeah, but that ain't ever the way it works out. Them two can't get along. Any time they try to work together, sooner or later there's a ruckus."

"Yeah, sometimes brothers are like that," Scratch agreed. He pushed his chair away from the table. "Well, maybe Miz Abigail's calmed down a mite by now, and she can tell me just what chores need doin' around here."

Ponderosa used a final piece of biscuit to sop up the rest of the gravy on his plate. "Yeah, and I'll show you where that harness is, Bo. Come on out to the barn with me."

It was an uneventful morning for the Texans. Scratch had hoped to spend most of it with Abigail, but he was disappointed. She had him repairing some shelves in the kitchen while she spent the morning in the office, going over the stage line's books.

Bo did his work in the tack room inside the barn, mending harness for the teams while Ponderosa perched on a three-legged stool and kept him company. The old-timer filled a pipe with some particularly noxious-smelling tobacco and puffed away on it after Bo lit the pipe for him. He talked at length about his days working for the Butterfield Stage Company with Will Sutherland, and also about how they had come here to Red Butte together to start the new stage line.

"Will wanted to make me a partner in the line, but I turned him down flat," Ponderosa said. "For one thing, I didn't have no money to put into it. Money never has had a habit o' stayin' in my pockets for too long. Will offered to make me a partner anyway and let me pay him back outta my share o' the profits, but I wouldn't hear of it. I don't want to be beholdin' to anybody, and I sure didn't want the headaches o' actually bein' responsible for anything!" Ponderosa threw back his head and laughed. "I expect you an' Scratch can understand that, bein' the fiddle-footed galoots that you are."

"We haven't let much grass grow under our feet these past thirty or forty years," Bo admitted with a smile. He didn't mention that once he'd had a fine little ranch between Victoria and Halletsville, with plenty of good grass growing underneath his feet. He'd had a wife and children, too, until the fever took them, and then the ranch didn't mean anything without them.

If not for his friend Scratch, he wouldn't have made it through that tragic time. So it made sense that they'd ridden together ever since.

"I told Will I'd be glad to work for him, though," Ponderosa went on. "Things went pretty well at first, until some o' the mines started to peter out and those other settlements folks talked about startin' around Chino Valley and Cottonwood never came to anything. Then Jared Rutledge got uppity and on the prod 'cause he wanted to be the big skookum he-wolf in these parts and own the stage line. Will turned him down flat."

"Yeah, I've been wondering about something Gil said along those lines," Bo said. "Did Rutledge offer to buy the line again after Will Sutherland died?"

Ponderosa nodded. "Yep, he sure did. Showed up too soon to even be decent about it, if you ask me. Poor Will was barely cold in the ground before Rutledge was pesterin' Miz Abigail to sell out to him. She tried to be nice about it at first—she can't hardly be no other way, you know—but Rutledge wouldn't take the hint. She finally told him that she wouldn't ever sell the stage line, that it'd be disloyal to her husband's memory if she did, since Will worked so hard to start it up. Rutledge is the sort o' fella who don't like it when somebody tells him no. He don't like it even a little bit."

"And it was after that Rance Judson and his outlaw gang showed up," Bo mused.

"Yeah. 'Bout a month later they pulled their first job, if I recollect right. First job around here, I should say. They'd pulled some holdups over in New Mexico Territory and up in southern Colorado, round Pueblo. That's how come folks in these parts were able to figure out who they were. Judson's an ugly-lookin' fella, and his face is on plenty o' wanted posters. The gang wears masks most o' the time, but a few people got a look at Judson's face an' recognized him."

"There's a certain type of owlhoot who wants his victims to know who he is," Bo said. "Frank and Jesse James and the Younger Brothers never went to any great pains to keep their identities secret."

Ponderosa puffed hard on the pipe and sent a cloud of smoke into the air around his head. "That's just what I'm sayin'! Judson's proud o' being a no-good desperado, and he don't care who knows it!"

Bo thought about everything Ponderosa had told him, and after a moment he asked, "What do you know about Jared Rutledge?"

"What do you mean, what do I know about him? I know enough not to like the high-handed polecat!"

"He was already here in Red Butte when the Sutherlands moved here and started the stage line, right?"

"Yeah. He hadn't been here for too long, though. He'd been runnin' his freight wagons for a month or two."

"And you don't know where he came from before that?"

"Got no earthly idea." Ponderosa frowned. "Say, what're you gettin' at, Bo?"

"Mrs. Sutherland said she thought there might be a connection between Rutledge and Rance Judson. I'm wondering if they knew each other before Rutledge moved here."

"You mean maybe Rutledge was an outlaw, a member o' Judson's gang!" Ponderosa clamped his teeth on the stem of his pipe and slapped his thigh. "Doggonnit, you might have somethin' there! How would you go about findin' out somethin' like that?"

Bo shook his head. "I don't know. There's no telegraph line here, so I can't wire the authorities in New Mexico Territory and Colorado to ask them about Judson's gang. I suppose I could write some letters and mail them. I know a few lawmen over there who might be willing to do me a favor."

He didn't mention that some of those lawmen had arrested him and Scratch before finding out that they were really hell on outlaws. Some of the star packers the Texans had crossed paths with still considered them to be worthless, troublemaking saddle tramps, but there were a few Bo thought of as friends.

"Writin' letters and gettin' answers would take a while," Ponderosa said, "but that might be the only way to go about it, all right. You could send the letters in the pouch on the next eastbound stage."

"And guard them myself," Bo said with a chuckle.

"Yeah, you could see to it they got turned over to the postmaster at Cottonwood. Sounds like somethin' that'd be worth doin'."

"I'll write the letters tonight," Bo said with a nod.

Ponderosa regarded him shrewdly. "You're the sort o' fella that likes to get to the bottom o' things, ain't you?"

"Scratch says that I can't abide a mystery. I reckon there's some truth to that."

"I got a feelin' Jared Rutledge is gonna be sorry you ever come to Red Butte."

Bo wondered if Rutledge already felt that way, and if Rutledge was worried enough to send somebody with a rifle into that clump of trees across the street to get rid of a potential problem before it developed.

It was an interesting question, and one that Bo intended to answer before he and Scratch left Red Butte.

CHAPTER 11

Bo was finished mending harness by the middle of the afternoon, and since Scratch was still busy in the house, working on a recalcitrant butter churn now, Bo strolled down the street to Marshal Tom Harding's office. He found the lawman inside, cleaning one of the rifles from the rack on the wall.

"Howdy, Creel," the lawman said with a nod. "I thought maybe you'd left town."

"Why's that?" Bo asked as he perched his hip on a corner of the desk.

"Hasn't been any general mayhem so far today."

Bo smiled. "Contrary to what you might think, Marshal, sometimes Scratch and I visit a town where nobody tries to kill us at all."

"What town would that be?"

Bo thumbed back his hat and chuckled, then said, "I was wondering what you could tell me about Rance Judson."

"Judson? Why? Are you thinkin' about going after the bounty on his head?"

"I had more in mind keeping him from attacking any more of Mrs. Sutherland's stagecoaches."

Harding grunted and replaced the rifle in the rack. "Good luck with that. Nobody's been able to corral that son of a buck yet." He turned to the desk and pawed through a welter of papers on it. "I'll do better than tell you about Judson. I'll show you what he looks like."

After a moment, Harding found the paper he was looking for and slapped it faceup on the desk in front of Bo. It was a wanted poster, and staring up from it was a craggy visage with a large, somewhat misshapen nose and a thick black mustache.

"That's Rance Judson," Harding said. "Picture's ugly enough for a mama to use it to scare her kids, ain't it?"

"He's not what you'd call handsome," Bo agreed. "This reward dodger's from New Mexico Territory."

Harding nodded. "Yeah. He's wanted there and in Colorado for bank robbery, rustling, stagecoach holdups, and murder. Him and his boys have been busy."

That information jibed with what Ponderosa Pine had told Bo.

"And now Judson's wanted over here, too."

"Yep. There's five hundred dollars on his head, and two-fifty for any of his men. I expect the amounts will go up every time they pull a job and get away with it."

"Ponderosa was telling me that Judson was identified by several people who saw him without his mask while he was carrying out crimes."

Harding sat down behind the desk and waved a hand dismissively. "Judson doesn't care about things like that. He's proud of being an outlaw. Always has been. I've read newspaper accounts of some of the holdups he was responsible for over around Taos and Santa Fe, and he didn't always wear a mask there either. So it's nothing new. Why do you find that interestin', Creel?"

"Just trying to find out as much about him as I can," Bo said with a shake of his head. "Sounds like a proud man. Arrogant even."

"I'd say that's true."

"You know anything about the other members of his gang?"

"Not really. I imagine they're just typical hardcases and gunnies."

Bo nodded. "But they're good at giving the slip to the law. The county sheriff took a posse after them, didn't he?"

Harding hitched his chair forward and said, "Yeah, but he didn't have any luck. You head north on the other side of Hell Creek and it's nothing but badlands all the way to the Verde River. Get in that mess of gullies and buttes and a man could wander around for days without finding his way out. Probably die of thirst if he was lucky, starve to death if he wasn't. Nobody knows much about it except a few stubborn old desert rats who spent years lookin' for gold in there without ever findin' any."

"It sounds like Judson knows his way around the badlands all right, if he's able to hide out and lose posses in there."

Harding shrugged. "I guess that's true enough. Wouldn't surprise me, though, if one of those old prospectors was a member of his gang. Fella could've given up huntin' for gold and decided to steal it instead."

That made sense to Bo. It was certainly a possibility.

He didn't really care *how* Judson had been able to locate a hideout in the badlands, though, only that the boss outlaw had done so.

It would go a long way toward solving Abigail Sutherland's problems if somebody could find that hideout and lead the law to it, he thought.

"North of Hell Creek, you say?"

"Yeah." Harding lifted a finger. "Now listen, Creel. If you go poking around up in the badlands, you'll be puttin' your life in danger, and I can't help you. My jurisdiction runs out at the edge of town."

"You've given me all the help I wanted, Marshal," Bo said. He straightened from casually leaning on the desk and nodded to Harding. "Be seeing you."

The lawman blew out his breath in a frustrated sigh and returned Bo's nod without saying anything.

Bo left the marshal's office and walked back toward the edge of town and the stage line headquarters. He found Scratch sitting in one of the rockers on the front porch, smoking a quirly.

"Wondered where you'd gotten off to," Scratch said.

Bo took the other rocker and replied, "I was talking to the marshal."

"What about?"

"Rance Judson."

"Find out anything?"

"That there's a five-hundred-dollar reward for him over in New Mexico Territory. Add up all the bounties on his head in various places and it probably comes to a pretty good amount."

Scratch frowned. "We ain't bounty hunters, though."

"No, but I was thinking that if we collected those rewards, we could buy ourselves enough supplies to last for a good long time and give the rest of it to Mrs. Sutherland to help keep her business going. And of course, it would be a good thing for the stage line if Judson and his gang were behind bars where they belong."

"Or dead," Scratch said.

Bo nodded slightly to acknowledge the validity of that point.

"So, are we goin' after the varmint?"

"Not right away. We've got that run to Chino Valley and Cottonwood to make in a couple of days, plus whatever else Mrs. Sutherland needs us to do. But I figure we'll be around here for a while, so there might be a chance to take a *pasear* up to the badlands and have a look around."

Scratch grinned. "I like the way you think, old hoss. We ain't had us a good tussle with a bunch o' outlaws in a long time."

"Yeah, it's been a few months since we came near to getting our danged fool heads shot off," Bo said dryly.

"Say whatever you want, pard, at least life don't get borin' very often around us."

"I could use a little more boredom."

"You lie, Bo Creel."

Bo grinned. "Yeah, I guess I do."

They hadn't seen much of Gil during the day, and nothing of Dave. According to Ponderosa, that was nothing uncommon, at least where Dave not being around was concerned.

"He'll come draggin' in late tonight, drunk as a skunk," Ponderosa predicted. "And that'll give Gil one more thing to pick at him about."

Supper was fried chicken, and it was just as good as the roast beef the night before. Abigail and Gil seemed to have gotten over their argument that morning, or at least if they hadn't, they didn't mention it. The fact that Dave wasn't there, also not mentioned, hung in the air like the ominous feeling before a thunderstorm.

"Ponderosa tells me that you did an excellent job with the harness, Bo," Abigail said after a while. "And I know you did fine with the chores I gave you, Scratch."

"I was glad to do it, ma'am," Scratch said. "Anything else you have that needs doin', you just let me know."

"Well . . . the corral fence isn't in very good shape. Maybe tomorrow both of you could see what you can do with it."

Bo nodded. "Of course. Be glad to."

"Good thing you fellas came along," Ponderosa said. "Place is startin' to shape up again."

Gil didn't look too pleased at the praise being heaped on the heads of the Texans, but he didn't say anything. After supper, he took a lantern and went out to the barn for another look at the horses, he said. Bo figured he was actually going out there to sulk.

After clearing away the dishes, Bo and Scratch didn't step out onto the porch to smoke, as they had the night before. Whoever had taken those shots at them was still out there somewhere, and when somebody wanted to kill you, it made sense not to make the chore any easier for him. Instead, they sat with Ponderosa in the office, the old-timer behind the desk on which a lamp burned and the two Texans on the leather-covered sofa.

Bo went over what he had learned from Marshal Harding, then asked, "How much do you know about the badlands, Ponderosa?"

"Not a blasted thing except that it's smart to stay out o' there. I ain't one o' those desert rats the marshal told you about. Never wasted a single day o' my life prospectin' for gold. For ninety-nine outta every hundred men who try it, it's a fool's errand. Always had better things to do with my time."

"Do you know anybody else in Red Butte who might be familiar with that part of the country?"

Ponderosa scowled in thought and scratched at his whiskers with his good hand. "You might talk to old Hezikiah," he said after a moment. "I've heard that he did some prospectin' up in that hellhole when he was younger. Don't go thinkin' he could help you look for Judson's hideout, though. He had a bad spell of apoplexy here a while back and can't get around no more. He can still talk, though."

Bo nodded. "Where can I find him?"

"His boy runs the general store. Ol' Hez is there most days, sittin' by the pickle barrel."

"Maybe we'll have a talk with him."

Before Bo could say anything else, footsteps sounded on the porch. Someone knocked on the door. Even though it was unlikely that a would-be killer would just walk up and knock like that, both Bo and Scratch moved their hands closer to their guns as they stood up and turned toward the door.

"Who's there?" Ponderosa called. "The office is closed!"

"I know," a man's voice replied. "It's Dr. Chambers."

Ponderosa looked surprised. He pushed himself to his feet and went over to the door, opening it to admit the local sawbones. "Somethin' wrong, Doc?" he asked. "Nobody sick here, as far as I know."

"Well, I thought I'd check on that wound of yours while I'm here, but that's not the real reason I came," Chambers said. He was a small, neatly dressed, middle-aged man with a salt-and-pepper goatee. He looked at Bo and Scratch and went on. "You must be those Texans I've heard so much about."

"We're from Texas, all right," Scratch said. "We've sent a little work your way, too."

"Yes, I know." Chambers turned back to Ponderosa. "Is Gil here?"

"Out back in the barn, I reckon," the old-timer replied with a jerk of his head. "You need to see him?"

112

"I just thought someone should let him know that Dave is about to get into trouble down at Sharkey's. He's trying to pick a fight with some of Jared Rutledge's men."

"Aw, hell!" Ponderosa exclaimed. "Don't that boy have any sense at all?"

"It looked to me like he'd been drinking," Chambers said. "I don't know for certain what's going on, though. I just heard a commotion in there as I was passing by and looked through the door. Dave was jawing at a couple of Rutledge's men."

"Were Dave's friends with him?" Bo asked.

"Tall drink o' water called Angus and a fella named Culley who's about as wide as he is tall," Scratch added.

Chambers nodded. "Yes, I know who you're talking about, but I didn't see either of them. Dave appeared to be by himself."

"I'll go tell Gil," Ponderosa said. "I'm afraid I know what he's gonna say, though. He'll say if Dave got himself in a mess, it's his own damned fault and it's up to him to get himself out of it."

Bo lifted a hand and said, "Hold on," as Ponderosa turned to leave the office. "Scratch and I will go down there and see what we can do. There's no need to say anything to Gil."

"Or to Miz Abigail," Scratch said. "It'd just worry her."

"You're sure?" Ponderosa asked with a frown.

The drifters were already reaching for their hats. "We're sure," Bo said.

They left the stage line headquarters, walking quickly along the darkened street toward the main part of the settlement and Sharkey's Saloon. Scratch said, "I'm startin' to think this whole family attracts trouble just like we do, Bo."

"It's beginning to look like it," Bo agreed. He hoped that they reached the saloon before Dave got himself into too big of a mess.

That hope appeared to be dashed, though, because they were still about twenty yards from the batwinged entrance to Sharkey's when shots suddenly erupted from inside the place.

CHAPTER 12

Bo and Scratch broke into a run that carried them quickly to the saloon. Bo was first through the door, slapping the batwings aside. Scratch was right behind him. Bo went right, Scratch went left, putting some distance between them in case they were running into a gunfight.

But the shots had stopped after that initial burst of three or four. Dave Sutherland stood with his back to the Texans, stiff and straight. He had a gun in his hand, and it was leveled at two men who also had drawn their weapons and pointed them at Dave.

Everybody else in the saloon had cleared out from around them, and the bartender, Claremont, was hunkered behind the bar, peeking over the hardwood with wide, frightened eyes.

Dave didn't turn around when Bo and Scratch burst into the saloon. He couldn't afford to take his eyes off the men he was facing. If he did, they would probably open fire on him again, and this time they'd be likely to ventilate him.

Bo and Scratch knew what had happened here almost immediately. Nobody was lying dead in the sawdust, and it even appeared that no blood had been spilled. When angry men who had been drinking slapped leather, it wasn't uncommon for all the shots to miss their targets. Powder could be burned and lead flung, but nobody was hit because of poor, hurried aim and whiskey-blurred vision. That seemed to be the case here.

The men facing Dave were two of the hardcases who had been with Jared Rutledge the night before, Bo and Scratch realized. There was no telling what had started the fight, but likely it had something to do with the hostility between Rutledge and Abigail Sutherland, although the Texans were a little surprised that Dave would take up for his mother. So far, he hadn't really seemed to care all that much about his family.

What was important now was defusing the situation before somebody was hurt—or killed. Bo said, "Why don't you fellas all put those guns down? There's been enough shooting."

"Get out of here, Creel," Dave snapped. "This is my business."

"Not hardly it ain't," Scratch said. "We work for

your ma, and we don't want to see her cryin' over your hide when it's got three or four bullet holes in it."

It took an effort for him not to say "worthless hide" instead, but he managed not to.

"You old codgers get out of here," one of Rutledge's men said. "This is between us and the kid."

Bo shook his head. Neither he nor Scratch had pulled iron, but their hands hovered near the weapons, ready to hook and draw.

"If you figure on dealing again," Bo said, "we'll be taking a hand in the game."

The tension in the saloon stretched until it felt like something was about to snap. Bo and Scratch had experienced that sensation many times before. It was usually followed by the roar of guns.

This time, though, the moment was broken by the arrival of Marshal Tom Harding, who shouldered through the batwings with a shotgun in his hands. He barked, "All right, damn it, everybody freeze!"

That struck Scratch as a little funny. He chuckled and said, "Nobody's movin', Marshal."

"You know what I mean," Harding said, sounding a little flustered now. He tried to regain control of the situation by saying, "Dave, put that gun down! Hitchens, Rawley, you, too! I'll throw the whole lot of you in jail if you don't holster those irons!"

Slowly, Rutledge's men began to lower their weapons. Dave followed suit, but not until the other two men had moved first. Bo and Scratch relaxed a little but remained watchful. Rutledge's gunnies might be trying to pull some sort of trick.

That wasn't the case. They actually holstered their guns, and so did Dave. Marshal Harding circled around to the side so that he could cover all three of them easier and demanded, "All right, what happened here? I heard shots."

"That kid's crazy!" one of Rutledge's men said. "He came in here on the prod and started in on Rawley and me!"

"That's not true," Dave protested. "I just wanted to have a drink in peace. They're the ones who picked the fight."

Harding heaved a sigh. "This is gettin' to be a habit, and I don't like it." He glanced at Bo and Scratch. "And I should've known you two would be mixed up in it, too."

Bo shook his head. "We didn't get here until after the shooting started, Marshal. We came in and found the three of them holding guns on each other."

Scratch added, "Looked like they did some blazin' away at each other but didn't hit much of anything."

From behind the bar, Claremont said, "That's not true! A couple of bottles of good whiskey got broken, and there's a hole in the front wall. It's just luck the window didn't get busted!"

Bo sniffed. Now that Claremont mentioned it, the smell of spilled rotgut was indeed a little stronger than usual. He hadn't noticed it first because of the tang of gunpowder in the air.

"Are you tellin' a straight story this time, Claremont?" Harding asked.

If the bartender noticed the marshal's sarcasm, he gave no sign of it. He nodded and said, "I sure am."

"Who started the fight?"

"I couldn't tell you that. I was down at the other end of the bar. All I know is that all three of 'em were jawing away at each other and getting pretty loud about it. Then, before you know, they were grabbing for their guns and everybody else scattered and hunted for some cover. I got down behind the bar myself."

"What was the fight about?"

Claremont snorted. "What's it always about? The Sutherlands just don't get along with Mr. Rutledge and his men. I don't reckon Dave is any different from the rest of the family."

"All right, I've heard enough," Harding declared. He motioned with the Greener's twin barrels. "Creel, Morton, take their guns."

Scratch looked at the marshal in surprise. "What?"

"You heard me. Get their guns while I cover 'em. All three of 'em are gonna spend the night in jail for disturbin' the peace and dischargin' a firearm in town."

"Marshal, we're not your deputies," Bo pointed out.

"I know that, damn it, but I got a right to ask the citizens for assistance in performin' my duties as a lawman, don't I? Now get the blasted guns!"

Hitchens took a step backward. "Nobody takes my gun," he growled.

"Well, then, I'll just blow you in half instead,"

Harding said. "Rawley's standin' close enough to you that the buckshot'll probably kill him, too, or at least hurt him mighty bad. But it's your decision, Hitchens."

"For God's sake, Hitch!" Rawley said, unable to keep the fear out of his voice. "Turn over your gun, man!"

Hitchens grimaced and hesitated, but finally he jerked his head in a nod and said in a low, angry voice, "All right."

Harding looked at Bo and Scratch. "Well?"

Bo stepped forward, coming alongside Dave. He held out his hand and said quietly, "Give me your gun, Dave."

"Take it," the young man replied with a sneer.

Bo plucked the revolver from its holster. Meanwhile, Scratch had advanced to disarm Hitchens and Rawley, watching the two hardcases very closely as he did so just in case either of them tried to make some grandstand play.

Neither of them wanted to attempt that with Marshal Harding's shotgun covering them, however, so Scratch was able to take their guns without any trouble. When the three men were disarmed, Harding motioned with the Greener again and ordered, "Head down to the jail. If you try to make a break for it, I'll drop you, sure as hell." To Bo and Scratch he added, "Creel, Morton, you come along, too, and bring those guns."

Dave gave a disgusted snort and led the procession

out of the saloon and down the street toward the squat adobe building that housed the marshal's office and a small cell block in the rear. Hitchens and Rawley came next, then Harding, and finally Bo and Scratch. Men who had been in the saloon for the futile gunfight came out onto the boardwalk to watch the prisoners being taken to jail. The few other pedestrians who were still out and about at this hour paused to watch the little parade, too.

The jail had only two cells that faced each other across a short corridor. A stout wooden door with a small barred window in it separated the cell block from Harding's office. The marshal put Dave Sutherland in the right-hand cell, Hitchens and Rawley in the one to the left. He slammed the doors solidly behind them.

"You gonna keep us in here all night?" Hitchens asked.

"Damn right I am."

"There's only one bunk in this cell!"

Harding gave him a tight, humorless grin. "You can flip a coin to see who gets it and who gets the floor," the marshal said. "Now settle down. You cause a ruckus back here, I'll get a bucket of water and throw it on you, just like I would a dog that won't behave."

Dave laughed at that. He stretched out on the bunk in his cell and tipped his hat down over his eyes.

Bo and Scratch watched the exchange from the doorway between the office and the cell block, then stepped back as Harding emerged from the corridor, the shotgun tucked under his arm now. Harding closed and locked the door, then put the shotgun in the wall rack. He turned to Bo and Scratch and gave them a curt nod.

"I'm obliged to you for your help. Just put those guns you took away from 'em on the desk. I'll give them back in the morning when I let those boys out."

"Might be a good idea to release them at different times," Bo advised.

Harding snorted. "You don't need to tell me how to do my job, Creel. I've been the marshal here for eight years. I know what I'm doin'." He sat down behind the desk and went on in a friendlier tone. "I thought I'd probably let Dave go first. Somebody ought to be here to take him down to his ma's place and make sure he gets there all right. His brother maybe."

"We haven't been around here for long," Bo said, "but I can't see Gil doing that. I'm not sure he cares what happens to Dave."

"What time are you plannin' to let him go?" Scratch asked. "We'll be here when you do."

Harding shrugged. "That's all right with me. Around eight o'clock, I guess."

Bo and Scratch nodded. "Does the fact that you're releasing Dave first mean that you think he wasn't to blame for what happened tonight?"

"Not necessarily." Harding shrugged again. "But in my experience, Dave isn't likely to start a fight when he's by himself. It's different when Angus and Culley

121

are with him. They're troublemakers from way back. No, I figure Hitchens and Rawley started in on him, just like Langdon, Simms, and Bartlett did with you fellas last night. Rutledge's men are always lookin' for some way to get at the Sutherlands, short of open war."

"It may come to that," Bo warned.

Harding regarded him and Scratch warily and said, "I know, now that you two have signed on with the Sutherlands. Before you came to Red Butte, Abigail didn't really have any way to fight back. Gil's no gunfighter, and neither is Dave. Ponderosa Pine has plenty of sand, but he's old."

Scratch chuckled. "So are we."

"There's a difference," Harding said, "and you know it."

There was nothing to say to that. After a moment Bo said, "We'll be here at eight o'clock in the morning to take charge of Dave . . . if he'll let us."

Harding nodded. "Fine."

The Texans turned toward the door of the office, which opened at that moment to let Jared Rutledge stalk in angrily. "I hear you've got two of my men locked up, Marshal," he said without preamble.

"That's right. Hitchens and Rawley are back there in the cell block, charged with disturbin' the peace and firin' off their guns."

Rutledge put a hand in his pocket. "I'll pay whatever fines are against them—"

Harding held up a hand to stop him. "There ain't any

fines against them. They're spendin' the night behind bars. That's it."

"They were supposed to take a freight wagon to Cottonwood for me tomorrow morning," Rutledge said with a frown.

"They'll be released from custody at nine o'clock. What they do after that is none of my business, as long as they don't break the law again."

"I'm not sure they'll feel like making that trip after spending the night in jail."

"Send somebody else, then" Harding said. "That's your lookout, Mr. Rutledge, not mine."

"Damn it, I'm short-handed already because of what these two drifters did last night," Rutledge burst out, flinging a hand toward Bo and Scratch, "and you didn't lock *them* up!"

"They didn't try to shoot up Sharkey's place."

"What about Dave Sutherland? I'm told that he was there, too, and that he started the fight!"

"I don't know who started it, but Dave was part of it, so he's locked up for the night, too." Harding folded his hands together over his belly as he leaned back in his chair. "I try to be fair in enforcin' the law."

Rutledge didn't like it, but after a moment he nodded and said, "Nine o'clock?"

"That's right."

"I'll be here to see that it's not a minute later."

"You do that, Mr. Rutledge," Harding said.

After Rutledge was gone, Bo said, "You're coming pretty close to making an enemy of that man, Marshal."

"I know it. I don't like it, but I can't help it either. I swore to uphold the law and keep the peace here in town. Rutledge is the one who keeps pushin'."

"Maybe so," said Scratch, "but if it comes to a showdown, who will the citizens support, you or the man who brings in all their supplies?"

Harding shook his head and sighed. "I hope I never have to find out."

CHAPTER 13

Ponderosa was waiting on the front porch of the stage line headquarters when Bo and Scratch got back there a short time later. He came down the steps to meet them and said, "I heard shootin' a while ago. Where's Dave?"

"In jail," Scratch replied.

"But he's all right," Bo said. "He and a couple of Rutledge's men got in a fight, but no one was hurt. Marshal Harding locked all of them up for the night."

"Who'd the boy tangle with?" Ponderosa asked.

"Some fellas named Hitchens and Rawley."

Ponderosa let out a low whistle of surprise. "Dave's mighty lucky not to be dead. Those two are fast on the draw."

"Fast ain't the same as good," Scratch said. "It don't matter how quick you can get your gun out if you can't hit what you're shootin' at."

"They'd all been drinking, too," Bo said. "Still, I agree with you, Ponderosa . . . Dave's lucky."

"But his luck may not last if he keeps on gettin' into trouble," Scratch said.

Ponderosa nodded. "I know, I know. Guess I better go in and tell Miz Abigail what happened. She's already a heap worried."

"I thought you weren't going to say anything to her," Bo said.

"I couldn't help it. She heard Doc Chambers talkin' and wanted to know what he was doin' here at this time o' night. I never have been able to lie to a woman, 'specially that one."

"What about Gil?" Bo asked. "Does he know?"

"He came in and heard about it, too."

"But he didn't come to find out what had happened to Dave."

Ponderosa shook his head. "Nope. He sure didn't."

It was a damned shame the way families fractured sometimes. Neither Bo nor Scratch could even imagine an hombre being so unconcerned about the fate of his own brother. It went both ways, though. Dave didn't seem to care what happened to the stage line.

The three men went into the office and found Abigail sitting tensely at the desk. Before she could say anything, Ponderosa told her, "Dave's all right. He got in a ruckus with a couple o' Rutledge's men, but nobody was hurt. The marshal locked 'em all up, though."

"Dave is in jail?" Abigail said.

"That's right, ma'am," Bo said.

Abigail started to get to her feet. "I should go see him . . ."

Scratch held up a hand to stop her. "No need for that, Miz Abigail. Bo and me were just there, and he's fine. He was stretched out on the bunk in one o' the cells, and he's probably asleep by now."

"Because he'd been drinking again," she said.

"They all had been," Bo said. "That probably helped start the fight."

Abigail shook her head. "It would have happened anyway. Bad luck has been following this family around ever since my husband got sick and died." She sank back in the chair and covered her face with her hands.

Bo and Scratch glanced at each other. They wanted to comfort her somehow, but neither man felt comfortable going to her, since they had known her for such a short time.

Ponderosa took care of it. He walked around the desk and gave her an awkward pat on the shoulder with his good hand. "Aw, now, Miz Abigail," he said, "there ain't no need to carry on so. Your family ain't jinxed. Ever'body runs into a string o' bad luck now and then. I'll bet yours is just about over."

Scratch was emboldened to say, "I'd like to think that Bo and me changed your luck for the better when we rode in, ma'am."

Abigail lowered her hands, wiped away the tears that had appeared in her eyes, and said, "I'd like to think so, too, Scratch . . . but so far things haven't worked out that way, have they?"

126

"Give it time, ma'am," Bo advised. "Scratch and I told Marshal Harding that we'd be at the jail in the morning when Dave is released. We'll have a talk with him and bring him back here."

Abigail managed to smile. "I don't think talking will do any good, but I'll appreciate the effort anyway, Bo." She got to her feet. "Now, if you'll excuse me, I think I'll turn in. It's been a long, trying day as usual."

She retreated to the family's living quarters. Bo, Scratch, and Ponderosa headed for the barn. The old-timer asked, "Are you really gonna have a talk with Dave?"

"I plan to try to," Bo said. "Somebody needs to talk some sense into him."

"Better take a two-by-four with you."

"Why?"

"Because that boy's just like a mule," Ponderosa said. "You'll have to whack him in the head with it a few times just to get him to pay any attention to you."

Despite Ponderosa's advice, neither Bo nor Scratch was carrying a two-by-four when they walked down the street to the marshal's office the next morning. They'd had breakfast at the stagecoach station a short time earlier. Abigail was still upset and worried, but had her emotions under better control than they had been the night before. Gil was flatly dismissive of his brother's problems.

"You can let him rot in jail for all I care," he had told Bo and Scratch.

Now, as they approached Harding's office, Scratch said, "If you ask me, Gil needs that wallop upside the head just as much as Dave does."

"Yeah, Abigail's got her hands full with those two," Bo agreed. "When I stop and think about it, though, some of the worst fights I've ever seen have been between brothers, so I guess it's not too much of a surprise that Gil and Dave don't get along."

"Yeah, but even when brothers don't get along, they'll usually close ranks against outsiders who cause trouble for their family."

"Usually," Bo said, "but not always."

They stepped up onto the boardwalk in front of Harding's office and went inside. The marshal was behind his desk. Tendrils of steam rose from the coffee cup in front of him. He picked it up, gave Bo and Scratch a nod of greeting, and took a sip.

"More coffee in the pot on the stove, if you'd like a cup," he offered.

Bo shook his head. "No, thanks. Prisoners give you any trouble during the night?"

"Well . . . Dave didn't. He mostly slept, I think. Hitchens and Rawley kept bitchin' until I had to threaten 'em with a bucket again, and then they settled down, too. Ain't heard a peep outta any of 'em so far this mornin'."

Harding took another drink of coffee, then set the cup down and stood up. He took a ring of keys from a nail in the wall and unlocked the cell block door. As he swung the door open, Hitchens called from the left-hand cell, "Hey, when do we get something to eat?"

"I don't recall sayin' anything about feedin' you," Harding replied.

"That ain't fair," Rawley protested. "You can't lock us up and then starve us."

"Don't worry, you'll be out before you starve. If you get a little hungry between now and then, it won't kill you." Harding went to the door of the right-hand cell and thrust a key into the lock. "On your feet, Dave."

Inside the cell, Dave Sutherland was sitting on the bunk, holding his hat in one hand and raking the fingers of the other through his tousled brown hair. He winced every time someone spoke, a sure sign of a wicked hangover. After rubbing his temples for a second as if they were pounding, he stood up shakily and said, "Could you tone it down a mite, Marshal?"

"Head hurting, eh?" Harding asked in a deliberately booming voice. "You're lucky that's all that hurts. You idiots could've plugged each other. Worse, you could've ventilated some innocent bystander with those stray bullets." The marshal swung the door open. "I talked to Ed Sharkey last night. It's gonna cost him two dollars to get that bullet hole patched in his wall, and he claims those two bottles of whiskey that got broken were full and worth a dollar apiece. I'm not sure he's tellin' the truth about that, so all I'm gonna collect from you in the way o' damages is one dollar, Dave. Pony it up."

Dave found a dollar coin in his pocket and slapped

it in Harding's outstretched palm as he shuffled out of the cell.

"Hey, we're next!" Hitchens yelped as the marshal turned back to the office without unlocking the door of the other cell.

Harding shook his head. "Nope, your release papers ain't been processed yet. It'll still be a while before you get out of here."

"Release papers! You didn't have no release papers for Sutherland!" Hitchens gripped the bars of the door tightly and shoved his flushed, furious face up close to them.

"You might as well sit down and shut up," Harding snapped. "You'll get out of here when I'm good and ready to let you out, not before!"

"You're gonna be sorry for treatin' us like this, Marshal," Rawley warned from where he sat on the bunk. "You won't get away with it. Mr. Rutledge'll see to that."

"If Jared Rutledge has a problem with the way I do my job, he can take it up with the town council. I work for them."

"Maybe that's just what he'll do!" Hitchens shouted as Harding left the cell block. The heavy wooden door slammed shut behind him.

That made Dave wince in pain, too. Ever so carefully, he settled his hat on his head.

Harding hung the keys back on the ring and then opened a drawer in the desk. He took out a revolver and handed it to Dave.

"Here you go. It's unloaded." Harding fished some bullets out of the drawer and handed them to Dave as well. "You'd be smart to leave it that way for a while. Less chance of you getting yourself killed that way."

Defiantly, Dave thumbed the cartridges back into the Colt's cylinder before he holstered the weapon. "Am I free to go?" he asked in a surly voice.

"Yeah. Creel and Morton came by to make sure you get back to your ma's place all right."

Dave glanced at Bo and Scratch. "I don't need no damn nursemaids," he said. "Especially not a couple of ancient ones."

"Now listen here," Harding said. "I don't want any more trouble between you and Rutledge's bunch. You go with Creel and Morton and stay away from Sharkey's. Steer clear of Rutledge's freight yard, too."

"You can't tell me what to do as long as I'm not breaking the law, Marshal."

Scratch said, "Maybe not, but I can turn you over my knee and give you a paddlin', boy, if you want to act like a spoiled little brat."

Dave's face flushed as he took a step toward Scratch. "Nobody talks to me like that—"

Bo moved between them. "Take it easy, kid. Why don't you show some sense for a change? You may not realize it, but we're on your side."

"The hell you say. You work for my mother."

"That ought to be pretty much the same thing," Scratch said.

"Ought to be doesn't mean it is."

Dave turned and started toward the door.

"See you later, Marshal," Bo said over his shoulder as he and Scratch followed the young man out.

Dave stalked stiff-legged down the street, clearly still angry. Bo and Scratch followed. For a second, it appeared that Dave was going to stop at Sharkey's, which was open despite the early hour, but then he wiped the back of his hand across his mouth and went on.

"He was thinkin' about a little hair o' the dog what bit him," Scratch said to Bo in a low voice.

"Yeah," Bo agreed, "but he decided against it. Maybe that's a good sign."

Abigail and Ponderosa were on the front porch of the stage line headquarters, watching Bo and Scratch approach with Dave. Abigail couldn't stand it and came down the steps to greet her son. Dave didn't pull away when she hugged him.

"Are you all right?" she asked as she stepped back to look him over.

"I'm fine," he answered. "I just spent a night in jail, that's all. And I'm hungover."

"Come on inside. There's some breakfast left . . ."

Dave grimaced. "I'm not very hungry, Ma. But I could use a cup of coffee."

They went into the building. Ponderosa lingered on the porch and asked Bo and Scratch, "How'd that talk you were gonna have with the boy go?"

"We never really got a chance to talk to him," Bo said.

"Marshal Harding had a few choice words for him, though," Scratch put in. "They didn't seem to take."

Ponderosa sighed. "I was afraid o' that. Dave's at the age when he don't want to listen to anybody, especially somebody who's tryin' to talk sense to him."

"Where's Gil?" Bo asked.

"Don't know. He left a while ago, said he had better things to do than hang around here and watch his ma fawn over her no-account son. He's probably around town somewhere."

"Sounds like a mighty bitter young man."

"Yeah. He wasn't like that before Will died. Oh, him an' Dave didn't get along too well even then, but it was different. Losin' his pa hit Gil mighty hard."

Scratch thumbed his hat back on his head. "Wonder what chores Miz Abigail needs us to do today."

"Nothin', far as I know," Ponderosa replied. "You fellas got so much accomplished yesterday, you're plumb outta chores for today. Reckon you can just take it easy and rest up for that stage run tomorrow. Coach is scheduled to roll out at nine o'clock."

Scratch looked over at Bo. "You want to handle the team or ride shotgun?"

"I don't reckon it matters to me."

"I'll take the guard's job then," Scratch said with a grin. "More fun for me that way if those owlhoots try to jump us again."

The Texans were taking it easy and smoking in the rocking chairs on the front porch a short time later when the sound of hoofbeats from somewhere out back caught their attention. They stood up and went to the edge of the porch, looking around the corner of the building in time to see a mounted figure riding in the direction of the red sandstone butte that loomed over the settlement.

"That looks like Dave ridin' off," Scratch said.

Bo took his pipe out of his mouth and nodded. "It *is* Dave. I wonder where he's going. As far as I know, there's not much in that direction, once you get around the butte."

Scratch ground out the butt of his quirly under his boot heel and said, "I reckon there's one way to find out."

"You mean we should follow him?"

"Don't have anything else to do today, do we?"

"No," said Bo, "I reckon we don't."

"And I know how bein' curious about something just eats away at you."

Bo knocked out the dottle from his pipe on the porch railing. "Let's saddle up and ride," he said.

CHAPTER 14

They managed to get their horses ready to ride without Ponderosa or Abigail seeing what they were doing. That was good, because they didn't want to worry Abigail any more than she already was where Dave was concerned, and Ponderosa would have been inquisitive. The old-timer might have even insisted on going with them.

As it was, they were able to swing up into their saddles and send the dun and the bay trotting toward the butte without any delays. Dave was out of sight now, but Bo and Scratch were both experienced trackers. They were confident that they would be able to pick up his sign without much trouble.

That proved to be the case. Dave had skirted the butte to the east and then continued to head almost due north. The fresh hoofprints were like signposts to the eyes of Bo and Scratch. The trail mingled briefly with some other tracks that were a day or two old, but it wasn't hard to pick out the ones made by Dave's horse.

The Texans hung back and were careful not to skyline themselves, just in case Dave was checking his back trail. They didn't have any real reason to think that might be the case; it was more a matter of habit on their part. When you were following an hombre, it was usually a good idea not to let him know you were behind him.

"Where the devil's he headed?" Scratch mused as he and Bo followed Dave's tracks along a sandy wash. "There ain't any settlements in this direction, is there?"

"Nothing this side of Williams, and that's got to be at least forty or fifty miles from here," Bo said. He pointed to the spot where the tracks left the wash. "Anyway, he's starting to veer east now."

"Lord, there's *nothin'* out there!"

"Nothing but the badlands," Bo agreed.

The gray slopes of the Santa Marias and the green ranching country in the foothills were behind them now as they rode east into a broken, arid wasteland. At the edge of it they crossed a narrow stream.

"That's got to be Hell Creek," Bo said. "We're upstream, a good ten miles from where it crosses the stage road between Chino Valley and Red Butte."

"Yeah, the springs that feed it are probably up here somewhere," Scratch said. "I've seen streams rise before in canyons like this."

The ground was harder and rockier now, which made it more difficult to follow Dave's trail. He knew where he was going, but Bo and Scratch didn't have that advantage. Still, their keen eyes were able to make out the occasional hoofprint, the overturned rock, the bright splash on stone where a horseshoe had nicked it. Little things like that told them they were still on the trail.

"You've got an idea what the boy's doin' up here, don't you, Bo?" Scratch asked after a while.

Bo's face was grim as he nodded. "I talked to Marshal Harding about Rance Judson's gang. Their hideout is somewhere in these badlands. The one time that the county sheriff took a posse after them, the trail petered out in here."

"You think Dave's tryin' to hunt down those outlaws?"

"I think Dave is *meeting* those outlaws."

Scratch reined in and looked over at his partner. "You're sayin' that he's one o' the gang?"

"It would explain some things," Bo said.

"Like what? Judson's bunch has held up Miz Abigail's stagecoaches in the past. You can't believe that crazy talk of Rutledge's about her bein' tied up with those owlhoots!"

"Not Abigail, no," Bo said with a shake of his head. "I don't believe she wants anything except to make a success of the stage line that her husband started. But Dave hasn't shown any indication that he gives a damn about the stage line, or about the rest of his family for that matter."

Scratch rasped a thumbnail along his jawline and frowned in thought. "Yeah, that's true, I reckon. He could be workin' with Judson. I liked it better when I thought Rutledge and Judson was mixed up together, though."

"That could still be the case," Bo pointed out, "whether Dave is working with the gang or not."

"Now that don't make any sense at all. What about that shoot-out last night between Dave and those two gunnies who work for Rutledge?"

"Nobody was hurt, were they? The gunfight could've been staged just for show, to make sure everyone in Red Butte is convinced there's no connection between Dave and Rutledge."

Scratch shook his head. "Now you're makin' my brain start to hurt. You got too many folks conspirin' together, Bo. I can't keep all of 'em straight."

"I'm just throwing out ideas," Bo said as he hitched his horse into motion again. "Could be that none of them are right. We'll likely know more when we find out exactly where Dave's going."

"Yeah," Scratch agreed as he got his mount moving again, too.

The trail led through switchback canyons, along dusty arroyos and hogback ridges. At one point Scratch said, "I hope you know your way back outta here, Bo, because I'm plumb turned around."

"We'll get out," Bo said. "If we're still in here when it gets dark, we can steer by the stars."

"Yeah, and fall in a ravine that we don't see until it's too late."

Bo shrugged. "Yeah, there's that chance, too."

They spotted another butte in the distance, shorter and broader than the one that towered over the settlement of Red Butte. Something about it drew Bo's interest, and as he realized that Dave's tracks were leading in the general direction of the butte, he pointed toward it and said, "I think that's where he's headed."

"You reckon the gang's hideout is somewhere around that butte?"

"Formations like that usually have caves in their base, and sometimes tunnels that lead up to the top. A group of well-armed men could stand off a small army from a place like that as long as they had plenty of food, water, and ammunition."

Scratch rubbed his jaw. "Yeah, it'd be about as good as a fort, wouldn't it? We can't just waltz up and ask if Dave's there talkin' to Judson, though."

"No, we'll have to be careful approaching it—" Bo began.

The sudden whipcrack of a shot put a period to his statement. At the same time, a bullet whined between the two riders, missing both of them narrowly.

The Texans had been bushwhacked many times before in their adventurous careers. They knew what to do when somebody started shooting at them. They split up and headed for cover as fast as they could.

At the moment, they were riding up what appeared to be a blind canyon, toward a boulder-littered slope at the far end. Dave Sutherland's tracks led this direction, so Bo and Scratch knew there had to be a way out of the canyon, even though it wasn't apparent yet.

There were clumps of rock along both walls of the canyon, too, so Bo headed right and Scratch yanked his horse around and galloped to the left. More shots rang out. Sand and gravel spurted from the floor of the canyon around the hooves of the running horses as slugs plowed into the ground. Puffs of powder smoke from the rocks at the far end revealed where the riflemen were hidden.

None of the hurried shots found their targets. Bo and Scratch reached the walls of the canyon and left their saddles, dragging Winchesters from saddle boots as they did so. Slaps on the rump sent their horses galloping back around a bend in the canyon, putting them out of the line of fire. Bo crouched behind a boulder, while Scratch took cover behind a small shoulder of rock that jutted out from the left-hand wall of the canyon.

"You hit?" Scratch called across to his trail partner.

"Nope," Bo replied. "How about you?"

"Fine as frog hair!" Scratch thrust the barrel of his rifle around the rock and cranked off three rounds as fast as he could pull the trigger and work the lever, then ducked back as the hidden gunmen returned his fire.

That gave Bo a chance to loose some shots at the bushwhackers. He sent several slugs screaming into the field of boulders that littered the slope at the end of the canyon. The shots echoed back, along with the vicious whine of ricocheting bullets.

"Think I heard somebody yell," Bo called to Scratch as he lowered himself into a crouch again.

"You must'a tagged one of 'em!"

"Or came close enough to make him jump anyway."

Both of the Texans had extra ammunition in their pockets, so they were confident they could put up a good fight, even though they were pinned down here. Eventually, though, their cartridges would run out.

An even bigger danger was the possibility that the bushwhackers might send someone circling around to come up the canyon behind them. Then they would be caught in a cross fire and their chances of getting out of this ambush alive would be reduced to almost nothing. They couldn't afford to wait for that to happen.

"Reckon we should make a run for it?" Scratch asked.

Bo looked back along the canyon the way they had come. It was a good thirty yards to the bend around which the horses had disappeared. To get there, he and Scratch would have to turn their backs to the would-be killers and sprint for safety, gambling that they could reach the bend before the riflemen brought them down.

Bo had taken some mighty big risks at the poker table in the past, but this seemed like a sucker bet. "I don't think we'd stand a chance," he called to Scratch.

"Can't just sit here all day."

"Don't I know it."

Bo's eyes searched for any other possible avenue of escape. After a moment, he spotted something intriguing farther down the canyon. A minute's study convinced him that he might be on to something.

"I'm going to keep those varmints busy for a minute," he told Scratch. "While I'm doing that, take a gander at the rimrock on your side of the canyon, about fifty yards in front of us."

Scratch nodded in understanding. When Bo popped up from behind the boulder a second later and started peppering the rocks where the riflemen were hidden with bullets from his Winchester, Scratch looked around the rock that was giving him cover and gazed at the place Bo had indicated. He saw several large boulders perched rather precariously at the upper edge of the canyon wall.

Return fire from the bushwhackers forced Bo to crouch down again, and Scratch pulled back into cover as well. "You talkin' about those boulders up there, look like they're about ready to fall?"

"That's right," Bo said. "There are some smaller rocks right underneath the one in front. It looks to me like if they were dislodged, the rest of the boulders would come down."

"A rock slide like that would raise a heap o' dust," Scratch mused.

"And give us enough cover we could make a run for it," Bo said. "The problem is, the way the canyon wall juts out, I don't think either of us could hit those rocks from where we are."

"This idea o' yours ain't gonna do us much good then, is it?"

"But you might be able to draw a bead on them if you climbed part of the way up the canyon wall," Bo concluded.

Scratch's eyebrows rose in surprise. He tilted his head back to look up at the stone wall above him. "I ain't a blasted mountain goat!" he exclaimed.

"No, but I see a few footholds and toeholds you could use," Bo said. "I'm not saying it would be easy—"

"Good, because you'd dang near need to be a human fly to go up that wall!"

"But I don't see any other way out for us," Bo went on. "I'd give it a try myself, but I don't have any cover over here except on the ground. That shoulder of rock you're behind goes all the way up the canyon wall."

Scratch grimaced and muttered for several seconds, but finally he sighed and leaned his Winchester against the rocks and dropped his Stetson beside it. "All right, blast it!" he said. "But if I fall off'a this dang rock, it's your fault, Bo Creel!"

Bo just grinned and called, "Good luck."

"I'll need it," Scratch said.

He studied the rock wall for a moment longer, then reached up and grabbed a small place where he could get a good hold. He wedged a boot tip in a little notch and pulled himself up.

Bo continued exchanging shots with the hidden gunmen while Scratch began the slow, laborious climb. Bo wanted to keep the bushwhackers distracted so that maybe they wouldn't notice that Scratch wasn't shooting anymore. Once Scratch had climbed high enough, he would still face the tricky task of dislodging those smaller rocks supporting the larger ones with shots from his revolver. They were almost out of range of a handgun.

Scratch didn't get in a hurry. That could prove to be dangerous when climbing a rock face with no rope or other equipment. He tested each foothold and handhold before he put much weight on it. Slowly he rose five feet, then ten, then fifteen and twenty.

When Scratch was about thirty feet above the canyon floor, Bo called, "Give it a try now!"

If Scratch wasn't high enough yet, their plan would

be revealed anyway—but the try had to be made sometime. Scratch made sure both feet and his left hand had secure holds, then reached down with his right hand and drew the ivory-handled Remington from the holster on that side.

"Be careful the recoil doesn't knock you off!" Bo advised.

"Easy for you to say, mister," Scratch muttered. He took a deep breath, then swung his arm, shoulder, and head around the jutting rock so that he had a clear shot at the target.

His eyes locked instantly on the smaller rocks he had to knock loose. Thrusting the revolver toward them and leaning against the canyon wall, he squeezed off three shots, pausing briefly after each one to be sure of his aim. The bushwhackers saw what he was doing and began firing at him.

Scratch was forced to pull back as bullets whined around his head and smacked into the canyon wall only inches away from him. He didn't have time to see whether or not his shots had had any effect.

Bo could see, though, and he let out a whoop as the large boulder in front of the others perched on the rimrock shifted slightly. "You did it, Scratch!" he shouted. "You did it!"

But then, a second later, the boulder ground to a halt again. It appeared to be as immovable as ever. Bo's spirits fell, and if he had been a man given to cussin', he would have turned the air blue with profanity at that moment.

"Bo!" Scratch said. He had holstered his gun but hadn't started climbing down yet. "What happened?"

"Looks like it didn't work—" Bo began.

That was when the boulder gave another sudden lurch and then plummeted from the rimrock, followed by half a dozen more huge rocks it had been supporting. With a grinding, rolling roar, the boulders slid down the side of the canyon, taking hundreds of smaller rocks with them and creating a large, billowing cloud of dust that filled the canyon from one side to the other.

CHAPTER 15

The dust cloud rolled toward Bo and Scratch, but hadn't reached them yet as Bo ran out from behind the rocks where he had taken cover and Scratch began climbing down the canyon wall. Even though it was more dangerous to do so, Scratch moved faster now, knowing that the time he and Bo had to make their getaway was limited. He swung from handhold to handhold, feeling like a danged monkey as he did so.

Bo heard shots whining through the dust, but knew that the bushwhackers were firing blind now. He and Scratch just had to trust to luck that none of those wild bullets would hit them. Their chances were better this way than any other he had been able to think of.

Running in a crouch, he crossed the canyon and reached the spot where Scratch had left his rifle and hat. Bo had barely grabbed them up when Scratch thudded to the ground beside him, having let go and dropped the last few feet.

"Are you all right?" Bo asked as he thrust the Winchester and Stetson into Scratch's hands.

"That landin' rattled these old bones a mite," Scratch admitted, "but I can still run!"

He proved it by dashing back down the canyon toward the bend that would protect them from the bushwhackers' shots. Bo was right beside him. Another slug ripped through the air between them, but then they reached the bend and careened around it.

If the horses had kept going, the Texans might again be in deep trouble. But fortune still smiled on them. The animals had come a stop only a short distance down the canyon and despite the crash of gunshots nearby, were cropping contentedly at some of the clumps of sparse grass that grew here and there in the rocky canyon floor.

Bo whistled for his horse. The dun lifted its head and moved skittishly a few feet toward him. The bay followed suit when Scratch called out to it. The Texans ran down the canyon to the horses, caught up the reins, and swung into the saddles, sliding the Winchesters into the sheaths as they did so.

"Now where?" Scratch asked.

"Back the way we came!" Bo said.

The chance still existed that they might run into some of the bushwhackers' allies, but there was no other way out of there.

They followed the twisting canyon until it petered out. Bo and Scratch tried to retrace their trail, but it was difficult. Within a short time they were turned around in the maze of gullies, canyons, and ridges. But there seemed to be no pursuit and they didn't run into anybody else who wanted to kill them, so there was that much to be thankful for anyway.

Even if they were lost.

After a while, they reined in and pulled out their bandannas to mop sweat off their faces and the back of their necks. The sun was high overhead, beating down fiercely from its zenith and baking the badlands in its heat.

"You reckon it was some o' Judson's gang that took those shots at us?" Scratch asked.

"That's the only thing that really makes any sense," Bo replied. "I'm more convinced than ever that their hideout is either on top of that butte we saw, or somewhere around it. That canyon must be the only good way to get there, so Judson posted guards in those rocks to take care of anybody who came along and might discover it."

"That means they let Dave Sutherland pass," Scratch said, "because we didn't hear no shots until they opened up on us." His face was grim as he put that together in his mind.

Bo's expression was equally bleak. "Yeah. If there was any doubt that Dave is tied in with the gang somehow, it's gone now, at least as far as I'm concerned."

"Yeah, me, too." Scratch shook his head. "This is gonna just about kill his ma."

"That's why we're not going to tell her."

Scratch's forehead creased in a frown. "Not tell her?" he repeated. "Her own son's workin' with the owlhoots who're about to run her stage line outta business, and we ain't gonna tell her?"

"Not until we know for sure what's going on," Bo said. "I'm not saying that we have to give Dave the benefit of the doubt, because that pretty much went away when those rannies started shooting at us. But I'd still like to hear his side of the story before we say anything to Abigail. In fact, it would be best if Dave himself told her about it."

"Yeah, I guess," Scratch conceded. "One problem, though."

"What's that?"

"We gotta get outta this godforsaken wilderness and back to Red Butte first."

Bo chuckled. "We'll find our way out. We've been in worse places than this."

"Yeah, maybe . . . even though I don't remember when."

They started their horses moving again, making their way through the barren breaks. From time to time, they caught a glimpse of the mountains in the distance, so they had a general idea of the direction in which they were going. As the sun moved from its position directly overhead, that helped, too.

Sometime in the middle of the afternoon, they came

to a tiny trickle of water in the bottom of an arroyo. As they reined in to look at it, Scratch asked, "You reckon that's Hell Creek?"

"More than likely," Bo said, "but I know one way to be pretty sure." He dismounted and hunkered on his heels next to the narrow stream, dipping up some of the water in his hand. He sniffed it, then took a taste and grimaced. "Full of sulfur. That's Hell Creek, all right."

"Then all we have to do is follow it downstream and sooner or later it'll take us out of here."

"That's right," Bo said as he mounted up again.

Following Hell Creek proved to be easier said than done, because in places the stream flowed through clefts in the rock that were too narrow for men and horses. Whenever that happened, Bo and Scratch had to circle around and locate the creek again farther downstream. The stream meandered through the rugged terrain, flowing first one direction and then another, but finally it began veering southwest and then turned almost due south. When it reached that point, the Santa Marias and their foothills were visible again, so Bo and Scratch knew where they were. They could even see in the distance the towering edifice of red sandstone that marked the settlement's location.

After crossing Hell Creek, they stopped and turned in their saddles to look back at where they'd been. "Reckon we could ever find the place again?" Scratch asked.

Bo nodded. "We can find it . . . but maybe we won't

have to. Maybe once Dave realizes that the jig is up, he'll be willing to lead a posse in there."

Scratch snorted. "I'll believe that when I see it."

They hitched their weary horses into a trot that carried them south toward Red Butte.

The guards at the bottom of the tunnel waved Dave past, and the ones at the top didn't stop him either. He didn't like the winding passage through the butte; it always spooked him a little, and it would have been even worse without the lanterns placed in niches carved in the stone walls every now and then to provide some light. For some reason, even though he was going up, it always felt to Dave like he was on a downward slope instead.

A slope into Hell?

He pushed that thought out of his mind as he emerged into the brilliant sunlight atop the butte. He reined in for a moment and squinted until his eyes adjusted to the brightness. Then he jogged forward again, toward the half-dozen adobe cabins that had been built up there sometime far in the past.

Rance Judson and his men hadn't built the jacales. They'd already been here when the outlaws moved in and adopted this place as their hideout. Dave had no idea who was responsible for them. Some of the old Spaniards who had come up here from Mexico seeking gold maybe. There was grass and water atop the butte, enough for the gang's horses, but not enough to support any sort of ranch.

The outlaws had fixed up the abandoned cabins, which had fallen into a state of disrepair, and built a pole corral for their horses from the ruins of a corral that had been there previously. They added thatched-roof *portales* in front of the cabins so that they could sit in the shade and catch some of the breeze that always blew up here. They'd put up an awning to shade the spring as well, so that the water was fairly cool where it flowed out of the rock, even though it did stink of brimstone and taste like it, too.

All in all, it was the best hideout he'd ever seen, according to Rance Judson, and the boss outlaw had seen plenty. If a posse ever came within rifle range, marksmen on the butte's rim could wipe them out with ease.

Judson was waiting under the *portal* in front of his cabin, sitting in a chair he had rocked back against the adobe wall behind him. A cigarillo that looked like a short length of twisted black rope was between his lips. A jug of whiskey sat on the ground beside him, handy for occasional sips when the urge hit him. His dark brown hat was pushed to the back of his head, revealing waves of thick, greasy black hair. His bushy eyebrows sat on a low-slung ridge of bone above his deep-set eyes, and his prominent nose showed the bends and bumps of having been broken several times in the past and set inexpertly. "Ugly" was the first word that sprang to mind whenever anyone looked at Rance Judson, and yet his face had a rugged power to it that was strangely compelling. Ugly or not, he never had any trouble attracting women—whenever there were any women around to attract.

He hadn't brought any out here into the badlands, although it would have been simple enough to ride down to Mexico and fetch back some whores. Judson's reasoning was simple enough: Men who got liquored up whenever there were women around always got into fights over those women. So he'd given his men a choice. They could have whiskey, or they could have whores, but not both.

The outlaws had voted overwhelmingly for whiskey. Time enough for whores when they were all rich men, spending the rest of their lives south of the border, safe from the law.

Lazily, Judson lifted a hand in greeting as Dave reined to a halt in front of the cabin. "Young Sutherland," he said around the cigarillo as Dave dismounted. "What brings you up here?"

"I came to talk to you, Rance." Dave stepped into the shade. "You could've killed my brother the other day."

Judson shrugged. "We were shooting high, just as we agreed."

"Then how did Ponderosa Pine wind up with a bullet through his shoulder?"

"Accidents happen," Judson said with a smile that didn't reach his eyes, which remained coldly reptilian. "Like maybe you *accidentally* led a couple of hombres up here to the hideout."

Dave's eyes widened in surprise. "I didn't lead anybody out here. I kept a close eye on my back trail, just like always."

"Didn't you hear the shooting after you passed through the canyon?"

"Yeah, but I didn't figure it had anything to do with me."

The front legs of Judson's chair thumped against the ground as he sat up straight. He spat out the cigarillo, picked up the jug, took a drink. "Two men rode up that canyon about fifteen minutes after you did. The guards opened fire on 'em, but they got away."

Dave tried to keep the worry he felt from showing on his face. He knew that Judson had set up an elaborate signaling system with mirrors, so that the guards posted all around the hideout could report in any time there was trouble. To an experienced eye, the flashes of light were just as good as electrical signals over a telegraph wire.

"Maybe it was just a couple of riders who happened to come that way," Dave suggested. "They might not have anything to do with me."

"Looked like older gents," Judson said.

"Damn it!" Dave couldn't contain the exclamation. "Creel and Morton!"

Judson nodded. "That's what I figure, too."

"You know about them?" Dave asked with a frown.

"I keep up with what's going on in Red Butte," Judson said. The cryptic answer didn't surprise Dave. He had speculated before now on whether the outlaw leader had spies in the settlement besides him. It seemed clear that that was the case. Judson went on. "Who are they?"

"Just a couple of shiftless saddle tramps. They're the ones who interfered the other day when you were chasing the stage. And then my mother went and hired them to help out with the stagecoach runs."

"I figured as much. They may be old, but they're still gun-handy, aren't they?"

"I don't know." Despite Dave's sullen reply, he *did* know that Creel and Morton could take care of themselves, both with guns and fists. He had seen proof of that with his own eyes.

"They followed you out here," Judson went on, "and they got away from my men. Pretty slick for a couple of old pelicans, if you ask me."

"It won't happen again," Dave promised.

"Damn right it won't. You won't be comin' out here again."

For a moment, Dave felt his guts turn cold with fear. Judson was perfectly capable of shooting him and tossing his body off the butte for the coyotes and the buzzards, and Dave knew it.

But he thought he was still worth something to the outlaws, so he said, "I'll do whatever you tell me, Rance, but I still want to help. Haven't I tipped you off whenever Rutledge's coach was carrying anything worthwhile?"

"I've got other sources of information," Judson said with a casual wave of his hand.

That made Dave think about how his mother always

insisted there was some connection between Rutledge and the outlaws. Was it possible that Rutledge was setting up the robberies of his own stagecoach? That didn't make any sense . . .

Unless Rutledge was splitting the loot with Judson, the same way Dave had gotten a share of the profits from the holdups of the Sutherland stages.

Dave figured he should steer the conversation away from Creel and Morton and the fact that they might have followed him out here. "Look," he said, "we agreed that nobody would be hurt if I helped you hold up our coaches. You already broke your word when Loach and Jenkins were killed a while back." Dave didn't care all that much about the driver and shotgun guard who had been gunned down during one of the robberies, but their deaths had really upset his mother.

Judson uncoiled from the chair like a striking snake. He grabbed the front of Dave's shirt with both hands and hauled the startled young man up on his toes.

"Listen to me, you little pissant," Judson growled. "There's only so much you can do to control the situation when the bullets start to fly. People get hurt. People get killed. That's part of it, you damned fool. You saw what happened at that bank over in Chino Valley."

Dave had seen, all right, and the thought of it still sickened him. That had been one of the jobs where he had gone along as an actual member of the gang, a masked, gun-wielding outlaw just like the others.

But he didn't kill anybody that day. Hell, he didn't

even fire his gun into the air. He had watched in horror, though, as Judson and some of the others had gunned down a couple of innocent men who'd tried to stop them. The killings hadn't been absolutely necessary, but the outlaws hadn't even hesitated.

"You're the one who wanted to work with us," Judson went on. "When we came to you and asked you if you were willin' to help us hold up your ma's stagecoaches, you said yes. You didn't give a damn then, so long as you got your cut, so don't go gettin' on a high horse now. You're an outlaw just like the rest of us. We get caught, you'll hang just like the rest of us. You understand?" Judson gave him a shake.

Dave's head bobbed up and down in a nod. "Y-yeah, sure, Rance," he managed to say. "I . . . I just don't want anything to happen to my brother."

"Should'a thought of that before you decided to betray him and your ma," Judson said with a sneer. He gave Dave a shove that sent the young man stumbling back against one of the posts that held up the thatched roof of the *portal*.

"Sorry, Rance," Dave panted. "I mean it. I'll do whatever you say."

"Then stay in Red Butte until we contact you again. And steer clear of Creel and Morton. I don't trust those two old meddlers."

"I will, Rance. You can count on that."

Judson reached down to the ground, picked up the jug, and took another swig. After he wiped the back of his other hand across his mouth he said, "It shouldn't matter too much anyway. Your ma's coach is goin' out again tomorrow, ain't it?"

"Yeah, first thing in the morning." Dave caught his breath as a realization hit him. "Creel and Morton are taking the run."

"I thought maybe they would be, but I'm glad to hear it." A smile split Judson's face, but didn't make it any less ugly. "Those two old troublemakers won't be comin' back to Red Butte. Not alive anyway."

CHAPTER 16

It was dusk by the time Bo and Scratch got back to the settlement, with shadows gathering in the streets and lamps being lit in the buildings. They hadn't eaten since breakfast, since they hadn't expected to be gone so long and hadn't taken any supplies with them. As Scratch's belly rumbled from hunger, he said, "I'm starvin' here, Bo. My belly thinks my throat's been cut."

Bo laughed. "Well, pretty soon you'll be able to reassure your belly that your throat's just fine."

As they brought their horses to a halt in front of the stage line office, Ponderosa Pine stepped out onto the porch and said, "There you fellas are. Miz Abigail an' me was thinkin' we might have to send out a search party to look for you. Where you been all day?"

"Just taking a look around the countryside," Bo replied. "The time sort of got away from us. We didn't realize it would be so late before we got back."

"We ain't too late for supper, are we?" Scratch asked, a note of desperation creeping into his voice.

Ponderosa threw back his head and laughed. "Naw, don't worry about that. Miz Abigail would'a waited for you anyway, at least for a while."

"Are Gil and Dave here?" Bo asked as he swung down from the saddle.

"Gil is. Ain't seen Dave all day." Ponderosa lowered his voice and glanced behind him, as if to make sure that Abigail wasn't in hearing range. "He's probably dead drunk somewhere, or else holed up in some whore's crib."

"Yeah, I guess," Bo said.

But he and Scratch knew better. Dave hadn't returned to Red Butte yet because he was still out there in the badlands somewhere, rendezvousing with Rance Judson. They didn't know that for a fact, but both Texans were convinced of it anyway.

"Supper'll be on the table in a minute," Ponderosa went on. "Need a hand puttin' your horses up?"

"No, we can take care of them," Bo said. "We'll wash up and be right in."

They led the horses around back to the barn, put them in a couple of empty stalls, unsaddled and rubbed them down, then left them with plenty of grain and water. The day had been a long one, and the dun and the bay were worn out.

Bo and Scratch felt pretty much the same way. A long day in the saddle took more out of them now than it had when they were younger . . . not to mention being shot at and almost killed.

They used the back door when they entered the building this time, which took them in through the kitchen. Abigail Sutherland greeted them with a smile as she stood over the stove, her face flushed a little from the heat. A few tendrils of dark hair had escaped from the bun that was pulled together at the back of her head, and they fell fetchingly around her face. She blew one of them away from her eyes and said, "You boys must be hungry. You've been gone all day."

"Plumb starvin', ma'am," Scratch said.

"Well, go on in the dining room and sit down. We have stew tonight, and it's almost ready."

"Yes, *ma'am!*" Scratch replied with an eager grin.

As they came into the dining room, they saw that Gil Sutherland and Ponderosa were already seated at the table. Gil frowned at them and said, "Where have you two been? I was afraid you'd decided to move on and didn't tell anybody."

"Not hardly," Bo assured him. "We just rode around some, getting familiar with these parts. We're still planning on taking that stage run tomorrow."

Gil grunted. "Good. You'll have a pretty full mail pouch and three passengers."

"Passengers, eh?" Scratch said as he lifted his eyebrows. "That's sorta uncommon these days, ain't it?"

"It's been a while," Gil admitted. "Thatcher Carson and his wife and little boy are headed over to Cottonwood. Mrs. Carson has a sister who lives there, and she's ailing. Mrs. Carson and the little boy are going to stay for a while, and Thatcher wouldn't let them travel alone. So he'll be coming back on the return trip with you."

"We won't get lonely then," Bo said. "What does this fella Carson do?"

"Keeps the books for the Pitchfork Mine. That's the only one of the mines still operating."

"He's a pretty good hombre for a fella who comes from back East," Ponderosa put in. "A lot o' gents in his position would just do their job and then leave when the time comes, but Thatcher moved his wife and boy out here and says he's gonna make Red Butte their home."

Bo nodded. "We'll take good care of him and his family."

Abigail brought in the pot of stew and began filling bowls with the savory, aromatic concoction. She had cornbread to go with it, and as Scratch put it, "Ma'am, this cornbread is so sweet and moist, it pert' near melts in your mouth."

"I'm glad you like it, Scratch. Eat hearty, gentlemen. You'll need your strength for tomorrow. It's a long run to Cottonwood."

Everyone dug in. They were all aware of the empty place that had been set for Dave, but no one mentioned the fact that he wasn't there. Evidently, that was a common enough occurrence that it wasn't remarkable anymore.

After the meal was over and everything had been

cleaned up, Gil sat in the office with Bo and Scratch and went over all the details of the job that awaited them the next day. As far as the Texans could tell, there was nothing unusual about it, other than the potential threat from Rance Judson's gang of outlaws. There hadn't been any Indian trouble in this part of the territory for several years, and the stage road from Red Butte to Chino Valley and then on to Cottonwood was clearly marked and easy enough to follow.

"We've done this sort of work quite a few times in the past, Gil," Bo told the young man. "Don't worry, we can handle it."

"I'll worry until you get back," Gil said with a shake of his head. "Can't help it, with all the trouble that's gone on in recent months. I told my mother I'd take the run myself and let one of you be the shotgun guard, but she insisted that I need the rest."

In truth, Gil looked rather haggard and hollow-eyed. He had taken on a great deal of responsibility after his father's death, and it appeared to be weighing heavily on him.

"Miz Abigail's right," Scratch said. "Just let us do the worryin' for a while."

Gil gave them a faint smile. "I'll try," he said, "but I'm not sure how successful I'm going to be."

When he was satisfied that Bo and Scratch knew what they were doing, the Texans bade him and Abigail good night and walked to the barn to get some rest. Ponderosa was already there, sitting on a three-

161

legged stool and awkwardly trying to pack his old briar pipe one-handed.

"Lemme give you a hand with that, old-timer," Scratch offered.

Ponderosa snorted. "Old-timer, is it? You two ain't no spring chickens your own selves."

"And haven't been for quite a while," Bo agreed as he pulled up another stool and took out his own pipe.

Once Scratch got Ponderosa's pipe going, he rolled a quirly for himself, and the three men sat there smoking quietly for a while, surrounded by the night and the smell of the stable and the small noises made by the horses as they shifted around in their stalls.

Finally, Ponderosa said, "What'd you two fellas really do all day? That business about ridin' around and sightseein' was just a line o' bull."

Bo sighed. "I was afraid you'd see through that, Ponderosa. We rode out to the badlands to see if we could find any sign of Rance Judson's hideout. I'd talked to Marshal Harding about it and knew that Judson and his bunch hole up out there somewhere."

Ponderosa thought about that answer for a moment and seemed to accept it. "You find anything?" he asked.

"Just some o' the ugliest, driest, hottest country this side o' hell," Scratch said. "And I don't mean Hell Creek, 'cause we were on the other side of it."

Ponderosa puffed on his pipe and blew out a cloud of acrid smoke. "What was you plannin' on doin' if you found the hideout?"

"There are a lot of rewards out on Judson and his men," Bo said. "That money would be coming to us if we led the sheriff and a posse out there."

"Yeah, but did you ever stop to think that if you'd found the hideout, Judson and his varmints might try to kill you? What if you'd rode right in on 'em?"

Scratch said, "Don't reckon we'll ever know. We didn't find the blasted place. Did good just to find our way outta that hellhole."

"Damn right. If you'd got lost in there and died o' thirst, it wouldn't have been the first time that happened to some hombres unlucky enough—or dumb enough—to get theirselves in that fix."

Silence reigned again for a while.

Finally, Ponderosa tamped out his pipe and said, "Ah, I'm turnin' in. Mornin's gonna come early, so you fellas better get some sleep, too."

"We will," Bo said. He and Scratch had spread their bedrolls up in the loft. Ponderosa had a cot in the tack room.

The drifters climbed the ladder, took off their boots and gunbelts, and crawled into their soogans. They didn't go to sleep right away, though, and after all these years they were attuned enough to each other's moods to know that. After a while, Scratch said, "I been thinkin'."

"About what?" Bo asked.

"You ever consider settlin' down again?"

Bo didn't answer for a moment. Then he said, "Not really. Oh, the thought crosses my mind now and then, of course, but it never stays around for long. After what happened . . ."

Both of them knew he was talking about the family he had lost in Texas. That was the sort of pain a man shouldn't have to bear more than once in his life, if that.

"I been thinkin'," Scratch said again. "When we come into the kitchen tonight and Abigail was standin' there at the stove . . . well, I don't think I ever saw anything so pretty in all my life, Bo. I got to wonderin' what it would be like to see such a pretty sight ever' day for the rest o' my life."

"I know what you mean. That would be mighty nice, all right."

Scratch turned his head to look in the direction of where Bo lay in the darkness, several feet away. "Dadgummit, you ain't gettin' sweet on her, too, are you? You just said you didn't want to settle down again!"

"I said the thought crosses my mind from time to time, too."

"Well, I seen her first," Scratch muttered.

"I believe we both saw her at the same time."

"I *said* somethin' first!"

"You said something to me," Bo pointed out. "You haven't said anything to Abigail about how you feel, have you?"

"No, but neither have you. I know you ain't, 'cause we been together just about all the time since we rode into Red Butte."

Bo shifted around some in his blankets and said, "Listen, Scratch, I'm not going to fight you over Abigail. For one thing, we've been partners way too long for that, and for another, you've saved my life more times than I can count. Besides, settling down wouldn't ever work out for me. It might be something to dream about every now and then, but that's all." He chuckled. "Anyway, it's not like you need my blessing to court Abigail. You're a grown man and she's a grown woman."

"Yeah. I reckon what I'm really worried about is . . . if I settle down here and help her run this stage line, what're you gonna do?"

"I expect I'll amble on somewhere else after a while, just like we usually do."

"By yourself?"

"I'm a grown man, too, Scratch," Bo pointed out quietly.

Scratch pondered on that for a while, then said in a voice that was finally growing sleepy, "Abigail's got that trouble with Judson and one son who's proddy and another who's maybe crooked. There's an old sayin' about how a fella shouldn't ought to get mixed up with a woman who's got more problems than he does."

"Could be that works the same way from the woman's side," Bo said.

"Yeah, I reckon. Seems fair, don't it? How in the hell do folks ever get together anyway, what with all the trouble in the world?"

"They find a way," Bo said. "One way or another, they find a way."

Scratch's only reply, a moment later, was a quiet snore.

They were up early the next morning. Fortified by a big breakfast and a couple of pots of strong, black coffee, Bo and Scratch got the stage ready to roll, backing the big, strong horses that made up the six-horse hitch into their harnesses. Ponderosa "supervised," watching closely and telling them everything they did wrong, at least to his way of thinking. Bo and Scratch amiably complied with his suggestions.

While they were doing that, Gil walked down to the post office and returned with the mail pouch that contained letters going to Chino Valley, Cottonwood, and all points farther along. He placed it in the boot under the seat, closed and locked the latch.

"Be careful with that," he said as he handed the key to Bo, who tucked it into the pocket of his black coat.

"Don't worry," Bo told Gil, not for the first time. He didn't figure the words would do much good, but he said them anyway.

With that done, Bo climbed onto the seat and drove the coach around the building, swinging it around so that it was facing east and bringing it to a stop in front of the adobe station. It wasn't quite time for the scheduled departure, and the passengers hadn't arrived yet.

Scratch walked through the building and came out

onto the porch carrying not only the shotgun that Ponderosa usually took along on these trips, but also his own Winchester. "Can't have too many guns," he said.

"Better to have 'em and not need 'em than need 'em and not have 'em," Bo quoted, although he had no idea who had originally come up with that bit of wisdom.

Scratch set the rifle and the shotgun on the floorboard, then opened the door on the side of the coach that faced toward the building. Abigail, Gil, and Ponderosa gathered on the porch. Abigail had a hopeful expression on her face this morning, although concern lurked in her eyes, too. Dave never had come home the night before. According to what Ponderosa had told Bo and Scratch, this wasn't the first time that had happened, but it still worried Abigail.

Right now, though, she was smiling as she said, "Here come the Carsons."

Bo and Scratch looked along the street and saw three people approaching. The man wore a gray tweed suit and a hat of a darker gray shade. He was slender and in his thirties, with dark hair and a lean, intelligent face. He carried two valises. His wife was a little younger, a pretty blonde tending toward plumpness. The little boy with them was around eight years old and had inherited his mother's fair hair and good looks. He stared up in awe at the horses and at the two tough-looking Texans.

Scratch gave them a big, charming smile and tugged on the brim of his Stetson. "Mornin', folks," he said in a booming voice. "Ready to hit the trail for Cotton-wood?"

"We certainly are," Thatcher Carson replied. "If you'll show me where to put these bags . . ."

"I'll do better'n that," Scratch said. "Lemme take 'em. I'll put 'em right back here in the rear boot where they'll be safe."

"I hope we'll *all* be safe," Carson said as he handed over the bags. "I don't mind telling you, I'm a little worried about this trip. We wouldn't be taking it if my wife's sister weren't so ill. If those bandits try to hold up the stage—"

"Don't you worry about bandits," Scratch interrupted. "I'm Scratch Morton, and that hombre handlin' the reins is Bo Creel. We been fightin' bandits longer'n you been alive, young fella. We've tussled with owlhoots from the Mississippi to the Pacific Ocean, and from the Rio Grande to the Milk River way up yonder in Montana. We've swapped lead with bank robbers, train robbers, rustlers, renegade Comanch', gunrunners, Mexican *bandidos,* river pirates, and ever' other kind o' no-good varmints you can think of."

Thatcher Carson swallowed hard. "So what you're saying is that the two of you . . . attract trouble?"

From the driver's seat, Bo said, "What my partner there is saying, Mr. Carson, is that we're still here and all those lawbreakers aren't. We'll keep you and your family safe. You have my word on that."

Carson nodded. "Thank you, Mr. Creel. I suppose

that will have to be good enough. Come along, Claire. You, too, Noah."

The little boy was even more awestruck after Scratch's recital. His father had to speak to him again before he finally climbed into the stagecoach after his mother. Carson boarded last, his weight making the coach sway a little on its thoroughbraces as he climbed in.

Scratch slammed the door and hauled himself up onto the box next to Bo. He picked up the shotgun and held it across his knees, at the same time resting a foot on the Winchester's barrel to keep it from sliding around.

Bo reached for the brake lever and released it. "See you tomorrow evening," he called to the three people on the porch as he lifted the reins. Abigail lifted a hand to wave farewell, as did Ponderosa with his uninjured arm. Gil's hands were in his pockets, and he didn't move them, nor did he lose his dour frown.

Bo and Scratch were both grinning in anticipation, though, as Bo called out to the horses and slapped the lines against their backs. The team surged forward, pulling against its harness, and the stagecoach lurched into motion, rolling down the road out of Red Butte.

CHAPTER 17

It had been a while since Bo had driven a stagecoach, but the knack came back to him quickly. It was just a matter of adjusting to the rhythms of the team, knowing when to shout at them, when to slap their backs with the leathers, when to pop the whip above their ears. The rocking of the coach was different from the gait of riding a horse, but within a few miles after leaving Red Butte, it felt as natural as air and water.

The road was crushed caliche in some places, hard-packed dirt in others. The hooves of the team raised dust everywhere, so Bo and Scratch both pulled their bandannas up to cover nose and mouth and keep the dust out.

"We look like *bandidos* our own selves," Scratch commented as the stage rolled along.

"Masked hombres, that's us," Bo agreed.

Inside the coach, Claire Carson and her son Noah rode on the rear seat, facing forward, while Thatcher Carson had the backward-facing seat. They had pulled the shades over the windows to keep out the sun glare and some of the dust, but it was impossible to keep out all the dust. The temperature rose quickly inside the coach, too. Claire smiled bravely, though, whenever her husband looked at her.

"Can I ride up on the driver's seat with Mr. Creel and Mr. Morton?" Noah asked.

"I don't think there's room for you, son," Carson said.

"And it might be dangerous," Claire added.

"Aw, it wouldn't be!" Noah protested. "And I don't take up much room."

Carson shook his head. "We won't hear any more about it, Noah, do you understand?"

The boy subsided, looking down at the floor of the coach and muttering under his breath.

Up top, Scratch turned his head to look behind them at the plume of dust that followed the coach. "Anybody who's lookin' can see that for miles around," he said.

Bo nodded. "I know. But there's no way to avoid it unless I pull these horses back to the slowest walk possible. Then it would take us darned near a week to get to Cottonwood instead of a day."

"Yeah, I reckon. You think anybody's watchin'?"

Bo looked around, feeling the hair prickle a little on the back of his neck. "I wouldn't be a bit surprised," he said.

"Think they'll hit us?"

"Don't know. Could be nothing."

Scratch shook his head. "I'd feel better about this if there wasn't a woman and a kid in there." The easygoing confidence he had displayed earlier had been replaced by a relatively rare show of concern, now that he and Bo were alone here on the driver's box. When it was just the two of them facing trouble, Scratch could laugh in the face of death and usually did. But the responsibility of protecting the Carson family weighed just as heavily on him as it did on Bo.

"Keep your eyes peeled," Bo advised.

Scratch didn't say anything, just gave a curt nod.

Nothing had happened by the time they crossed Hell Creek and reached the first relay station, which was nothing more than a corral, a shed, and an adobe jacal where the hostler lived. The man helped them switch the teams, then the stage rolled on. Scratch pulled his turnip watch from his pocket, flipped it open, and checked the time.

"We're on schedule," he reported. "Ought to make Chino Valley a little after noon, just like we're supposed to. If nothin' happens between here and there, . of course."

"Of course," Bo agreed, his voice as dry as the dusty stage road.

The terrain was flat for the most part, with only the occasional gentle rise. A few buttes and mesas were visible in the distance, both north and south of the road. From time to time, the coach rattled across plank bridges built over dry washes. A greenish-purple line on the horizon far to the east represented the mountains just beyond the Verde River, which curved down from the northwest. Cottonwood was in the foothills, right on the river. The stagecoach would reach it late that afternoon, barring any delays.

Despite the taut-stretched nerves that both Bo and Scratch were experiencing, the next leg of the trip passed without incident, other than meeting a freight wagon headed toward Red Butte. The two men on the box scowled at Bo and Scratch as the two vehicles passed, and even though the Texans didn't recognize the men, they noticed the hostility.

"Those fellas seemed to know who we are," Scratch said.

Bo nodded. "They must work for Rutledge. He's the only one carrying freight into Red Butte as far as I know. They've probably seen us around town, even though we didn't pay any attention to them."

"That'd be my guess," Scratch agreed. "At least they didn't start shootin' at us."

"They wouldn't do that without orders from Rutledge, and I'm guessing that he's not to that point in his war with Abigail . . . yet."

Bo didn't have to elaborate. Both of them knew that if the situation in Red Butte continued to deteriorate, gunplay would break out sooner or later.

The stagecoach reached Chino Valley while the sun was almost directly overhead. It was a small but bustling settlement on the road between Prescott and Williams. The station here was larger, with a barn and corral and an adobe building where passengers could get something to eat and rest for a while. There was even a short bar on one side of the big main room. Scratch eyed it thirstily as they came in, but Bo shook his head. It would be a long, hot afternoon, and they didn't need any whiskey muddling their minds even more than the heat and dust already would.

Several Mexican hostlers worked here, as well as

the station manager. The hostlers would tend to changing the teams. The manager's wife, a stout Mexican woman, had already dished up beans and tortillas for the Carson family, who sat on a bench beside the long table that dominated the room. Bo and Scratch sat down on the other side of the table, and the woman brought plates of food for them.

"Got any chilies?" Scratch asked. "The hotter the weather, the hotter the peppers, I always say."

The woman smiled and nodded. *"Sí, señor. Un momento."*

She came back with a bowl full of stubby green peppers. Scratch picked one up, took a bite off the end, and chewed. His eyes began to water, but he nodded in satisfaction and said, "Mighty good, ma'am. *Gracias.*"

When everyone had eaten, rested for a short time, and then walked around a little to stretch their legs— or in the case of Mrs. Carson, her "limbs"—the passengers boarded the coach again and Bo and Scratch climbed onto the box.

In a low voice, Scratch said, "The way that kid was shovelin' in the beans, I'm glad I'm ridin' up here and not in there. Gonna be a long way to Cottonwood for those folks."

Bo just chuckled and picked up the reins.

A siesta would have been nice, but there was no time for that. The passengers would probably doze off, despite the heat and dust and rocking motion of the coach, but Bo and Scratch had to remain alert. The suspicion that there could be somebody waiting up ahead to ambush the stagecoach and kill them made that fairly easy.

No other passengers had gotten on at Chino Valley, so it was still just the five of them. They would reach another relay station around mid-afternoon, change horses again, and then push on to Cottonwood, arriving there not long before dusk. Bo and Scratch would spend the night at the station there, then start back to Red Butte in the morning. The plan called for Thatcher Carson to go with them, leaving his wife and son in Cottonwood for the time being. He would return for them later, after his sister-in-law's medical crisis had passed.

The mountains were actually visible on the horizon now, not just the line they had been earlier. The landscape was gradually changing. There were more hills, although they were still small and rolling, and the browns and tans and reds of the mostly arid country behind them had begun to shade toward green as the vegetation increased. The arroyos they crossed over now sometimes had a little water in them.

The road still ran mostly straight, curving only to avoid hills and ridges. As the coach approached two such hills, low, rocky prominences flanking the trail to north and south, the prickling sensation on the back of Bo's neck suddenly increased. "I don't like the looks of that up yonder," he said. "Those hills are tailor-made for an ambush. Better get your rifle."

"I was just thinking the same thing," Scratch said as

he bent over to trade the shotgun for the Winchester that still lay on the floorboard at their feet.

Just as Scratch leaned forward, Bo heard the wind-rip of a bullet passing close by, followed instantly by a high-pitched whine as the slug ricocheted off the brass rail that ran around the coach's roof. Reaching for the rifle had saved Scratch's life, because the slug had torn through the space where his head had been a heartbeat earlier.

Scratch heard the bullet, too, and knew what had happened. He snatched up the Winchester and brought it to his shoulder as he straightened. His eyes saw the puff of smoke just above one of the rocks on the hillside to the left. He fired twice in that direction, his hand a blur as it worked the rifle's loading lever between shots.

Meanwhile, Bo hauled back hard on the reins and called out to the horses as he began turning them. Running away from trouble went against the grain for him, but he knew that he would be risking the passengers' lives even more if he plowed ahead stubbornly and tried to race the stagecoach through the gauntlet between those two hills. He suspected that several bushwhackers were hidden up there behind the rocks.

"Wouldn't do that if I was you!" Scratch called, and as Bo twisted his head around to look behind them, he saw why his partner said that.

Half a dozen men on horseback were pounding toward them, a couple of hundred yards back up the road. Powder smoke already spurted from the guns in their hands, even though the range was too far for Colts to represent any real threat.

The attackers would close in quickly, though, so Bo couldn't go back the way they had come. The terrain was too rugged to head out across country with the stage.

Straight ahead was the only way open to them.

Right under the guns of those bushwhackers, who were firing from both hills now as Bo cracked the whip and sent the team lunging forward again. "Keep 'em busy as you can!" he shouted to Scratch.

Inside the coach, Claire Carson cried out in fear, and then clutched her son closer to her at the sudden stop and then the jolting start. Her husband's jaw tightened and his face grew pale as he began to hear the popping of shots over the thunderous pounding of hoofbeats.

"Thatcher, what is it?" Claire asked.

"We're under attack," Carson answered, his expression grim.

"By outlaws?" Noah yelped. He managed to sound scared and excited at the same time. "Or maybe Injuns?"

"Outlaws almost certainly," Carson replied. "The Indians haven't been a threat around here for several years." He reached under his coat and brought out a pistol that he carried in a shoulder holster.

His wife gasped at the sight of the gun and said, "Thatcher!"

He managed a bleak smile. "Don't worry, dear. I know how to use it. I deal with enough money and gold at the mine that I carry a gun most of the time."

"You never told me that!"

"I didn't want to worry you."

Claire was worried now, that was for sure. She looked positively terrified. She hugged Noah close against her, even though he looked like he wanted to wriggle free and stick his head out the window so he could see what was going on.

Up on the box, Bo had the horses moving faster than they had so far on this journey. The animals stretched out in a gallop, leaning forward and straining at their harness. Bo popped the whip and shouted at them. Speed was their only real chance now. It was a lot more difficult to hit a swiftly moving target.

Beside him, Scratch kept up a continuous fire, swiveling to right and left so that he could pepper both hillsides with .44/40 slugs. Powder smoke rolled over the slopes now as the bushwhackers poured lead down at the stagecoach. Scratch figured there were at least half a dozen riflemen hidden on each hill, and he didn't hold out much hope of actually hitting any of them with his shots. They had good cover behind those rocks. But he wanted to come close enough to make them duck every now and then and slow down their volleys.

And it was always possible that one of his slugs would find the mangy hide of a bushwhacker. Stranger things had happened.

Bullets whipped all around the Texans and chewed splinters from the coach roof. Bo hoped the Carsons were keeping their heads down. As he sent the old

Concord jolting and careening into the trail directly between the two hills, he realized something—the riflemen weren't shooting at the horses. Their fire seemed to be directed for the most part at him and Scratch. If this was a regular holdup, they would have been more concerned with stopping the coach, and killing the leaders of the team would have accomplished that in a hurry.

The possibility that he and Scratch were the real targets was intriguing, but Bo didn't have time to ponder it now. He kept popping the whip and shouting. The coach was drawing past the hills now; the bushwhacker lead came more and more from behind. They had run the gauntlet and come through alive and possibly even unharmed. He hoped the same was true of the passengers.

"You hit?" he shouted at Scratch.

"Nope! You?"

"Not yet!" Bo turned to glance over his shoulder again. The horsebackers were still behind them and had narrowed the gap some. Not only that, but now mounted men were emerging from the rocks and coming down the hillsides to fall in behind the other riders and join in the pursuit. A few of the riflemen were still up there, firing after the stagecoach. Another bullet spanged off the brass fittings.

They wanted him and Scratch dead, all right, Bo thought, and they were going to be stubborn about it, too.

This chase had just begun.

CHAPTER 18

Scratch twisted around on the seat and saw the pursuers thundering after the coach, too. "I'll try to discourage the varmints!" he shouted as he brought the rifle up. He braced an elbow on the coach roof, but that didn't do much to steady his aim, the way the vehicle was bouncing around.

Scratch began firing anyway, emptying the Winchester of its remaining rounds in a hurry. He was firing blind for the most part because of the dust cloud boiling up from the coach's wheels and trailing behind the Concord. But he caught glimpses of the riders through gaps in the dust, and during one such fleeting look he was rewarded by the sight of a horse tumbling down and sending its rider sailing through the air.

"Got one!" Scratch whooped. "Don't know if I hit man or horse, but both of 'em went down!"

"Either way, that's one less chasing us!" Bo responded as he continued urging the team on to its greatest speed.

Scratch began reloading the Winchester with cartridges from his pocket, thumbing the rounds into the loading gate with deft, practiced ease, even on top of a wildly jouncing stagecoach.

Inside the coach, Thatcher Carson leaned forward, getting ready to stick his head and arm out the window so he could take part in the running fight. Claire still had one arm around Noah, but her free hand shot out and grabbed her husband's sleeve, pulling him back.

"Thatcher!" she cried. "What are you doing?"

"I should help Mr. Creel and Mr. Morton fight off those desperadoes," Carson explained. "I'm a decent shot. I've practiced quite a bit, out at the mine."

"But you might be wounded! Or even killed!"

Carson looked at several holes in the coach where sunlight slanted through. "We've already run that risk," he said. He and his wife and son had all crouched as low as they could while bullets were punching through the roof and sides of the coach and humming through the heated air like bees. "I probably won't be in as much danger now as we all were just a short time ago."

Claire hesitated, then let go of his arm. "All right," she said. "But be careful."

That was just like a wife, Carson thought wryly . . . telling her husband to be careful when he was about to trade shots with a gang of bloodthirsty outlaws.

He took his hat off, slid closer to the window, and leaned out. Since he was riding in the front seat, facing backward, he didn't even have to turn around. All he had to do was stick his arm and head out the window and start firing at the pursuers. The wind whipped through his hair, leaving it in wild disarray as he squeezed off several shots.

Bo and Scratch heard the crack of Carson's pistol from the coach window. "That Eastern dude's gettin' in on the fun," Scratch said with a grin. "I don't reckon he'll hit much of anything, but you never know."

The horsemen were only about fifty yards behind the stage now, close enough so that Scratch could tell they wore masks. Despite that, he had no doubt they were Rance Judson's men. Whether or not they had any connection with Jared Rutledge—or with Dave Sutherland, for that matter—Scratch didn't know and didn't particularly care. Bo could figure all of that out when the time came. Right now, Scratch just wanted to ventilate as many of the ornery buzzards as he could.

Beside Scratch on the seat, Bo longed to draw his Colt, turn around, and blaze away at the pursuers just like his partner was doing. All of his attention had to remain focused on driving the stagecoach, though. He had to keep the team under control, yet still moving at top speed. If they ran away wildly, there was no telling where the coach might wind up. It could leave the road and crash in a gulley or overturn.

Scratch saw another of the riders clutch at a shoulder and fall back. The wounded hombre was out of the fight. But that still left almost a dozen men chasing the stagecoach.

Thatcher Carson had emptied his pistol. He ducked back inside the coach, dug fresh cartridges out of his coat pocket, and began fumbling them into the cylinder, trying not to drop any of the bullets as he did so. On the opposite seat, Claire and Noah still looked frightened, but pride was visible on the boy's face, too, along with excitement. This was the most action-packed few moments of his young life, and he was looking at his father with new eyes. His pa was no longer just a dull fellow who spent his days adding up long strings of figures in account books. Now he was a gunfighter!

Carson stuck his head and arm out the window again, and saw that the masked riders had drawn even closer. A bullet struck the coach roof just above Carson and showered splinters down on him. He cursed and ducked back for a second, and Claire let out a terrified cry.

"Thatcher! Are you hurt?"

"I'm fine," he told her through gritted teeth. Squinting against the dust and wind that stung his eyes, he leaned out the window again, thrust the pistol toward the outlaws, and squeezed off a couple of shots.

Amazingly, one of the men in the front rank of riders tumbled from his saddle. The man behind him tried to avoid trampling him, but as a result that man got his horse tangled with another man's mount, and suddenly they were down, too, the horses rolling and flailing their hooves in a welter of dust. Carson couldn't see what happened to the riders, but he was sure it couldn't have been anything good.

Up on the seat, Scratch was reloading the Winchester again when Carson fired, and he glanced up in time to see several of the pursuers take a wicked spill. He let out a yell and reported to Bo, "That dude's a fightin' fool! He just knocked two or three of 'em down!"

"Maybe we've got a chance after all!" Bo said. "How close are they?"

"Mighty close!"

"See if you can do some damage with that scattergun!"

Scratch reached down to the floorboard and picked up the shotgun, which he had been holding in place until now with a foot. He set the Winchester down instead and called to Bo, "Put one o' those big clodhoppers o' yours on this rifle!"

Bo complied as Scratch started to climb over the back of the seat onto the roof.

"What the devil are you doing?"

"Gettin' a little closer!" Scratch replied. On his belly, he slid along the roof of the stagecoach until his head was over the rear boot.

Blinking and squinting against the dust, he made out the shapes of several pursuers closing in on the coach. They probably thought they could get close enough to grab hold, climb on, and throw him and Bo off.

They were in for a buckshot surprise, Scratch thought with a savage grin.

The dumb varmints were bunched up close together, so he let them draw nearer and nearer until finally they were close enough to spot him lying on top of the coach with the Greener pointed in their direction. He saw their eyes widen in shock and they started trying to pull away, but they were too late. His fingers contracted in the triggers, and both charges of buckshot blasted out of the twin barrels with a double geyser of flame.

The devastating load of lead tore through men and horses alike. The men were swept out of the saddle and crashed to the ground looking like bloody rag dolls. The horses managed to gallop on for a few yards before collapsing.

Scratch broke the shotgun, dumped the empties, and shoved fresh shells into the barrels. He snapped the weapon closed and unleashed another double load of buckshot, but the other outlaws had seen what happened and were already falling back. The second shotgun blast knocked one man out of his saddle, but that was all.

Now there were only about half a dozen of the pursuers left, and they might be thinking better of continuing the chase. Scratch called to Bo, "Pass me up the Winchester!" Bo did so, and Scratch took the rifle and began trying to convince the remaining pursuers that it wasn't worth continuing. Shots rolled out from the Winchester.

That did it. The masked riders peeled away, slowing down and abandoning their pursuit. They had already paid a high price in their attempt to kill the Texans, and none of the others wanted to throw their lives away.

"They're fallin' back!" Scratch told Bo. "Better not slow down for a ways, though!"

"I don't intend to!" Bo said. He wanted to go on

putting as much distance as he could between them and the outlaws.

Scratch crawled back to the front of the coach and slid down onto the seat, bringing the shotgun and the Winchester with him. He leaned over and called to the passengers, "Hey! You folks all right in there?"

"We're fine!" Thatcher Carson replied. "What happened to those men?"

"They gave up an' lit a shuck outta here! We fought 'em off, Mr. Carson!"

Inside the coach, Thatcher Carson nodded in satisfaction and slumped back against the seat. Claire screamed when she saw blood dripping from the fingers of his left hand.

"Thatcher! You're hurt! Driver! Driver! Mr. Creel! Please stop!"

Bo heard the woman's frightened cries and pulled back on the reins a little, slowing the team but not stopping it. He said to Scratch, "See if you can find out how bad he's hurt."

Scratch nodded. He swung off the seat, reaching down and placing one boot on the foot rail that they used when climbing onto the coach. He hung on to the rail around the roof with his hands.

"Hey, kid," he called through the window, "open that door!"

Noah Carson slipped out of his mother's grasp and twisted the latch on the door. It swung open. Scratch got his other foot inside the coach, shifted a hand to the door, and hauled himself inside. He wound up sprawled on the floor at Mrs. Carson's feet and said, "Beg pardon, ma'am." He pulled himself onto the seat next to Carson. "Lemme take a look at your arm, partner."

"It's nothing," Carson insisted. "Just a scratch."

"Reckon I'd be a better judge o' that than you, friend, that bein' my name and all." Scratch saw where the bloodstain started on Carson's upper arm. He pulled out his folding knife, opened it, and cut away the sleeves of coat and shirt. Mrs. Carson gasped as she saw the bloody bullet hole in her husband's arm.

"It looks worse'n it really is, ma'am," Scratch told her after a quick examination of the wound. "Bullet went in and right back out, didn't take nothin' with it but a little chunk o' meat. We'll plug up the holes to stop the bleedin', and your husband'll be fine. Ought to see a doc at Cottonwood and let him clean it up good, though."

"Of course." Claire was still pale and shaken, but she had the presence of mind to ask, "Would you like for me to tear off some of my petticoat to use for bandages?"

"That'd be just about perfect. I'll avert my gaze."

It didn't take long to get Carson's wounded arm patched up. As Scratch tied the last of the makeshift bandages in place, he saw that the Easterner had passed out. Mrs. Carson noticed, too, and asked anxiously, "Is he—"

"Just fainted from loss o' blood," Scratch assured

her. "He spilled a heap of it. But he'll be fine with a few days' rest."

"But he was going back to Red Butte tomorrow. He had something important coming up at the mine."

"Reckon that'll just have to wait. I expect the sawbones in Cottonwood won't want him travelin' for a little while."

Mrs. Carson didn't say anything else about that. Instead, she said, "Trade places with me, Mr. Morton. I'd like to sit next to my husband."

"Sure thing, ma'am."

Once they had traded places, Claire pillowed her husband's head against her bosom. That made Carson a lucky hombre, Scratch thought, even if he *did* have to get shot first.

Scratch found himself sitting next to the little boy, who looked up at him and said, "I heard some really loud noises up on the roof."

"That was me shootin' a shotgun," Scratch told him.

"Did you get any of the miscreants?"

"The what? Oh, them fellas who was chasin' us? Yeah, I blasted three of 'em outta their saddles the first go-round, but only got one the next time."

"You killed four men, just like that?"

"Noah!" his mother scolded. "You shouldn't sound so . . . enthused about it."

Scratch thumbed his hat back and said, "Well, ma'am, when some hombres are tryin' their darnedest to kill me and I get around to killin' them first, I'm usually a mite enthused about it my own self." When she frowned at him, he went on hurriedly, "But we, uh, best not talk about that, youngster. Or the fact that your pa did for some o' the varmints, too."

"Really?"

Scratch nodded. "He sure did." He leaned closer and added, "Tell you about it later, when we get to Cottonwood."

From the driver's seat, Bo called, "Everything all right in there?"

"Yeah!" Scratch replied. "Need me to climb back up there?"

"No, I'll let you know if I see any more trouble headed our way."

Scratch grinned at Noah. "Feel a mite like royalty, ridin' inside this way." He made a shooing motion with his hand. "Carry on, driver, carry on."

Noah laughed, and even Claire smiled a little at the Texan's antics.

They reached another relay station shortly after that, so Scratch's ride didn't last very long. Thatcher Carson regained consciousness while they were stopped to change teams, but he wasn't awake for very long before falling into a natural sleep as he leaned against his wife. Bo and Scratch warned the hostler at the relay station to be on the lookout for the men who had ambushed the coach, although neither of them thought the outlaws would try to follow them on to Cottonwood.

Running the horses so hard had actually gained a

little time, so the stagecoach arrived at its destination a few minutes ahead of schedule. Cottonwood was a nice little town on the western bank of the Verde River. The stream was lined with the trees that gave the settlement its name. Wooded hills surrounded it.

There was a deputy sheriff's office at Cottonwood, although the county seat was at Prescott, a good long ways to the southwest. It didn't take long for news of the attack on the stagecoach to get around town, and when the deputy, heard he came down to the stage station to talk to Bo and Scratch.

They had already taken Thatcher Carson to the local doctor's office and turned him over to the physician. They answered the deputy's questions, telling him about the ambush and stating bluntly that they thought Rance Judson was behind it.

"That damned Judson," the lawman said bitterly. "We've been tryin' to corral him for months now with no luck."

Scratch opened his mouth to say something, but before he could, Bo said, "You can ride out there and try to pick up their tracks if you want."

The deputy rubbed his grizzled jaw. "Well, I'll have to wire the sheriff first and see what he wants me to do. Might take a posse out there tomorrow. Too late in the day now to start followin' a trail anyway."

When the deputy had gone back to his office, Scratch said to Bo, "You know he's not gonna go after Judson's bunch. How come you didn't tell him where we think that hideout is?"

"Because we don't know for sure yet, and if the hideout *is* on top of that butte, any posse that came within rifle range would likely be slaughtered. We need to find out more before we call in the law."

"In other words, we're gonna give Judson even more reason to want us dead than he had when he come after us today?"

"That's about the size of it," Bo replied with a smile. "What's the matter, don't you like having a target painted on your back?"

Scratch just snorted and said, "You'd think I'd be used to it by now, wouldn't you?"

CHAPTER 19

The stage station in Cottonwood was larger and more comfortably appointed than the one in Chino Valley. It not only had a dining room, but also a couple of rooms in the back furnished with cots where the driver and shotgun guard could sleep. The manager was a tall, spare man named Olmsted who had been working for the Sutherland Stagecoach Line ever since it began. Like Will Sutherland and Ponderosa Pine, he had worked for Butterfield's Overland Express at one time.

"If you ask me," Olmsted said over dinner in the station dining room that night, "the sheriff ought to put a dozen deputies armed for bear in one of these coaches and run it back and forth until Judson's gang jumps it and gets the surprise of their lives."

"I reckon it'd be a mite crowded inside that coach," Scratch said with a smile.

"And for another thing," Bo added, "the sheriff would have a hard time doing that without Judson finding out about it ahead of time. I've got a feeling Judson has spies here in Cottonwood, as well as in Chino Valley and Red Butte. I never heard of a really successful outlaw who didn't have some of the common people helping him, either for a share of the loot or just because they admire him."

Olmsted shook his head. "There's nothin' admirable about Rance Judson. He's a killer and a thief."

"So were Frank and Jesse James, but that didn't stop people from lending them a hand whenever they needed it."

The station manager shrugged, unable to argue with Bo's point. "I still say that somebody needs to do something about Judson and his gang, before they ruin things for everybody in these parts. The settlements will never grow without reliable stagecoach and freight service unless the railroad comes through, and I don't see that happening any time soon."

Neither did Bo. Cottonwood, Chino Valley, and Red Butte would have to grow considerably before a railroad would find it profitable enough to put a line through this area.

"Somebody will put a stop to Judson's gang sooner or later," he said. "And Scratch and I will be doing our best to see that the stagecoaches get through safely."

Bo paused. "You mentioned freight lines. Have Jared Rutledge's wagons been hit fairly often?"

"Often enough that it's worrisome," Olmsted replied. He gave a snort. "Although why I'd worry about a skunk like Rutledge who wants to put Mrs. Sutherland out of business is beyond me. I guess I just feel sorry for the folks in Red Butte who'll be without supplies if Rutledge gives up and moves on somewhere else."

Scratch said, "Rutledge didn't strike me as the sort o' hombre who'd give up very easy. Seemed about as stubborn as a mule, in fact."

"Oh, he is, he is," Olmsted said. "He wants the stage line and the mail contract, as well as his freight business. But no matter how stubborn a fella is, he can't just go on losing money forever."

Bo leaned forward. "Rutledge is losing money?"

"Well, I don't know for sure—he doesn't share his account books with me or anything like that—but the way his freight hauling has fallen off since Judson's gang moved into the area, I don't see how he could be *making* any money. He never made anything on that one stagecoach of his, with its one run each week. He does that just to spite Mrs. Sutherland, if you ask me."

Bo and Scratch looked at each other, and both Texans were frowning in thought. Abigail Sutherland was convinced that Jared Rutledge was tied in somehow with the outlaws, but from everything Olmsted had said, that sounded mighty far-fetched. Really, nothing they had come across since riding into these parts indicated that Rutledge would come out ahead by siding with Rance Judson.

Unless he was after something completely different that nobody knew about yet.

That was something to consider, Bo mused, but at the same time he couldn't rule out the possibility that Abigail was wrong about Rutledge. Rutledge might be just much a victim of Judson's depredations as she herself was.

Coming up with a way to bust up Judson's gang and capture or kill the outlaws would go a long way toward hashing out the whole problem. That would likely drive Judson's allies, if he had any, out into the open.

Bo, Scratch, and Olmsted chewed over the situation for a while longer without really coming to any conclusions, and then Bo and Scratch withdrew to the sleeping rooms in the back of the station and turned in. Scratch had made a few noises about wanting to hunt up a saloon and get a drink first, but the day had been a long, tiring one, and in the end weariness won out over his thirst.

Both of the drifters passed the night quietly in deep, dreamless sleep.

The aroma of strong, black coffee filled the station when they got up the next morning. As they sat down to the big breakfast of flapjacks, bacon, eggs, and fried potatoes that Olmsted had prepared, Bo asked, "Will there be any passengers on the run back to Red Butte?"

"Not from here," Olmsted answered. "Might pick up somebody in Chino Valley, for all I know. And it's always possible some pilgrim could try to catch a ride at one of the relay stations, but that only happens once in a blue moon. There'll likely be a full mail pouch for you, though. I was about to head down to the post office to pick it up. It'll still be a while before the hostlers have the coach ready to roll."

"Good," Bo said with a nod. "That'll give us a chance to check on Mr. Carson and see how he's doing this morning."

Even though the lack of passengers was bad news for Abigail, Bo and Scratch were both sort of relieved they wouldn't have anybody traveling in the coach on the return trip. The outlaws might decide to jump them again, and they preferred just looking out for themselves, rather than having to worry about the safety of innocent passengers.

They left the station and walked down the street to the doctor's office. The medico, a short, fat, mostly bald man, told them that Thatcher Carson had gone on to his sister-in-law's house the night before, where he would be staying for a few days while he recuperated from his arm wound and while his wife cared for her ailing sister.

"Whoever patched up that arm did a good job of it," the doctor added.

"That'd be me," Scratch said.

"Have you any medical training?"

"Me?" Scratch laughed. "Not hardly. Just had to

tend to a heap o' bullet wounds in my time, includin' some in my own carcass."

"Then that practical experience served you well, sir. The injury wasn't that serious in itself, but Carson could've bled to death if you hadn't been there to help."

The Texans got directions to the place where Carson was staying, then started to leave the doctor's office. Scratch paused and asked, "Whatever the sister-in-law's got that made her sick . . . it ain't catchin', is it?"

The sawbones guffawed and shook his head. "Not unless you grow some female parts, Mr. Morton."

Scratch looked scandalized by the very idea and departed quickly, followed by a chuckling Bo.

They found the house without any trouble. It was a neat, two-story frame dwelling on a side street, with a picket fence in front and a couple of pine trees in the yard. Noah Carson answered Bo's knock on the door and burst out in a big grin at the sight of the two Texans on the porch.

"Ma!" he called over his shoulder. "It's Mr. Creel and Mr. Morton!"

Claire appeared, smiled at them, and said, "Please, gentlemen, come in."

Bo and Scratch took their hats off, and Bo said, "Morning, ma'am. We just came by to see how your husband's doing. The doctor told us he was here."

"That's right. Thatcher's injury wasn't serious enough to require that he stay at the doctor's. He's in the kitchen having breakfast. Would you care to join us?"

"Thanks, ma'am, but we already ate."

"Wouldn't mind another cup o' coffee, though," Scratch said.

"Of course. Follow me."

As they went through the neatly kept house to the kitchen, Noah trailed behind them and asked, "Has anybody shot at you yet today?"

Scratch laughed and said, "No, not today. It ain't like somebody shoots at us every single day."

"It just seems like it sometimes," Bo said.

"Yeah, sometimes we go a week or more without gettin' into a gunfight."

Noah's eyes widened even more than they already were. "A gunfight every week . . . I can't even imagine."

"And you never shall," his mother put in with a stern frown. She brought them into the kitchen, where Thatcher Carson was sitting at a table with his wounded arm in a black silk sling.

He smiled at Bo and Scratch and said, "I thought I heard Noah mention your names. How are you today?"

"We're fine," Bo replied. "Question is, how are you?"

"My arm's rather stiff and sore," Carson admitted. "Hurts like blazes at times, in fact. But I suppose that's to be expected when you've been shot."

"It ain't ever what you'd call a pleasant experience,"

Scratch said. "Doc says you're gonna be fine with a little rest, though."

Carson frowned. "Yes, I just hope that's not too much of a problem for Claire. Now she has to care not only for her sister, but for me as well."

"I'm used to it," she said with a laugh. She poured coffee for Bo and Scratch, placed the cups on the table, and told them to sit down.

As they did, Carson went on. "It's a problem for the superintendent at the mine, too. I really need to be there."

Bo took a sip of the coffee, which was a little better than that brewed by Olmsted at the stage station, and said, "Surely the place can get along without you for a little while."

"Under normal conditions, yes, but right now—" Carson stopped short and shook his head, as if realizing that he was about to say more than maybe he should. "Never mind. You men shouldn't have to concern yourselves with my problems. You've done enough for me already, just by saving my life and the lives of my family."

Bo and Scratch looked at each other for a second. They were in agreement that the attack on the stagecoach the day before hadn't been a simple holdup. The outlaws were bent on killing the two of them. So, in one way of looking at it, *they* were partially to blame for the bullet hole in Carson's arm. The targets on their backs had attracted plenty of trouble already, and Thatcher Carson had gotten in the way of it.

"We're just glad we were there to help," Bo said. "Is there anything else we can do?"

Carson took another drink of coffee, set his cup down, and said, "As a matter of fact, there is. I've written a note for Mr. Flynn, the superintendent at the Pitchfork. Would you mind delivering it to him? I suppose I could put it in the mail pouch, but I thought if you could take it to him personally, that would speed things up."

"Why, sure," Scratch said. "We'd be glad to, wouldn't we, Bo?"

"That's right," Bo said with a nod. "As a matter of fact, I've been a mite curious about that mine. I wouldn't mind taking a look at it, and delivering your note will give us a good excuse to do that, Mr. Carson."

"Excellent! I appreciate it, gentlemen. Claire, if you could fetch that envelope from the dresser in the bedroom . . ."

"Of course, darling. I'll just look in on Helen, too, while I'm upstairs, if that's all right. It won't take but a minute."

After Claire had left the kitchen, Carson said, "Are you sure you have time to wait like this?"

"Stage ain't leavin' without us," Scratch assured him with a grin.

"You think those outlaws are gonna try to hold up the stage again today?" Noah asked.

Bo shook his head and said, "I sure hope not. Yesterday was bad enough."

"Yeah, and you won't have my pa with you today to help fight 'em off if they do. He killed some of 'em, you know."

Carson motioned with his good hand for the boy to be quiet. "Remember, Noah, we said we weren't going to talk about that," he said.

"Yeah, but I think it's really good. It's not every kid who's got a pa who gunned down some owlhoots."

Carson winced. "Please don't let your mother hear you talking like that. She's already upset enough about everything that's happened."

"I'll be quiet," Noah said, "but you've gotta keep your promise and get me a gun one of these days, so you can teach me how to shoot."

"You'd probably be better off having someone like Mr. Creel or Mr. Morton teach you."

"It's not likely we'll be around Red Butte that long," Bo said.

Noah looked surprised. "Why not?"

"Hombres like us, we're what you call fiddle-footed," Scratch said. "That means we don't like to stay in one place for too long. Always got to be movin' on after a while."

"Well, I hope you don't leave Red Butte before I get back there," Noah said.

"There's a good chance we'll still be there for a while yet," Bo told the boy. For one thing, he didn't think the whole mystery surrounding the Judson gang's hideout, and what had brought them to these parts in the first place, would be cleared up right away.

He and Scratch weren't going to ride on and leave the situation dangerously unsettled.

Claire Carson returned to the kitchen a moment later with a square, sealed envelope that she handed to Bo. He slipped it into his coat pocket and said, "We won't put this in the mail pouch, Mr. Carson. It'll go straight to Mr. Flynn at the mine just as soon as we get a chance to ride out there. Probably be tomorrow morning, since we won't get back to Red Butte until almost nightfall."

Carson nodded. "That'll be fine. Thank you." He shook hands with both of them, using his good hand. Bo and Scratch drained the rest of their coffee, told Mrs. Carson they were much obliged and that they hoped her sister got to feeling better soon, and then left the house after tousling Noah's hair and waving so long to the boy.

"Sort of interestin'," Scratch mused, "the way Carson was actin' like something was goin' on out at that mine."

"I was thinking the same thing," Bo replied as they walked toward the stage station.

"You reckon it could have anything to do with this whole mess involvin' Judson, Rutledge, and Miz Abigail?"

"Right offhand, I don't see how it could, but anything's possible. I've got a hunch that *something* is tying it all together."

"Maybe that note Carson wrote to the mine superintendent would explain a few things," Scratch suggested.

"That envelope is sealed."

"Envelopes can be steamed open."

Bo shook his head. "It wouldn't be right."

"We been known to bend the law a time or two when we had to, when something needed done and there wasn't no other way to do it."

"This isn't like that," Bo insisted. "Carson put his faith in us to deliver that note, and I'm sure if he intended for us to open it and read it, he would have said so."

"But he didn't say *not* to."

"You're just an old reprobate, you know that?"

Scratch chuckled. "I been called worse. Many a time, in fact."

"But we're still not opening that letter."

Scratch just shrugged. He'd go along with Bo . . . for now.

CHAPTER 20

The hostlers had the fresh team hitched up by the time the Texans returned to the stage station, and Olmsted had the mail pouch he had gotten at the post office. Bo and Scratch watched him stow it in the box under the driver's seat and fasten the lock. Neither of them said anything about the message Thatcher Carson had given to them to be delivered to the superintendent of the Pitchfork Mine.

As they climbed onto the box, Scratch asked, "Are you handlin' the team again?"

"Seemed to work out all right yesterday," Bo said. "I don't see any reason to change."

"Me neither." Scratch settled himself on the seat, rested the shotgun across his knees, and lifted a hand in farewell. "So long, Olmsted."

"Be careful, you two," the station manager called as Bo lifted the reins.

With a slap of leather and a holler, Bo started the team moving. With the Verde River so close, the streets in Cottonwood were watered on a regular basis, so the stagecoach didn't raise much dust as it rolled out of the settlement, heading west.

It was hard to leave the green, tree-covered slopes of the foothills behind and head back out into the mostly arid flats. Even though the temperature wasn't really that much different, it just *seemed* cooler and more pleasant in Cottonwood.

But the way to Red Butte lay westward, and so did their responsibilities for now, so Bo and Scratch headed west, swaying on the seat as the stagecoach rocked gently back and forth. The eyes of both men were constantly moving, roving back and forth over the landscape around them as the terrain flattened out and grew more barren of vegetation. They were looking for any sign of an ambush.

The day before, Judson's gang had wanted them dead. It seemed likely the outlaws still had that goal in mind.

Nothing unusual had happened, though, by the time they reached the first relay station. The switch over of the teams took place without incident. Bo got the fresh horses moving, and the stagecoach continued on its way toward Chino Valley.

As they rode, the Texans raised their voices so they could hear each other over the rattle of hoofbeats and the creaking and rumbling of the wheels, and discussed everything that had happened since they first heard the gunshots signaling the attack on the stagecoach in which Ponderosa Pine had been wounded. It didn't help much. Bo and Scratch both sensed there was something they didn't know yet, something that would tie everything together and make it all make sense.

By the time they reached Chino Valley at midday, the sun was beating down with full force. The Texans had shucked their jackets, and sweat stuck their shirts to their skin. They were thankful for the shade that their broad-brimmed hats cast.

As Bo hauled back on the reins and brought the team to a stop in front of the Chino Valley stage station, he saw a man sitting on the ground, knees drawn up as he leaned against the wall of the building. A quirly dangled from his lips, and a saddle sat on the ground beside him. He wore an old gunbelt with a black-handled revolver in the holster. The brim of his battered old hat was pulled down so that Bo and Scratch couldn't see his eyes at first, but then he lifted his head and tipped it back so he could look at the coach. The man, who was dressed in worn range clothes, began climbing to his feet.

The station manager emerged from the building and raised a hand in greeting. "Howdy, boys," he called up to the Texans. "Any trouble between here and Cottonwood?"

"Not this mornin'," Scratch answered. "Trip was smooth as silk."

The implications of Scratch's words sunk in on the station manager, causing him to frown in concern. "What happened yesterday?"

"Judson's gang jumped us," Bo replied as he set the brake and wrapped the reins around the lever.

"Good Lord, not again! Were either of you hurt?"

Scratch shook his head. "Not us. But that fella ridin' inside the coach took a bullet through the arm."

"You mean Mr. Carson from Red Butte? Dadgum! Was he hurt bad?"

"He'll be all right," Bo said. "He's staying in Cottonwood for a few days to recuperate before he goes back to Red Butte, though. That's why we don't have any passengers today."

"Well, you got one now," the station manager said as he jerked a thumb over his shoulder toward the lean cowhand who'd been sitting against the wall. "That fella bought a ticket a little while ago."

"Yeah, but now I'm not sure whether I want to go or not," the man said with a grin as he ambled closer. "I've been listenin', and it sounds like this coach is a magnet for trouble."

"We'll make it through just fine, mister, don't you worry about that," Bo said, trying not to let his voice get stiff with anger at the cowboy's mocking words.

The man stepped over to the coach and poked a finger through one of the bullet holes in the side of it near a window. "I don't know. This coach looks like it's been through a war. Or at least a battle."

"Those holes'll be patched up once we get back to Red Butte," Scratch snapped, feeling the same sort of instinctive dislike for the stranger that Bo did.

"I'm sure they will," the man said. "I didn't mean any offense, fellas. Name's Cochran. I'd be obliged if you'd let me ride to Red Butte with you."

"Don't have much choice, seeing as how you bought a ticket already," Bo said. "We'll be leaving as soon as we've had something to eat and the team is changed."

Cochran nodded. "Fine. All right if I put my saddle back in the boot?"

"Yeah, go ahead."

Bo and Scratch climbed down from the seat while Cochran stowed his saddle. He followed them into the station.

The station manager's Mexican wife had food waiting for them, this time bowls of a thick, savory stew instead of beans and tortillas. Cochran didn't eat anything, just lounged at a table in the corner and smoked.

In a quiet voice, Bo asked the woman, "Did that hombre eat earlier, before we got here?"

She shook her head. "No, señor. I think maybe he only have enough money for to buy a ticket to Red Butte."

Bo nodded and took another couple of bites, then said to Scratch, "I don't like to see a fella going hungry, even when I don't particularly like him."

"I was thinkin' the same thing," Scratch admitted.

"Well, as long as we're in agreement . . ."

Bo got up from the bench alongside the table and walked toward Cochran. The cowboy regarded him curiously.

Bo inclined his head toward the table where he and Scratch were eating. "Why don't you come join us, mister?" he asked. "The señora's got a whole pot of that stew, and it's mighty good."

Cochran shook his head. "No, thanks. I'm all right."

"If it's a matter of money, Scratch and I will stand you a meal. We don't like to see anybody go hungry."

The man's lips curved in a thin smile. "That's mighty kind of you."

"Not trying to be kind," Bo said, growing a little impatient. "That's just simple human decency."

"That's true." Cochran came to his feet. "I'm much obliged, Mister . . . ?"

"Creel. Bo Creel. That's Scratch Morton."

"Good to meet you."

Cochran followed Bo back over to the long table. Scratch had already motioned for the station manager's wife to bring another bowl of stew. She had it sitting on the table with a spoon next to it, waiting for Cochran when he got there.

He nodded to Scratch, then sat down and began to eat. Bo resumed his seat.

"Fella with a saddle but no horse has usually had a run o' bad luck," Scratch commented after a few moments.

Cochran nodded and swallowed a mouthful of stew. "That's true enough," he said. "I was on my way to Red Butte when my horse stepped in a damned hole and broke its leg. Had to shoot the poor bastard."

Bo and Scratch both nodded. They'd had to put down horses that had had similar unfortunate accidents, and it was always a hard thing to do.

"Was just lucky for me it happened only a couple o' miles outta the settlement here," Cochran went on. "I was able to get my saddle off and hoof it on in, but I got to tell you, even that's a long walk for a fella like me who ain't used to travelin' shank's mare."

The Texans understood that sentiment, too. Most cowboys felt like any job that couldn't be done from horseback was a job that just wasn't worth doing. They walked as little as possible, so when they were forced to, it was a real chore.

"Ridin' the grub line, are you?"

"Yeah. I heard there are some good spreads over on the eastern slopes of the Santa Marias, and I'm hopin' that one of them will be hirin'." Cochran shrugged. "If not, I'll try the mine they got over there. I've turned my hand to minin' a time or two in my life. Not as good at it as cowboyin', but anything that puts grub in the ol' belly, right, boys?"

"I reckon," Bo said.

"Long as you got a saddle, you ought to be able to get a ridin' job," Scratch said. "Of course, it ain't roundup time right now, but maybe one of the spreads'll be lookin' for a man."

Cochran said, "I'll keep my fingers crossed," and kept eating.

After a few minutes, he paused and asked, "You fellas wouldn't happen to know any of the ranch foremen over in those parts, would you? I thought maybe you could put in a good word for me."

Bo shook his head and said, "Sorry. We haven't been in these parts for very long ourselves. We haven't gotten to know very many people yet."

"Oh. You ain't the regular driver and guard on this stagecoach run?"

"This is our first time to make it," Scratch said. "We've been from Red Butte to Cottonwood, and now we're on our way back."

"I get you. This stage line wouldn't need a good man, would it?"

Cochran didn't impress either Bo or Scratch as a particularly good man, but Bo just said, "You'd have to ask the owner about that."

"But you'd put in a good word for me with him, wouldn't you?"

"Owner's a her," Scratch said, without really answering Cochran's question about whether or not they would recommend that Abigail hire him. "Mrs. Abigail Sutherland."

Cochran's eyebrows rose. "A woman? Say, you ain't

joshin' me, are you? I never heard of a woman ownin' any business before, let alone a stage line."

"It's the truth," Bo said. "Her husband started the line, but he passed away a while back."

"Sorry to hear that." Cochran didn't sound all that sorry. "She probably does need help then. I'll be sure to talk to her if I don't catch on at one of the ranches around there. I think I'd rather work around stage-coaches than go back to minin'. Never did care for holes in the ground. Far as I'm concerned, there ain't no really good reason to go down in one of those until you're dead, know what I mean?"

They finished the meal, cleaning their bowls of the stew, and Bo gave the manager's wife a coin to pay for all three of them. As he was doing that, the manager came back into the station and reported that the fresh team was hitched to the stage.

"You fellas be mighty careful," he warned them. "Judson's bunch might jump you again. They can be mighty persistent varmints when they want to be."

"I'm not worried too much about it," Bo said. "If I remember the country between here and Red Butte— and I ought to, since we just traveled through it yesterday—there are a lot fewer places where that gang could spring an ambush. If they come after us, chances are we'll see them coming quite a ways off."

"Well, good luck anyway." The manager glanced at Cochran. "You sure you still want to go, mister? You can hang on to that ticket you bought and use it later, if you want."

Cochran shook his head. "I trust Bo and Scratch here. Anyway, from what I've heard, it's liable to be just as dangerous another time as long as that outlaw Judson is on the loose."

"You got a point there," Scratch said. "Come on."

They went outside. Bo checked the harness on the horses, not because he didn't trust the hostlers who worked here, but simply because a man always checked the gear he was going to be using himself before he put his full trust in it. Satisfied that the team was hitched up properly, he climbed to the driver's seat.

Cochran reached up to open the coach door, but he paused before climbing in. "It's gonna be mighty hot and stuffy in there, fellas," he said. "Mind if I ride up top with you? I don't mind sittin' on the roof."

Bo and Scratch looked at each other, and Scratch shrugged. "It ain't very pleasant ridin' inside when the weather's this hot," Scratch said. "At least up top you can get some breeze."

"All right," Bo said with a nod. "Climb up, Cochran."

The cowboy grinned as he pulled himself to the driver's seat and then clambered onto the roof of the coach. He turned around facing front and sat with his knees pulled up, much like he had done when he was leaning against the wall of the station. He didn't have anything behind him now to brace him, though.

Scratch climbed onto the seat beside Bo and settled himself with the scattergun across his knees again. Bo untied the reins from the brake lever, released the brake, and got the horses moving with a slap of leather and a yell. The three men on the stage waved farewell to the manager and the hostlers as the stage rolled away from the station.

"I sure appreciate you payin' for that bowl of stew, Bo," Cochran said as they left Chino Valley. "I don't mind admittin' that I'm busted. Used the last of my *dinero* to buy my ticket on the stage. I was hopin' that when I get to Red Butte I could find somebody to stake me until I find a job."

Neither of the Texans responded to that hint. As far as they were concerned, they had done enough favors already for Cochran.

The cowboy seemed to be unable to keep his mouth shut for more than a few minutes at a time. Like a lot of men in solitary professions, when he was around other people he liked to talk. He rambled on to Bo and Scratch, telling them about places he had been, ranches where he had worked, and women he had known. Scratch could be pretty talkative himself at times, so he tolerated Cochran's long-winded gab and tried to show an interest. Bo just ignored it, for the most part.

They were back in the flat, arid country now. If the outlaws wanted to ambush the stage again, about the only place they could hide to do so would be in one of the dry washes that slashed through the terrain every so often. Bo kept a close eye on each of those arroyos as the stage approached it.

The coach's wheels rattled over one of the plank bridges about halfway between Chino Valley and the last relay station this side of Red Butte. Bo glanced both ways along the wash as they crossed it, but didn't see anything suspicious. The arroyo took a sharp bend about a hundred yards north of the stage road, though, so he couldn't see any farther than that in that direction.

His instincts warned him that anybody could have been hiding around that bend in the wash, so when the stagecoach was about fifty yards beyond the bridge, Bo glanced back, looking past the still-jabbering Cochran.

He wasn't really surprised to see horsemen lunging their mounts up the bank of the wash next to the bridge to start galloping after the coach. "Scratch!" he called. "Behind us!"

Scratch started to twist around and lift the shotgun, but before he could do so, Cochran put his left hand down on the coach roof to brace himself and used his right to yank the black-handled pistol from the holster on his hip.

"Hold it!" Cochran ordered in harsh tones. "Stop this coach, Creel, or I'll blow both of you old pelicans right off it!"

CHAPTER 21

Cochran's actions didn't really take Bo by surprise. He hadn't liked or fully trusted the so-called grub line rider right from the start, and it had occurred to him that if Judson wanted to attack the stage again, it might work better if the outlaws had somebody close to him and Scratch, to get the drop on them.

Because of that suspicion, Bo had started moving as soon as he looked back and spotted the outlaws coming after them. He snatched the whip from its socket at the same time as Cochran reached for his gun, and he struck with it even as the words were coming out of the gunman's mouth.

The short whip slashed across Cochran's face with all the power Bo could put behind it from his awkward position, half-turned on the driver's seat. That was enough to open up a wicked cut on Cochran's face that slanted from above his left eye, across the bridge of his nose, and down his beard-stubbled right cheek. Blood welled from it as Cochran screamed in pain and jerked back. The gun in his hand roared as his trigger finger contracted involuntarily, but Scratch had already slammed the barrels of the shotgun against Cochran's wrist and knocked the gun out of line. The bullet screamed off harmlessly to the side.

Scratch brought the shotgun back around and slammed the barrels against Cochran's jaw. The blow sent the treacherous gunman rolling toward the edge of the coach. Cochran's legs went off the coach, and he had to drop his gun and make a desperate grab at the brass rail to keep from plunging all the way off.

His momentum carried him all the way over the edge, and he wound up dangling on the side of the coach, hanging on to the rail for dear life as his booted feet kicked at empty air. They tried to find a purchase on the side of the coach, but kept sliding off.

Meanwhile Bo urged the team on greater speed, popping the whip and calling out to the horses. They were still relatively fresh, so they responded eagerly, straining against their harness. The coach began to bounce and sway more as it raced along the road.

"We could make better time if we didn't have any deadweight holdin' us back!" Scratch called to Bo over the thundering hoofbeats.

Bo glanced back and saw Cochran's fingers clinging to the rail. The gunman's head was below the level of the roof, so the fingers were all Bo could see of him.

He had seen enough a few moments earlier, when Cochran had drawn his gun and his face had turned ugly with evil. There was no doubt in Bo's mind that Cochran was a member of the outlaw gang now pursuing them—again—so he gave Scratch a curt nod.

Grinning, Scratch turned around and leaned back with the shotgun, slamming the twin barrels down on the fingers of Cochran's left hand, probably breaking one or two of them. Cochran howled in pain and let go with that hand. He had to know what was coming next, but instinct kept his right hand clamped around the rail.

Scratch brought the shotgun barrels down on those fingers, too, and with a desperate yelp that was swallowed up by the pounding hoofbeats, Cochran was gone. Scratch squinted back through the swirling dust and caught a glimpse of the man rolling over limply before coming to a stop in a motionless sprawl. It could be that Cochran had broken his neck when he fell, or he might be just knocked out. Scratch didn't much care either way.

With that chore taken care of, he swapped the shotgun for the Winchester, as he had the day before, and climbed onto the coach roof to open fire on the pursuers. The outlaws had gotten enough of Scratch's deadly accuracy with the rifle during the previous fight, so they gave up the chase fairly quickly this time, throwing a few last, futile shots at the coach as it sped away.

"I don't think any of that lead even hit us this time," Scratch said with a grin as he slid back down onto the seat. "Did you already know that no-good Cochran was workin' with Judson's bunch before he threw down on us?"

"Not for sure," Bo replied, "but I had an idea he might be. At first, I thought he was just a drifting cowhand like he claimed. I wouldn't have bought any grub for him otherwise. But it occurred to me a ways back that Judson might try a trick like that."

"Glad it did. That varmint looked mighty surprised when you caught him across the face with that whip."

"Did you see him after he fell?"

"Yeah. He bounced a time or two, but he didn't move after that."

Bo shook his head. He didn't feel any real regret that Cochran might have lost his life in the incident—the man was an owlhoot and a killer, after all, and had threatened to ventilate him and Scratch—but he didn't take any particular pleasure in the knowledge either.

Bo kept the team moving at a fast clip until the outlaws had fallen completely out of sight, and even after that, he didn't slow back to a normal pace until the coach had covered another mile or so. Then he let the horses walk and catch their breath.

The rest of the trip to the next relay station was peaceful. The hostler there didn't ask any questions, and Bo and Scratch didn't volunteer any information. They figured they would have to be telling what happened during the trip soon enough, when they reached Red Butte.

That took place shortly before dusk. Ponderosa was waiting on the porch for the stagecoach to arrive, and Abigail must have been inside the office because she emerged from the building even before the vehicle's wheels had stopped turning. Gil hurried around from the barn.

"Thank God you made it back safely," Abigail said, greeting the Texans as they climbed down.

"No thanks to Rance Judson," Scratch told her.

"That varmint and his gang o' desperadoes tried for us both times, comin' and goin'."

Abigail's eyes widened. "Were either of you hurt?" she asked.

"No, we were lucky," Bo said.

"'Pears that the coach wasn't so lucky," Ponderosa said. He came down the steps and poked a finger on his good hand through one of the bullet holes, just as the gunman calling himself Cochran had done back at Chino Valley. "They shot her up pretty good, looks like."

"That was yesterday," Bo explained. "They ambushed us in some hills this side of Cottonwood and came near to stopping us. We were able to fight them off, though, with some help from Mr. Carson."

Gil said, "I thought Carson was supposed to leave his wife and son in Cottonwood and come back with you today. Did he change his mind?"

"Those owlhoots changed it for him," Scratch said. "Plugged him in the arm durin' the fight."

"Oh, no!" Abigail said. "Was he badly hurt?"

"The doctor in Cottonwood said that he'll be fine. He just needs to rest up for a few days before he travels again," Bo said.

"What about Mrs. Carson and the little boy?"

Scratch shook his head and said, "Carson was the only one who got ventilated . . . if you don't count the coach. It's got some extra ventilation with all them bullet holes."

"Ponderosa and I can patch them," Gil said. His face

was grim. "We have another coach that can be used for the next run. In the meantime, someone needs to take the mail pouch down to the post office. I can do that if you'll unlock the box, whichever of you has the key."

Bo took the key to the driver's box, which Olmsted had returned to him just before the stagecoach left Cottonwood that morning, from his pocket and unlocked the driver's box. Gil reached inside and removed the mail pouch.

"Carson must have been glad you were coming right back here," he commented. "He probably wanted to write a letter to the mine superintendent since he wasn't able to return as scheduled."

"No, he didn't put a letter in the pouch, as far as I know," Bo said.

"Oh? Well, I guess he thinks that he'll be back soon enough that it doesn't really matter."

Gil slung the pouch over his shoulder and started down the street toward the post office. He called back, "Just leave the coach there. I'll drive it around to the barn and get the team unhitched when I'm done delivering the mail."

Bo lifted a hand in acknowledgment of Gil's offer.

Abigail said, "Come inside. I want to hear about what happened."

Bo, Scratch, and Ponderosa followed her into the office, where the Texans spent the next few minutes giving her a somewhat abbreviated version of the running battle the day before and the would-be ambush on the return trip. They left out some of the gorier details, such as the damage Scratch had done with that double load of buckshot at relatively close range.

"Did you tell the deputy in Cottonwood about what happened?" Abigail asked.

"We told him," Bo said, "but I don't reckon it'll do much good. It was too late to take a posse out yesterday evening, even if he could have gotten one rounded up, and Judson's bunch was long gone by this morning."

"'Cept for the ones who jumped you again," Ponderosa pointed out.

"Yeah, but they didn't make much of a stab at it once their little trick didn't work," Scratch said.

Ponderosa laughed. "Well, if nothin' else, you two are whittlin' down the numbers in Judson's gang. Keep this up for a while and maybe they'll decide that these parts ain't so healthy for 'em."

"I don't think there's much chance of that happening," Bo said. There was something else here that Judson wanted, something beyond some simple stage holdups. Bo was convinced of that . . . but he left that part of the thought unsaid.

"I'll bet after everything that's happened, these two fellas would like to wet their whistles," Ponderosa went on as he pushed himself to his feet.

Abigail smiled. "It will still be a while until supper, so if you gentlemen would like to go get a drink, that would be all right."

Scratch returned the smile. "That's pretty open-minded of you, ma'am. Most ladies don't understand how thirsty an hombre can get sometimes. No offense."

"My husband always said that a cold beer every now and then never hurt anyone. Go ahead. I'll see you later."

Bo, Scratch, and Ponderosa left the office and headed down the street toward Sharkey's. They met Gil on his way back from the post office and asked him to come with them, but the young man shook his head.

"I've got to get that team taken care of," he said as he went on toward the stage station.

"That young fella takes his job mighty serious," Scratch commented.

Ponderosa snorted. "Somebody's got to. Can't count on Dave for nothin'."

"Did he ever show up again?" Bo asked.

"Yeah, he come draggin' in sometime last night. He was around for a while this mornin', all sulled up like a bear with a sticker in its paw. Ain't seen him since then, though. No tellin' where he is now."

"Any trouble with Rutledge's men while we were gone?"

Ponderosa shook his head. "Nope. Things have been plumb peaceful. Be all right with me if they stayed that way."

"Us, too," Scratch said.

But both he and Bo knew just how unlikely that was. Trouble might have taken a brief holiday in Red Butte, but both of the Texans sensed that it was just waiting for the right time to explode again.

CHAPTER 22

Bo and Scratch looked around as they entered Sharkey's with Ponderosa. Several men who stood drinking at the bar were familiar, and the drifters pegged them as some of Jared Rutledge's men.

But the hardcases just sent unfriendly glances in the direction of Bo and Scratch, and then turned their attention back to their beers. They talked among themselves in low tones, but didn't give any indication that the conversation concerned the three men who had just entered the saloon.

"Reckon Rutledge gave 'em orders not to start any trouble?" Scratch asked in a low voice.

"It's possible," Bo replied. "Could be Rutledge wants to keep things on an even keel for a while, until he's ready to make another move."

"Wonder what that'll be . . . and when."

"We'll have to wait and see," Bo said.

He and Scratch and Ponderosa went to a table and sat down, keeping some distance between themselves and the gun-hung men at the bar. One of Sharkey's girls came over to the table and took their orders, then returned a few minutes later carrying a tray with three mugs of beer on it.

Rutledge's men finished their drinks and filed out of the saloon. Bo and Scratch relaxed a little. After the past two days, they were in no mood for another brawl or a gunfight. Even hombres who seemed to attract trouble like a lodestone attracted iron needed a few moments of peace every now and then.

It appeared that this respite wasn't destined to last very long, however, because only a few minutes later Jared Rutledge pushed through the batwings, looked around the room, and came toward their table as soon as he spotted them. The tall, powerfully built businessman had an intent expression on his rugged face.

"Uh-oh," Scratch said under his breath. "Looks like Rutledge is on the warpath."

"Take it easy," Bo advised. "Let's see what he wants."

Bo had to admit, though, that Rutledge looked like he was spoiling for a fight.

The freight line owner came to a stop in front of the table and gave a curt nod to the three men sitting there. "I want to talk to you," he said.

"I ain't sure you got anything to say that we'd be interested in," Ponderosa replied with a sneer.

Rutledge fixed the old-timer with a cold stare. "I wasn't talking to you, Pine," he said. "My business is with Creel and Morton."

"I don't recall us having any business with you, Rutledge," Bo said.

"Just hear me out, that's all I'm asking. And I'd like to talk to you privately."

"We trust Ponderosa," Scratch said. "Anything you want to say to us, you can say with him here."

"I'd rather not," Rutledge insisted.

Ponderosa gave a disgusted snort. "Don't waste your breath arguin' with this varmint, boys." He picked up his beer and drank the rest of it thirstily, then pushed to his feet. "I'll mosey on back to the station."

"You don't have to leave, Ponderosa," Bo said.

"I know that. I want to, though." Ponderosa looked pointedly at Rutledge. "The smell in here's worse'n usual this evenin'."

An angry flush crept into Rutledge's cheeks, but he didn't say anything. He was controlling his anger and dislike for Ponderosa with a visible effort.

Ponderosa started to leave, but paused after a step to look back at Bo and Scratch. "Just remember one thing while you're listenin' to what Rutledge has to say . . . His tongue's as forked as a snake's—or the Devil's."

The old man walked out of the saloon, seemingly oblivious to the glare that Rutledge sent after him.

Then Rutledge turned back to the table and asked, "Is it all right if I sit down?"

Scratch shrugged. "Free country, last time I checked."

Rutledge pulled back the empty chair across from the one where Ponderosa had been sitting. As he sat down, the girl who had delivered the beers earlier started toward the table, but Rutledge waved her away. He was interested in talking, not drinking.

"I heard that you ran into those outlaws between here and Cottonwood," he began.

"News gets around fast," Bo said. "Or maybe you already knew about it."

The tight rein that Rutledge was keeping on his temper looked like it almost slipped as he demanded, "What the hell is that supposed to mean?"

"Maybe you knew what was going to happen before it happened."

Scratch grinned and added, "I know what's gonna happen if you get much redder in the face, Rutledge. You're gonna bust a blood vessel, that's what."

"I don't like what you're implying, Creel," Rutledge said in a low, dangerous voice. "I don't have any connection with Rance Judson or his gang. I was just down at Hanson's store and heard him talking about the attacks on the stage."

Bo had to admit that Rutledge's claim sounded credible enough. Red Butte's post office was located inside Ole Hanson's general mercantile, and the Swede also served as the town's postmaster. Gil must have told Hanson about the outlaws jumping the stage; there was no secret about it, after all. And Rutledge could have easily heard Hanson talking about the incidents.

"All right," Bo said. "What else is on your mind, Rutledge?"

"You've seen for yourself what bad shape the Sutherland Stage Line is in. Its business has fallen off to almost nothing."

"Miz Abigail's coaches are still carryin' more passengers than yours is," Scratch pointed out, "and she's got the mail contract, to boot."

Rutledge snorted. "The government's going to take that contract away from her if the stagecoaches continue to get held up the way they have been lately. How long do you think Washington will put up with those disruptions of service?"

"And you figure that when Mrs. Sutherland loses the contract, you'll get it," Bo said. "That's a powerful motive for you to be causing trouble for her, it seems to me."

Rutledge had calmed down a little, but now he flushed again as Bo stopped just short of an outright accusation. "I don't have to do anything to cause her to lose that contract," he said. "It's going to happen naturally when the people in charge realize that running a stagecoach line is too big a job for a woman! That's why I offered to buy her out. I was trying to do her a favor, damn it!"

Bo leaned forward and said, "Wait a minute. You tried to buy out Will Sutherland when he was still alive, because *you* wanted to have the only stage line in these parts."

Rutledge met Bo's intense gaze squarely. "It's true I made an offer to Will," he said. "I knew there wasn't room for two stage lines, and I thought I could do a better job of it since I already had my freight route established. He turned me down flat. Stubborn man. Mule-headed actually." Rutledge shook his head. "But I went back to Abigail after Will died and made her an even better offer, since I figured she'd need the money to make a fresh start somewhere else. It never occurred to me that she'd be foolish enough to try to run the stage line by herself."

"She ain't by herself," Scratch said. "She's got her boys and ol' Ponderosa, and I reckon she had some other hombres workin' for her then, too."

Rutledge nodded. "She did, but they've all quit her one by one since those outlaws moved in and started causing so much trouble. Pine's an old man, and Gil's not cut out for a big job like that. Dave . . ." A contemptuous snort came from the man. "Dave's not worth a bucket of warm spit and never has been."

"So you expect us to believe that out of the goodness of your heart, you tried to buy the stage line from Mrs. Sutherland," Bo said. His tone made it clear that he didn't believe Rutledge.

"Sure, I thought I could turn a profit with the line, but blast it, I didn't want to see Abigail ruined!" One of Rutledge's hands clenched into a fist and thumped the table. "She'd already been through enough. She'd lost her husband. She didn't deserve to go through any more trouble, and I knew that's what the line would be for her. She ought to have better, a woman like her—"

He stopped short, leaned back in his chair, and glared at Bo and Scratch, who just sat there watching him silently.

After a moment, Rutledge went on. "I don't have to explain myself to a couple of saddle tramps. What I really came in here to do was to ask you if you had enough sense to go to work for me."

That took the Texans by surprise. Dryly, Bo asked, "Why would you want a couple of saddle tramps with no sense to work for you?"

Rutledge made a curt motion with his hand, dismissing what he'd just said. "You two have shown that you can handle trouble, both in those fracases with my men and in fighting off Judson's gang not once but twice."

"Three times," Scratch said. "You're forgettin' that first day when they were chasin' the stage with Gil and Ponderosa on it."

"All right, three times. It doesn't matter. You're good men in a fight. I like to have that sort of man on my side."

"We're working for Mrs. Sutherland," Bo said.

"Give notice," Rutledge snapped. "She can't keep going much longer. I happen to know that she's almost out of money."

"Got a friend at the bank, do you?"

"Never mind that. I've made you an honest offer. I want an honest answer. Once the Sutherland line has gone under, my business will be booming. I'll need men, good men. How about it?"

Bo looked across the table at Scratch. "What do you think?"

Scratch picked up his mug, drank the rest of the beer in it, and set it back down on the table deliberately as he drew the back of his other hand across his mouth. "I think I'd rather go find a hog waller somewhere and work for the hogs," he said.

Bo smiled. "To put it a little more diplomatically, Rutledge . . . no, I don't think I will at that. I'd rather work for the hogs, too."

Rutledge scowled at them. "You're making a mistake," he said. "I know you think that I'm somehow to blame for Abigail's troubles, but I'm not. I can see the writing on the wall, though. The Sutherland Stage Line is doomed, and if you stay there you'll go down with it."

"I reckon we're done talking here," Bo said.

Rutledge scraped his chair back and stood up. "Don't say that I didn't try to give you fair warning."

He turned on his heel and stalked out of Sharkey's.

Bo still had a little beer in his mug. He drank it and said, "Now that was interesting."

"What? The way that varmint had the gall to come in here and ask us to abandon Miz Abigail and go to work for him?"

"That . . . and the way he kept calling her Abigail and saying that she deserved better."

Scratch frowned across the table at his partner. "What in blazes are you sayin', Bo? You don't think ol' Rutledge has got himself a soft spot for her, do you?"

"He *did* sound sort of sympathetic toward her," Bo said.

Scratch shook his head. "He's been tryin' to run her outta business!"

"That's the way it looks to Abigail."

"You said yourself he might be tied in with that owlhoot Judson!" Scratch protested.

"And he might be. I haven't ruled that out."

"I'd come a lot closer to believin' that than I would that he's really worried about her," Scratch said. "A fella like that don't care about anything except his own self."

Bo stood up. "I reckon it'll all get sorted out sooner or later, one way or another. Right now, supper ought to be ready down at the station and I'm hungry. That bowl of stew we had at the Chino Valley station was a lot of miles and hours ago."

"A few gunshots, too," Scratch said, remembering Cochran and the latest attempt on their lives by Rance Judson's gang. As he and Bo left the saloon, Scratch went on. "You know, by practically accusin' Rutledge of being in on it with Judson, you might've made them targets on our backs even bigger, Bo."

In the gathering darkness, Bo smiled. "You can't clean out a hornet's nest without stirring up the hornets first," he said.

By the time full night had fallen, the rider was already waiting at the butte looming over the settlement. He heard the slow, steady approach of hoofbeats and rested his hand on the butt of his gun until a low whistle cut through the air. He returned the signal, and a moment later Rance Judson rode out of the shadows at the base of the sheer sandstone cliff.

"What does it take to kill two old men?" the rider from Red Butte coldly demanded without any greeting.

Judson spat and cursed. "Creel and Morton aren't typical old men. They're gun-handy and tough as whang leather. I never saw anybody quite as lucky as they are either."

"I'm beginning to think that luck has nothing to do with it."

Judson ignored the implications of that statement. "They weren't by themselves yesterday either. They had help."

"For God's sake! Thatcher Carson is no gunfighter. He shouldn't have been any threat to your men or anybody else."

"Anybody can get lucky," Judson insisted. "That's just what I was sayin'. Carson helped them out yesterday, and today the man I put next to 'em must've tipped them off somehow without meaning to."

"Did you ask him about it?"

Judson grunted. "You could ask Cochran all day, but you wouldn't get an answer. Snapped his neck clean as you please when he fell off that stagecoach."

The man from Red Butte took his hat off and rubbed a weary hand over his face. As he replaced his hat, he said, "All right, there's no point in arguing about it. Time's getting short now. If we can't get rid of Creel and Morton, we may just have to take our chances with them when the big payoff comes. Even if they're really as tough and lucky as you say they are, they're only two men. They won't be able to stop us."

"Damn right," Judson said. "We're fixin' to be rich men."

"But if you *do* get another chance to kill those blasted Texans . . . make sure they wind up dead next time."

CHAPTER 23

Supper was ready when Bo and Scratch got back to the stage station. Abigail called them into the dining room, where they found her standing by the table with a worried expression on her face.

"What did Jared Rutledge want to talk to you about?" she asked the Texans.

Bo and Scratch looked at Ponderosa, who stood there looking like butter wouldn't melt in his whiskery mouth. Obviously, he had come back here and told Abigail that they were talking to Rutledge down at Sharkey's saloon.

"Just more of the usual bluster," Bo said. "He told us that your stage line was going to go under and threatened us if we stayed around and tried to help you."

Those things weren't untrue; Bo just hadn't mentioned the other things Rutledge had said, such as offering them jobs and claiming that he had tried to buy out Abigail after her husband died because he felt sorry for her. For now, it seemed to Bo that it would be better not to go into those things.

Abigail's chin lifted defiantly. "We'll just see about that," she said. "Ponderosa, where's Gil?"

"Still out at the barn, I reckon. I'll go let him know supper's ready."

Ponderosa went out through the back door. Abigail looked at Bo and Scratch again and said, "Maybe you think Mr. Rutledge is right. Maybe it would be best if the two of you just rode on. After all, this isn't really your trouble . . ."

"No chance o' that, ma'am," Scratch told her with a smile. "This became our trouble as soon as we took cards in the game. Anyway, I see a big bowl o' chicken an' dumplin's on the table. We been eatin' better since we came to Red Butte than we have in a month o' Sundays."

Bo smiled, too. "Scratch is powerful fond of chicken and dumplings."

Abigail's tense stance relaxed as she laughed. "Sit down then and enjoy yourselves," she told them. "Gil and Ponderosa ought to be in soon."

"What about Dave?" Bo asked.

Abigail's smile disappeared. "He promised me that he would be here," she said. "But we're not going to wait for him. I've learned not to do that."

As she predicted, Gil and Ponderosa came in from the barn a few minutes later, but Dave didn't show up until long after supper was over. Bo, Scratch, and Ponderosa had already gone back out to the barn to turn in when the young man rode up. The Texans were sitting with Ponderosa just outside the tack room and having a last smoke. Dave gave them a surly look in the dim light of the lantern that hung on a nail by the tack room door.

"Need a hand unsaddlin'?" Scratch asked in a

friendly tone as he dropped the butt of his quirly on the dirt and ground it out with his boot heel.

"I can take care of my own horse," Dave said. He swung down from the animal's back and began undoing the cinches.

"How are Angus and Culley doing these days?" Bo asked. "Haven't seen them around much lately."

"Neither have I," Dave snapped. "I guess we've decided to part company."

"Not a bad idea. Those two were trouble."

Dave paused in his chore and looked back over his shoulder at Bo. "You don't know what trouble is, mister."

"Oh, I reckon we've been introduced a time or two." Bo put his pipe back in his mouth and puffed on it.

Dave just grunted and went back to unsaddling his horse. When he was finished, he rubbed the horse down and made sure that it had grain and water in the stall. Then he stalked out, heading for the station building.

"Fella takes good care of his mount," Scratch said. "Got to give him that much."

"Didn't appear to be drunk tonight either," Ponderosa said. "Maybe the boy's decided it's time to straighten up and grow up. I ain't a-gonna hold my breath waitin' to see it, though. Don't expect nothin' outta Dave. That's the only way you won't be disappointed sooner or later."

"Wonder where he's been," Bo mused.

"No tellin'."

The Texans glanced at each other, remembering what had happened when they followed Dave a few days earlier and ran into Judson's gang.

They had a pretty good idea where Dave had been tonight—and neither of them liked it.

The next stagecoach run to Chino Valley and Cotton-wood was still a few days away, so in the morning Bo and Scratch walked down to the marshal's office to talk to Tom Harding. Back at the station, Gil and Ponderosa were working on patching the bullet holes in the old Concord.

Harding looked up from his desk, where he was drinking coffee and reading a newspaper, when the Texans walked in. "Morning," he said pleasantly enough. "Anybody try to shoot you today?"

"No, but it's early yet," Scratch replied.

"You must have heard what happened," Bo said.

"I heard Judson's bunch jumped the stagecoach twice, once on the way to Cottonwood and once on the way back. Thatcher Carson wound up with a bullet in his arm." Harding gestured with his cup. "You fellas have a seat. Coffee on the stove if you want it."

Neither of them did this morning, having downed a couple of cups each at the stage station. Scratch picked up a ladder-back chair, reversed it, and straddled it, while Bo sat down on the battered old sofa and cocked his right ankle on his left knee.

"Carson doesn't have a bullet in his arm," Bo said.

"It went all the way through. Good clean wound that should heal up nicely."

"I'm glad to hear it. He's not a bad hombre for an Easterner."

"He was telling us about that mine he works for. The Pitchfork, right?"

Harding nodded. "Yeah. It's the only one still operating in these parts. They found the big vein there, and it hasn't played out yet."

"Pretty profitable operation, is it?"

"Oh, sure," Harding answered without hesitation. "It's owned by a syndicate with offices in Denver and San Francisco, and I reckon it makes plenty of money for the owners. I'm not sure why Carson would be braggin' on it, though. He hardly ever goes out to the mine itself. He handles the books and has an office here in town, right next door to the bank, in fact."

"We were thinking we'd ride out there and take a look at it," Bo said.

A frown creased the lawman's forehead. "How come?" he wanted to know. "It ain't for sale, I'm pretty sure of that."

Bo and Scratch grinned at each other. "Can you imagine either of us ownin' a mine, Marshal?" Scratch asked with a laugh. "We're just curious, is all. Carson said it was quite a setup."

"Oh, it is. Got all sorts of modern equipment. You boys ever do any mining?"

"A little," Bo said.

"Pick-and-shovel stuff," Scratch added. "Did a little panning for gold out in California, too."

"Well, this is nothin' like that," Harding assured them. "The Pitchfork is big business all the way. I guess it might be kind of interestin' at that."

"Can you tell us how to get there?" Bo asked.

"Sure. It's about five miles west of here, up in the foothills. There's a good trail, you can't miss it." The marshal chuckled. "The miners beat that trail into the ground, comin' into town to go to Sharkey's and the other saloons and bawdy houses."

"I don't recall seeing a lot of miners in town," Bo said. "Actually, I don't think I've seen any since Scratch and I have been here."

"Nope," Scratch agreed. "Plenty o' cowhands, but no miners."

Harding scraped a fingernail along his jaw. "Now that you mention it, they haven't been around the settlement much lately. I guess things are so good that Flynn's workin' everybody double time out there."

"Flynn?" Bo repeated.

"Theodore Flynn. He's the superintendent. Works for that syndicate I mentioned."

Bo nodded. "I see." He pushed himself to his feet. "Well, I reckon we'll be going."

Harding's eyebrows went up in surprise. "You're not even gonna ask me to go lookin' for those outlaws who jumped you?"

"Wouldn't do any good if we did, would it?" Scratch said.

"Well . . . I don't suppose it would. I don't have any authority out in the badlands, and I doubt if I could round up a posse to go with me. One man goin' out there after Judson by himself would just be committin' suicide, if you ask me."

"You're probably right, Marshal," Bo said.

Two men, though, might be a different story . . . especially if they were veteran troubleshooters from Texas.

"How come you never told anybody about that letter Carson wrote for Flynn?" Scratch asked as they rode out of Red Butte a short time later, heading west into the foothills toward the Pitchfork Mine.

"I got the feeling when he gave it to us that he'd prefer we kept quiet about it."

"He never said that."

"No, it's just a hunch that I have—"

"And your hunches usually turn out to be right," Scratch said. "Shoot, don't you reckon I know that by now?"

"By the time Carson gave us that message, we'd been through a gunfight with him," Bo went on. "That tends to make you trust somebody. And since he didn't send it in the regular mail but asked us to deliver it personally . . ."

"You don't have to convince me. Like I told you, I'll play along with whatever hunch you got, Bo, because chances are it's gonna turn out to be right."

Bo chuckled. "I appreciate the confidence. I hope it's not misplaced."

They rode on, not getting in any hurry as they followed the trail toward the mine. The trail was as easy to see as Marshal Harding had indicated that it would be, beaten down by the hooves of countless horses and mules as well as the wheels of heavily loaded wagons. On the way from the town to the mine, those wagons would be loaded with supplies for the miners; going the other way, the weight would come from ore wagons carrying gold, silver, and copper. Mostly copper, Bo reflected, since that was the dominant mineral in these parts, but a significant amount of gold and silver would be obtained, too, when that copper ore was refined.

He recalled being told that Judson's gang had raided one of the shipments from the mine. Chances were that hadn't been a very good haul for the outlaws. They might have gotten a few gold and silver nuggets, because those turned up from time to time in the mine shaft, too, but most of the shipment must have been copper ore, which wasn't worth a great deal unless you had the capability of refining it.

Still, it was hard to predict what a bunch of outlaws would do. Many of them were a little off in the head; otherwise they never would have taken to riding the owlhoot trail to begin with.

Just as in the approach to Cottonwood, the terrain here on the eastern slopes of the Santa Marias became more rugged and covered with trees. Bo and Scratch found the mine at the head of a narrow valley between two ridges, backed up to a good-sized hill. There were several large buildings made of logs—a long one that was probably a barracks for the miners, a mess hall with a cookshack adjacent to it, an office and living quarters for the superintendent and a couple of engineers, and a shedlike building where the ore that came from the mine was sorted. Steel rails led from that building to the gaping mouth of the mine itself, where they disappeared into that black hole in the side of the hill. Ore carts could be filled with the chunks gouged from the earth and wheeled along the tracks to the sorting shed.

Actually, the setup was even more advanced than that, Bo and Scratch saw as they came closer. There was a pulley arrangement with steel cables to pull the ore carts. It was powered by a donkey engine that sat at the far end of the sorting shed.

"First class all the way, just like the marshal said," Scratch commented.

"Yeah," Bo agreed. He saw a couple of dozen men working in the sorting shed, and more were going in and out of the tunnel. It was a busy place, and from the looks of that barracks, maybe as many as a hundred men were employed here, which made it even more puzzling why he and Scratch hadn't seen any of them in Red Butte.

They reined the dun and the bay to a halt in front of the building that they guessed housed the office. That was where they would likely find Theodore Flynn, the superintendent, although it was possible he could be in the mine itself or somewhere else around here. They were just about to swing down from their saddles when the door of the building opened and a man stepped out onto the narrow porch. He had a Winchester in his hands, and the weapon made a familiar metallic clatter as he worked the lever.

"Stay right where you are!" the man barked at Bo and Scratch. "Who are you, and what the hell are you doing here?"

CHAPTER 24

The Texans were startled by this unfriendly reception, but they'd had guns pointed at them plenty of times before. They didn't let it spook them. They just eased back into their saddles and Bo said, "Take it easy, mister. We're not looking for trouble."

"What we're lookin' for," Scratch said with a friendly smile, "is a fella name of Flynn. Would that happen to be you, mister?"

The man with the rifle frowned and lowered the weapon, but only slightly. It was still pointed in the general direction of the two visitors.

"That's right, I'm Flynn," he said. "And I won't ask you again. Who're you?"

"Bo Creel," Bo said. "This is Scratch Morton. We work for Mrs. Abigail Sutherland."

The frown on Theodore Flynn's face deepened. He was a tall man, lean almost to the point of gauntness, with a lantern jaw and a shock of iron gray hair. He bore a faint resemblance to the late President Lincoln.

"You're talking about the lady who owns the stage-coach line?" Flynn demanded.

Bo nodded. "That's right."

"Are you here on her behalf?"

"Nope," Scratch said. "We got a message for you."

"A letter actually," Bo said. He reached inside his coat, which prompted Flynn to lift the Winchester again. "Take it easy," Bo told the man as he slowly withdrew the square envelope that Thatcher Carson had given him in Cottonwood. "All I want to do is give this to you."

Flynn still looked suspicious. "Who's it from?"

"Thatcher Carson."

"Carson! He was supposed to be back from Cotton-wood yesterday."

Bo shook his head and said, "He couldn't make the trip. He was wounded when outlaws jumped the stage on the way to Cottonwood."

"Wounded!"

"Like to repeat things, don't you, mister?" Scratch drawled.

Flynn glared at him for a second, then turned his attention back to Bo. "How do you know about this? If that letter is for me, how did you get your hands on it?"

"Carson gave it to us and asked us to deliver it to you," Bo explained, sounding more patient than he actually felt. He didn't like being greeted at gunpoint, and he didn't much care for Flynn's overall attitude

either. But he was willing to cut the mine superintendent some slack . . . for now. "We were on the stage,
too. I handled the team, and Scratch was the shotgun
guard. Like I said, we work for Mrs. Sutherland."

"Oh. Well, I guess that makes sense." Still not
looking too happy about this visit, Flynn lowered the
rifle again, this time letting the barrel sag all the way
down until it pointed at the rough planks of the porch.
"Give me the letter."

"All right for us to dismount?"

Flynn jerked his head in a nod. "Go ahead. Got
coffee on the stove inside, if you'd care for a cup," he
added with grudging hospitality.

"That sounds pretty good after the ride out here
from town," Bo said. He and Scratch swung down
from their saddles and looped their horses' reins
around a short tie rail in front of the building.

Flynn waited for them as they climbed the three
steps to the porch. He thrust out his left hand. Bo put
the envelope in it, and Flynn grunted and jerked his
head for them to follow him into the building.

The door led into a sparsely furnished office. Flynn
wasn't the sort of man to go in for a lot of frills. You
could tell that by looking at his plain black trousers
and the black vest over a white shirt. Solid workman's
boots were on his feet. He placed the Winchester on a
scarred desk and motioned toward the potbellied stove
in the corner, indicating that Bo and Scratch should
help themselves to the coffee simmering in the pot
there.

While they poured cups of the thick, black brew, Flynn ripped open the envelope, took out a folded sheet of paper, and unfolded it to scan the words Thatcher Carson had written on it. His lean face remained expressionless, so there was no telling if the message contained good news or bad. Not that it was any of the Texans' business anyway.

Flynn put the letter on the desk next to the rifle and said, "I'm obliged to you men for bringing that out to me. Does anyone else know about it?"

Bo shook his head. "Nobody except Mrs. Carson. She was there when Carson gave us the letter."

"But you didn't say anything to anyone in Red Butte about it? It didn't go through the regular mail?"

"Nope," Scratch said. "We've had it with us ever since Carson handed it over yesterday mornin' in Cottonwood."

Flynn nodded and said, "Good. I appreciate your discretion."

"You want to tell us what this is all about?" Bo asked. Whether it was their business or not, it wouldn't hurt anything to ask.

Flynn opened his mouth like he was about to reply to the question, but then his lips snapped shut like a steel trap and formed a thin line for a moment. He shook his head and said, "Sorry. It's just Pitchfork business. Nothing interesting."

"All right," Bo said, his voice mild. He didn't believe for a second, though, that the missive from Carson didn't contain anything interesting or impor-

244

tant. A glance at Scratch told him that his partner felt the same way.

But they were men of their word. They had delivered the message to Flynn as promised, and that was the end of it.

"Anything else I can do for you?" Flynn asked.

Bo looked again at Scratch, who shrugged. "I reckon not," Bo said. He added, "Obliged for the coffee," even though the stuff was bitter and almost vile. Neither of the drifters finished what was in their cups.

Flynn followed them out of the office, leaving the rifle inside this time. As they reached the porch, the mine superintendent said, "Sorry for pointing that gun at you when you rode up. Didn't know who you were, and we've had some trouble with outlaws lately. This is the only mine still operating in the area, so we're sort of a target for thieves."

"Yeah, we heard talk in town about how Rance Judson and his gang hit the place once," Bo said. Flynn seemed to be a tight-lipped man by nature, but it might be possible to get him talking a little.

"That's right," Flynn said with a curt nod. "It's been a couple of months, but you never know when they might show up here again. My guards tried to fight them off. One man was killed and a couple more wounded."

"I reckon that's why you've been keeping all the miners out here lately instead of letting them go into town. In case Judson's gang shows up again, I mean."

Flynn hesitated, just for a second, then said, "Yeah, that's right."

"Seems odd that those outlaws would attack the mine like that," Bo mused. "I know there's gold and silver to be found in that copper ore, but seems like it would be more trouble to steal than it's worth until it's been refined."

"Well, they got into the office, too, and looted a handful of nuggets and the petty cash."

"Couldn't have added up to much."

Flynn's eyes narrowed in suspicion again. "You ask a lot of questions, Creel. And the answers aren't really any of your business."

Scratch laughed and slapped Flynn on the back. "Now you see what I got to put up with," he said. "Bo's just plumb curious about everything, and he never shuts up with the questions. But it don't mean nothin'. Half the time I don't think he even knows he's doin' it."

Bo nodded and said, "Sorry, Mr. Flynn. We spend so much time out on the trail by ourselves that when we get around new folks I tend to talk too much."

"That's all right," Flynn said with ill grace. "I just don't like anybody prying into mine business."

"Sure, I understand. Anyway, we need to get back to Red Butte."

Bo and Scratch untied their horses and mounted up. They lifted hands in farewell, turned the dun and the bay and rode back down the hill.

"That fella was about to get plumb spooked,"

Scratch said, pitching his voice low enough so that only Bo, riding alongside, could hear him.

"Yeah," Bo agreed. "I'm glad you stepped in like that . . . even though you're usually the one who can't ever keep his mouth shut."

Scratch laughed. "I figured you'd like that." As he grew more serious, he went on. "There's somethin' goin' on at that mine that ain't right."

"Yes, Flynn was hiding something. He was worried about more than just those outlaws. He looked like every nerve in his body was stretched tight as a barb-wire fence, and whatever was in the letter from Carson didn't make him feel any better."

Scratch rubbed his jaw and asked, "You think it's tied in with all the other hell-raisin' that's been goin' on around here?"

"I don't see how, except that Judson's gang hit the mine, too. But I've got a hunch—"

Scratch chuckled.

"—that it might be," Bo went on.

"How're we gonna find out?"

"Now, that I don't know," Bo admitted. "I was thinking, though, that we might go have another look for Judson's hideout. I'm convinced it's somewhere around that other butte we saw over in the badlands, the other side of Hell Creek. There has to be some other way in there besides through that canyon where those rannies shot at us."

"Maybe we could circle north of it and come in from that direction," Scratch suggested.

Bo nodded. "That's what I was thinking, too. But we'll take some extra water and some supplies this time, in case we're out there for a couple of days."

"Reckon it's safe to leave Red Butte for that long?"

"The trouble between Abigail and Rutledge seems to have settled down for now," Bo said. "I think we can chance it."

"You know how trouble is," Scratch warned. "Sometimes it just sits back in the weeds, waitin' for a good time to crop up again."

"We'll have to run that risk." Bo peered off into the distance. "I don't know why, but I have a feeling there's a showdown brewing. Maybe we can head it off if we can find a way to get a posse into Judson's hideout before all hell breaks loose."

It was the middle of the day before the Texans got back to Red Butte. Gil and Ponderosa were in the barn when they rode in.

"Where've you two been all mornin'?" the old-timer asked.

"Just out riding around," Bo replied as he and Scratch dismounted.

"You seem to do a lot of that," Gil said with a slightly suspicious frown.

Scratch slapped his bay on the shoulder and said, "These hosses don't take kindly to bein' penned up. Neither do me and Bo."

"You can ride on any time you want."

"Hold on, boy," Ponderosa said to Gil. "Don't go

248

runnin' these fellas off just yet. This shoulder o' mine ain't gonna be healed up for a while."

"I didn't mean anything by it," Gil said, but his sullen tone indicated that he still wasn't feeling very friendly.

Bo and Scratch shrugged off the young man's surly attitude. Gil probably felt like he had the weight of the world on his shoulders these days, what with all the troubles facing the stage line and the lack of help from his brother, and that was enough to make anybody a mite touchy.

"We didn't miss dinner, did we?" Scratch asked as he and Bo unsaddled their horses.

"No, Miz Abigail ought to have it ready any time now," Ponderosa told them.

As a matter of fact, it was only a few minutes later when Abigail came out to the barn and told them the midday meal was on the table. The men went inside eagerly.

As they ate, Ponderosa talked about patching the bullet holes in the stagecoach that morning. "I think me an' Gil got all of 'em," he said. "Judson's bunch must'a thrown a heap o' lead at you boys. That coach was about as shot up as I ever seen one. It's mighty lucky Miz Carson and the little boy weren't hit."

"We can't count on being that lucky every time," Gil said. "It's no wonder we don't have any passengers anymore."

"Don't worry," Abigail said. "It's all going to be all right."

Gil snorted. "No offense, Ma, but I don't see how you can be so sure of that."

"I just am, that's all."

Abigail sounded mighty certain, all right, which Bo and Scratch both noticed. Neither of the Texans could see any reason for her to be so optimistic, given the situation, but that was better than surrendering to doom and gloom, they supposed.

After the meal was over, they went back out to the barn with Ponderosa. Gil remained in the headquarters building, which was all right with Bo and Scratch. They had a few things to say to the old-timer.

As Bo filled an after-dinner pipe and Scratch rolled a quirly, Bo said, "I reckon we can trust you, Ponderosa."

"I hope to smile you can! Chances are I'd'a been buzzard bait that first day we met if you fellas hadn't come along when you did, since those outlaws would'a had to kill me to stop me from fightin'." Ponderosa gave the Texans a grim nod. "Tell me whatever you want. It won't go no further'n these ol' ears o' mine."

"We haven't been just riding around looking at the countryside," Bo said. "We've been trying to find Judson's hideout."

"And we figure we've got a pretty good line on it," Scratch said.

Ponderosa's eyes widened, and he ran the fingers of his good hand through his whiskers. "Tarnation! Are you boys undercover deputies or somethin' like that?"

Scratch grinned. "Us? Lawmen? Not hardly!"

"Although we have worn badges at times in the past," Bo said. "Right now, we're just trying to figure out a way to stop Judson and his bunch from making life miserable and dangerous for everybody from here to Cottonwood."

"What you're sayin' is you're the sort o' hombres who ain't happy unless you're neck-deep in trouble, that right?"

Bo chuckled. "Just about. We don't like outlaws."

"And we got a habit of stickin' up for folks who need help," Scratch put in. "Plus ol' Bo there, he plumb hates a mystery, and there's been some mighty odd things goin' on around here lately."

"Tell me about it!" Ponderosa said. "Seems like trouble's been comin' at us from all sides."

"Maybe all those different sources of trouble are connected," Bo said, "or at least some of them are. Scratch and I think we can figure it all out, especially if we can corral Judson some way."

"That ain't gonna be easy . . . or safe."

"We know, but we have to try."

"We need a couple of extra canteens and some food," Scratch said. "We're liable to be out on the trail for a day or two."

Ponderosa nodded. "I can wrangle that for you. What do you want me to tell Miz Abigail, though? She's bound to notice you ain't here, and she'll want to know where you've got off to."

"Tell her we've gone to do a little prospecting," Bo

said. "With all the mining that's gone on around here, it's not unreasonable to think that we might try to find a fresh vein. But tell her we'll be back to handle the next run to Cottonwood, too."

Ponderosa nodded. "All right. I reckon that story don't sound too fishy. She's a pretty sharp lady, though. She may not believe it."

"We'll deal with that later if we have to," Bo said.

"Wait here. I'll be back with the canteens and the grub."

Ponderosa went back into the building. When he was gone, Scratch said, "You didn't tell him about followin' Dave out there, or about bein' suspicious that the Pitchfork Mine is tied in with all this somehow."

Bo shook his head. "Time enough for that later. For now, we'll just concentrate on making sure we know where Judson's hideout is."

They got their horses saddled up again, and when Ponderosa came back a short time later with the canteens and a canvas bag full of food, Bo told him where they were going, detailing as best he could the route and the location of the butte where they thought the outlaw stronghold might be.

"Just in case we don't come back, you'll know where to tell the law to look for us," Bo added.

"The law, hell," Ponderosa said. "I'll be lookin' for you myself, soon as this shoulder o' mine's healed up enough I can ride. Damned if I don't wish I could come with you now."

"Don't start after us by yourself," Scratch warned.

"Those badlands are no place for a man alone, especially with Judson's bunch hangin' around. Get word to the sheriff in Prescott and stay after him until he sends a posse in there."

Ponderosa nodded his agreement, but his fierce expression made it clear that he would probably be riding with any posse that went looking for the Texans.

Ponderosa didn't ask how they had found the butte in the first place, which was just as well since Bo didn't want to tell him about Dave's likely involvement with the outlaws anyway. The old-timer just shook hands with them and said, "Good luck, fellas. I got a feelin' you'll be needin' it."

"We always need luck," Scratch said with a smile.

"Yeah, but this time you'll be headin' straight into the lion's den, just like that fella in the Bible."

"You mean Daniel?" Bo asked.

Ponderosa shook his head. "No, I'm talkin' about the fella who went in there before Daniel, the one you ain't never heard of . . . 'cause he got plumb ate up."

CHAPTER 25

When Bo and Scratch left Red Butte this time, they rode east along the road to Chino Valley and Cottonwood, just in case anyone was watching them. That was possible, since they suspected that Judson might have at least one confederate in the settlement. If that was the case, it wouldn't be so obvious that the

Texans were setting out in search of Judson's hideout again.

They followed the regular trail until they reached Hell Creek. After crossing the little bad-smelling stream on the bridge, they turned north and began following its eastern bank. Eventually, the creek would lead them to the spot where they had crossed it several days earlier when they were following Dave Sutherland. Bo and Scratch knew they would recognize that place, and from there they could figure out how they wanted to proceed.

As they headed into the badlands, Scratch said, "This country ain't got any cooler, or any prettier, since we were here the other day."

"No, and I don't expect that it will any time soon," Bo agreed. Both men had already shucked their coats, rolled them up, and tied them behind the saddles. Their shirt sleeves were rolled up over their forearms, and Bo had removed the string tie he usually wore and unbuttoned his collar.

"I been thinkin' about everything that's gone on, tryin' to put it together in some way that makes sense," Scratch said, "but it always winds up just goin' around and around in my head."

"We're missing the one thing that would tie it all together," Bo said. "And I've got a feeling that it's something we've already seen or heard, if we could just realize what it means."

"Maybe. I've about decided, though, that I ain't gonna worry about it anymore. You figure out who's to blame for all of it, point at the son of a gun, and I'll shoot him."

Bo laughed. "Deal."

It was past mid-afternoon by the time they spotted some familiar landmarks and realized that they had reached the place where they had crossed the stream before. Hell Creek had gotten narrower but not any less foul-smelling. They reined in, took a drink from their canteens, and poured water in their hats for the horses, who didn't seem to be in any mood to quench their thirst from the stream.

"I hope wherever those owlhoots are holed up, the water there stinks and tastes as bad as this creek does," Scratch said. "Varmints like that don't deserve any better."

"The sulfur in the creek won't kill you if you have to wind up drinking from it," Bo pointed out. "Some folks say that if you drink it long enough, you get used to it."

Scratch snorted in disbelief. "Yeah, you might get used to Hell if you were there long enough, too." He took another short swig from his canteen. "Where are we headed from here?"

"We'll keep following the creek north for another few miles," Bo decided. "Then we'll cut back to the east and see if we can spot that butte. We ought to be north of it by then."

"If we go that way far enough, we'll run into the Verde."

Bo shook his head. "We won't go all the way to the

river. That'd take a couple of days from here. I'd like to get that butte located by nightfall. Then maybe after dark we can work our way closer to it."

Scratch slung his canteen back on his saddle by its strap. "Sounds like a good plan to me," he said. "Let's get movin'."

They mounted up and rode on. The terrain was dry, ugly, and rough on both sides of the creek, which at times was nothing more than a narrow trickle through the rocks. Gradually the landscape began to lift to both east and west. That rise meant the stream bed cut deeper into the rocky ground.

The brimstone smell grew stronger. Scratch sniffed at the air and said, "What the hell is that?"

"So to speak," Bo said with a dry chuckle.

"What?"

"Smells like Hell."

"Yeah, it does."

A few moments later, they saw what was responsible for the stronger scent of sulfur in the air. They rode up a ridge and came out at the edge of a pool that had formed in a big hollow in the rock. It was perhaps twenty feet wide and forty feet from one end to the other. At the far end the waters of Hell Creek plunged down an eight-foot-tall waterfall, feeding the pool. The atmosphere around it was thick with that rotten-egg smell.

"Lord!" Scratch said. "Let's get on outta here."

Bo pointed across the pool at the waterfall. The stream emerged from a cleft in the rocks. The walls of that cleft rose some thirty feet from the level of the water.

"May be too narrow for us to get through there," Bo said. "We may have to leave the creek behind and strike out across country."

"That's all right with me. I'm gettin' mighty tired o' the smell anyway."

Bo hitched the dun into a walk and headed around the edge of the pool. "Won't hurt anything to have a look. We might be able to get through that way."

Sure enough, there was a game trail leading up into the cleft. It looked like the Texans' sure-footed mounts would be able to follow it. Bo dismounted and climbed up on foot to study the layout, leading his horse behind him. After a moment, he turned and called back down to Scratch, "We can make it. There's a ledge next to the creek that's big enough for us to ride single file."

Scratch didn't look too happy about that, but he dismounted and led his horse up the slope next to the waterfall. By the time he reached the cleft, Bo had already mounted up again and was waiting on the narrow ledge. Scratch swung up into the saddle, and they set out to follow the one-way trail alongside the stream.

The smell was worse than ever in the cleft, since there was no breeze. The creek appeared to be deeper here and definitely had a faster current. It leaped and chuckled along its rocky bed. The water had a faint yellowish tinge to it from the high sulfur content.

The cleft ran fairly straight, with only occasional bends. Bo and Scratch had no idea how long it was, but both of them hoped that they would soon be out of it. After a mile or so, though, there still appeared to be no end to the great slash in the earth that the creek had made sometime in the ancient past.

The looming walls, which in places seemed to be leaning in so that they overhung the trail, made the hoofbeats of the horses echo around the riders. The sound of the creek was unnaturally loud, too. After a few attempts at conversation, Bo and Scratch had fallen silent because their voices sounded so odd to them.

None of that, though, had prepared them for the deafening thunderclap of noise that assaulted their ears as a gun roared somewhere close by.

The shot was followed instantly by the high-pitched whine of a bullet ricocheting from the rock wall. Scratch had sensed as much as heard the slug whipping past his ear.

The Texans' horses were used to the sound of guns, but this was like being caught in the barrel of a cannon. As a second shot blasted, hard on the heels of the first, the animals spooked. The bay reared up and pawed violently at the air, while Bo's dun tried to turn around on the ledge, which was too narrow for such a maneuver.

Scratch yelled at his mount, which didn't help matters. Still reared up on its hind legs, the bay danced skittishly closer to the edge. As Bo fought to control his horse, he shouted, "Scratch, look out! The creek—"

The warning came too late, and there really wasn't anything Scratch could do anyway. With a shrill whinny of panic, the bay went over the edge, toppling into the creek and taking Scratch with it.

Whoever was behind them was still shooting, too, and by now the echoes were so loud and overpowering that it was impossible to think. Bo felt the dun leap underneath him as a slug burned across the animal's rump. When the horse came down, it was halfway off the trail. Unable to regain its balance, the dun followed Scratch's bay into the creek. Bo kicked his feet out of the stirrups and left the saddle as he followed his horse into the huge splash that resulted.

Bo went under the water, but he managed to grab a breath before he was submerged. He hadn't seen Scratch since his partner fell into the creek, and didn't know if Scratch had managed to get loose from the stirrups or not. Orienting himself, Bo gave a hard kick that propelled him in what he hoped was the direction where Scratch had disappeared.

The creek was murky and made seeing anything difficult. With two horses in the water, the danger of being struck by a flailing hoof was great. Bo peered around, trying to locate the animals in the yellow-tinged depths. He spotted one of them, and a few yards further on, Scratch was floundering around in the water, too.

Bo swam toward him, fighting the heavy weight of

his boots as they tried to pull him down. At the moment, though, that wasn't necessarily a bad thing. Whoever had taken those shots at them was still up there, and as soon as Bo and Scratch popped their heads above water, they might find themselves being used for target practice again.

A memory flashed through Bo's mind. As young men on the Texas frontier, sometimes he and Scratch had tossed some pumpkins into a fast-moving stream and then raced alongside it on horseback, blasting away at the floating gourds with Paterson Colts, the first revolvers they ever owned. Back then Texas had been a republic, and Bo and Scratch had belonged to a company of Rangers headed up by Captain Jack Hays. At that time the Rangers were the only line of defense the settlers had as they tried to make homes for their families in a mostly wild and untamed land. Those had been exciting times, fraught with danger, but Bo remembered them fondly . . .

He realized that he was sinking and his air was running out. He kicked hard again, stroked with his arms, and let the current carry him to Scratch's side. Scratch was still struggling. He could swim, but he had never been as comfortable in the water as Bo was. Bo remembered one time when they'd both wound up in the Brazos while it was in flood, and how Scratch would have drowned if Bo hadn't been there to fish him out.

With a grimace, Bo shoved the memories away for a second time. He knew how seductive they were, how easy it would be to give himself over to them, to go ahead and take a deep breath and go to the bottom and let the past have them both. Their best days were behind them now, and there came a time when you just had to stop fighting against the one foe who could never be defeated.

But not now. Not yet, damn it!

That thought went through Bo's mind like a bolt of lightning. He wrapped one arm around Scratch and kicked for all he was worth, propelling both of them toward the surface. The bushwhacker might be waiting up there, but that didn't matter anymore. They had to have air.

Their heads broke the surface. Even stinking of sulfur like it did, air had never smelled so sweet as it did then. Bo and Scratch both gulped down as much as they could, filling their lungs, and that helped combat the drag of their clothes and boots.

More shots blasted. Bo saw the bullets cutting into the water a few feet away. He kept his left arm around Scratch and with his right hand reached down to the holster on his hip, hoping that the Colt was still there.

It was. The thong over the hammer had held it in place. Bo slipped it free with his thumb and drew the gun. With those new-fangled metallic cartridges in it, a modern Colt could take a dunking like this and still work, something that couldn't be said of the old Patersons and Walkers. Despite the fondness that Bo felt for the things of his youth, he had to admit that some things were better now.

He added to the racket in the cleft by triggering two shots toward the figures he saw running along the ledge beside the creek. The current was carrying Bo and Scratch back downstream, in the direction they had come from. That had taken them right past the position of the two bushwhackers who had snuck up behind them. The sound of the creek and the echoes of the hoofbeats from their own horses had made it impossible for the Texans to know that they were being followed until it was too late.

Bo's shots both whined off the rock wall, but they came close enough to make the bushwhackers stop and duck. Bo got a good enough look at them to recognize them.

Angus and Culley, the two bullies from Red Butte who'd been with Dave Sutherland that first day!

Bo didn't see Dave, but that didn't mean the young man wasn't around somewhere close. Before Bo had time to think about it, he and Scratch went under again. This time they sunk so deep that Bo's feet hit the stream bed. He kicked against it and sent them bobbing back to the surface. Both Texans were spitting and sputtering and gasping for air as they came up.

Bo looked around, shaking his head to get the wet hair out of his eyes. He didn't see Angus and Culley along the ledge, and realized that the creek had carried him and Scratch around one of its occasional bends, taking them out of sight of the two would-be killers. Now was their chance to get out of the creek and deal with Angus and Culley on more or less equal terms.

If you could call it equal with him and Scratch being a lot like a couple of half-drowned rats . . . !

Bo stroked for the ledge. Scratch had calmed down some by now and caught his breath, and he was able to swim a little himself, instead of having to have Bo tow him to safety. When they reached the ledge, Bo helped Scratch climb onto its rocky surface, then clambered out of the creek himself. Water streamed from both Texans as they sat with their backs against the wall of the cleft.

"Best . . . check your guns," Bo said between gasps. "Angus and Culley are liable to . . . charge around that bend any time now."

"Angus and . . . Culley?" Scratch choked out. "Those varmints . . . from town?"

Bo nodded. "Yeah. I saw 'em on the ledge . . . while I was trying to make sure . . . you didn't drown."

"Me? Why . . . I was tryin'. . . to help you!"

The drifters grinned at each other. Scratch knew perfectly well that Bo had probably saved his life, and Bo knew it, too. But they were old friends, saddle pards from way back, and neither needed to say much for the other to know what he was thinking.

Anyway, it wasn't like Scratch hadn't saved Bo's bacon a heap of times, too.

Both of Scratch's ivory-handled Remingtons were in their holsters. He pulled them out and quickly checked them over, then nodded in satisfaction.

"I reckon they'll work," he said. "Now I just need somethin' to shoot at."

Bo had been listening intently as he thumbed fresh cartridges into his Colt's cylinder to replace the rounds he had fired. He shook his head and said, "I don't hear anybody coming."

He and Scratch instinctively had been pitching their voices low so that the cleft wouldn't be filled with echoes of what they were saying. It was possible that Angus and Culley were doing the same thing, but Bo doubted if the two men could make their way along the ledge without causing *some* noise. An Indian or another experienced frontiersman could manage that, but not a couple of town-living bullies.

Bo pushed himself to his feet and cat-footed toward the bend. Scratch followed him. Bo edged his head around the rock, halfway expecting to see Angus and Culley creeping toward them.

Instead, the cleft appeared to be empty.

The two bushwhackers had fled.

Bo shook his head and told Scratch, "They're gone. I guess they didn't want to come back this way."

"They were hopin' we were dead," Scratch said. "They figured either their bullets got us, or we drowned. But they didn't want to take a chance that we might still be alive and waitin' for 'em."

Bo nodded. "That's the way I read it, too."

"So . . . what do we do now?"

"Head back downstream and look for the horses, I

guess. We can't go back to hunting for Judson's hideout until we find them."

"Yeah," Scratch said. Neither of them mentioned what their fate would probably be if they couldn't find their mounts, or if the horses had drowned or been injured so that they couldn't be ridden. Their only chance would be to walk all the way back down the creek to the stage road. They wouldn't die of thirst, and they probably wouldn't starve to death in the time it would take them to make such a trek . . . but it would be a mighty hard journey anyway.

They would deal with that when and if they came to it. Their adventurous lives had taught them not to borrow trouble, but rather to deal with what was right in front of them. With that in mind, they holstered their guns and began trudging wearily south, following the ledge alongside Hell Creek.

CHAPTER 26

"They're dead, I tell you. I seen 'em both go under that last time. We hit 'em, and they either drowned or bled to death."

Culley just grunted. It was impossible to tell from his dull-witted face whether he agreed or disagreed with Angus's conclusion about the fate of Morton and Creel.

"Dave won't look down on us no more," Angus went on. "Him and his fancy owlhoot friends. Imagine him sneakin' off and joinin' Rance Judson's gang like that, without even tellin' us! Didn't he ever happen to think that we might be interested in ridin' with Judson and gettin' our hands on some of that loot?"

Resentment, jealousy, and admiration were all mixed in Angus's voice. Starting out, Dave Sutherland had been the one who'd wanted to tag along with him and Culley, not the other way around. He had looked up to them because they were tough.

But evidently not tough enough to suit Dave anymore, because over the past week he'd been spending less and less time with them, and he'd become more secretive about where he was going and what he was doing.

Angus knew, though, because one night when Dave was drunk, he'd let it slip about his connection with the Judson gang. He'd bragged about how he was feeding information to the outlaws and how he'd even gone along on some of the jobs they'd pulled. Dave hadn't taken part in any of the stagecoach holdups because, as he put it, even he had to draw the line somewhere. He wouldn't ride with the gang when they were robbing from his mother. But he'd tip them off when the stage was carrying something valuable, though. He didn't draw *that* line.

The thing of it was, the next time Angus and Culley had seen Dave, he'd acted like he didn't even say any of those things. Had he been so drunk that he didn't remember spilling his guts that way? After a while, Angus decided that was the only explanation that made any sense.

He'd been trying to figure out something he and Culley could do that would impress Dave and maybe even prompt him to take the two of them to Judson's hideout, so they could join the gang, too. That was when Angus had hit upon the idea of following those two troublemaking old Texans and killing them. That would serve a dual purpose: Dave would see that they deserved to be part of the Judson gang, and at the same time he and Culley would have their revenge on Creel and Morton.

It was perfect. They'd kept an eye on the Texans and followed them out to the Pitchfork Mine that morning, but the timing just hadn't been right for an ambush. Things had worked out much better this afternoon, with Creel and Morton following Hell Creek until the stream entered that knife-slash of a gully. Angus had been up there before and knew that once the Texans were on that narrow ledge, there wouldn't be any-where they could hide once the shooting started.

Problem was, things didn't work out exactly as Angus had envisioned them. Creel and Morton had fallen into the creek instead of being shot down on the ledge. The current, which was pretty swift inside the cleft, had swept them back downstream along with their horses while Angus and Culley were shooting at them. Angus was certain that they'd hit the Texans, as he'd told Culley, but the last they had seen of Creel and Morton, the old bastards were shooting at *them!*

So instead of following their victims around the bend in the creek, Angus had decided it would be all right to go on the way they were headed. They didn't have much choice in the matter anyway, since the ledge was too narrow for a horse to turn around. They could have headed back along the ledge on foot, but Angus had ruled that out. Another half mile or so and they would reach the end of the cleft. From there they could circle back around, pick up Hell Creek to the south, and find where the bullet-riddled bodies of those Texans had washed up. That was the way Angus saw it in his head, and by Godfrey, that was the way it was going to be!

"Gettin' tired o' this," Culley said as he rode behind Angus. Culley didn't say much, but when he did speak, he meant what he said. "Wanna be outta this hole in the ground."

"We will be soon," Angus assured him. "It's not much farther to where it ends. Less than half a mile."

Culley grunted. "Good. I don't like it."

"Well, don't you worry. It's almost over."

They continued on, following the ledge until the walls of the cleft began to lower on either side of them. The terrain smoothed out as the gigantic ridge that the cleft cut through sloped down and leveled off. The late afternoon sunlight seemed particularly bright to the two riders as they emerged from the long cut in the earth.

The glare was so strong, in fact, that Angus's eyes were dazzled at first and he didn't see the other men on horseback until he and Culley were right in front of them.

Angus jerked back on the reins, bringing his horse to an abrupt halt. He blinked rapidly, hoping that would help to clear his sun-blinded vision. He could make out six . . . no, eight . . . riders, sitting their saddles like they were waiting for something. Waiting for him and Culley? How was that possible? Nobody knew they were up here.

"Howdy, fellas," Angus called as Culley drew up alongside him. "Didn't expect to run into anybody out here in the middle of nowhere." He wished he could see the faces of the other men, but they remained nothing but dark silhouettes.

"You know Rance's orders," one of the men said. Since Angus couldn't really tell which of them the words came from, the voice seemed disembodied, like that of a ghost. But that didn't bother him too much because of what the man had said.

"Rance Judson?" Angus said, unable to keep the eagerness out of his voice. "We were just lookin' for him!" He was sure that once he explained about how he and Culley were friends of Dave Sutherland's, these men would take them right to the hideout . . .

Angus saw the men move, and he heard the cold metallic sound of guns being cocked. Alarm flared inside him. "Hold on a minute!" he said. "You don't understand—"

Instinct warned him that they weren't going to listen. His hand stabbed toward his gun as he yelled, "Culley, look out!"

It was too late for that shout to do any good, too late

for either of them. Angus still couldn't see the faces of the strangers, but he saw flame and smoke gush from the barrels of their guns. He felt the bullets thudding into his chest like hammer blows, felt himself being driven backward out of the saddle . . .

But he didn't feel it when he hit the stony ground, because he was already dead by then.

Bo and Scratch found their horses cropping at the sparse grass around the pool just below the waterfall, all the way back at the place where the cleft began. Scratch stared at the bay and the dun, who seemed none the worse for wear, and muttered, "Good Lord! You reckon they rode that waterfall down into the pool?"

Bo shook his head. "No, I figure they swam this far and then were finally able to climb out just before they got to the waterfall. The surface is closer to the same level as the ledge there."

"Yeah, you must be right. That's a lucky break for us."

"And for them," Bo said. "I don't think they'd have been able to go over that waterfall without breaking a leg . . . or two."

"Well, all I know is I'm mighty glad to see 'em. I wasn't lookin' forward to hoofin' it all the way back to Red Butte."

They made their way down the narrow trail to the pool. The horses watched them with the typically stolid, incurious gaze most horses wore.

"Reckon our extra clothes are any drier than what we got on?" Scratch asked.

"I doubt it. Now that we're out of that gully, the sun ought to dry what we're wearing fairly fast."

"Don't know if any o' that grub we brought with us'll be fit to eat."

"We'll salvage what we can," Bo said. He glanced at the sun, which was now low in the western sky, not far above the horizon. "Not as much daylight left as I thought there was. We'd better just camp here tonight and figure out what to do in the morning."

"Sounds good to me," Scratch said with a nod. "You think Angus and Culley will be comin' back this way?"

Bo frowned. "I don't know. After those shots we heard a while ago . . ."

They had still been walking along the ledge when they'd heard the faint popping of shots in the distance. The reports had echoed down the cleft, multiplying until it was impossible to tell how many shots were fired or by how many different guns. It had sounded like quite a volley, though. Bo and Scratch didn't know who had fired the shots, nor who or what the intended targets had been.

But they couldn't help but remember that Angus and Culley had been headed in that direction. Had the two bullies bushwhacked somebody else . . . or been ambushed themselves this time?

Bo and Scratch knew they would have to wait for an answer to that question, too. Right now, they were wet and a little banged up and tired, but they were alive.

They were alive, and they still had their horses and their guns.

For the time being, that was enough.

Dave had left Red Butte early that morning, before his mother and brother were awake. He had taken to avoiding them as much as possible, because he knew they would ask questions about where he'd been and what he had been doing. Especially Gil, who was a nosy son of a gun. That was because Gil wanted to be the boss of everybody, Dave thought. Gil had always thought he was smarter and better suited for running things than anybody else. He really felt that way when it came to his no-count little brother.

Well, Gil was in for one hell of a surprise one of these days, when he found out that Dave was smarter than any of them.

That day wasn't going to be too long in the future either, Dave had told himself as he approached the hideout. Rance had dropped a few hints that the big cleanup, the big payday, whatever you wanted to call it, wasn't far off.

The guards at the base of the tunnel waved him on through. Dave suppressed the uneasy feelings he always had when he rode into that dark hole and climbed to the top of the butte through the winding passage.

"Got any news?" Judson asked in a harsh voice from the *portal* in front of his cabin as Dave dismounted.

"Creel and Morton are still alive," Dave said.

Judson snorted in disgust. "Tell me somethin' I don't know! Those Texans are the luckiest old buzzards I ever saw. You know what they're plannin' to do today?"

Dave shook his head. "Sorry, Rance. I don't have any idea. I left early this morning and didn't even see them."

"Why ride all the way out here if you don't have anything useful to tell me?" the boss outlaw demanded with a scowl.

Dave felt a warm flush on the back of his neck. Judson didn't really take him seriously either, but at least he didn't look down on him as much as Gil did. "I thought you might have something you wanted me to do."

Judson shook his head and said, "There's nothin' goin' on right now. We're just waitin' for the right time to pull the next job."

"And when is that going to be?"

"When you need to know, I'll tell you," Judson snapped. "Same as what goes for everybody else around here."

Dave saw that he wasn't getting anywhere, and he didn't want to irritate Judson any more than he already had. He asked, "Is it all right if I hang around today and ride back into town this evening?"

"Suit yourself," Judson said with a magnanimous wave of his hand. "I think some of the boys are gonna get up a poker game after a while."

Sitting around and playing cards and drinking whiskey all day sounded better to Dave than riding back to Red Butte where Gil and his mother would do their best to put him to work. He wandered over to one of the adobe shacks and shot the breeze for a while with the outlaws who were gathered there, then settled down to play cards with them when they got the poker game going that afternoon.

Dave was out of his depth here and knew it, but he did his best and managed to win a pot every now and then. When he lost, the outlaws were willing to take his markers. He was into some of them for quite a bit, but he would settle up when the big payoff came. He was sure of that.

The men were playing on an old blanket spread out on the ground in the shade cast by one of the shacks, passing around a jug of rotgut as the game went on. Dave began to feel the whiskey. He wasn't drunk, but a warm, pleasant glow had crept into him and filled his body. He felt so good he barely noticed when the sound of shots in the distance drifted faintly to the top of the butte.

The other men had keener instincts than Dave did, though. They had lived on the cutting edge of danger for longer. They looked up at the sound of the shots, and one of them said, "Could be trouble."

After that one burst of gunfire, though, the shooting stopped. After a minute, another outlaw shrugged and said, "Couldn't have amounted to much, or whoever it was would still be burnin' powder."

"You think it was the fellas out on patrol?" a third man asked.

Dave frowned. "There's a patrol? Like in the army?"

Several of the outlaws laughed. "Sure, kid. Didn't you know that Rance used to be a sergeant a long time ago? Until he deserted, that is. But he still likes to keep some of the boys ridin' a big circle around the hideout most of the time, just to keep an eye out for bounty hunters or a sheriff's posse or somethin' like that."

Dave shook his head. "No, I didn't know. It sounds like a good idea, though."

Maybe the patrol had caught Creel and Morton trying to sneak out here and find the hideout, he thought. That sounded like something those meddling old pelicans would do. He felt a savage thrill go through him at the idea that the Texans might have gotten themselves killed. That would sure make Rance happy.

The sun was getting low in the western sky. Dave glanced up at it, then decided that he'd better call it quits when this hand was over. He wanted to make it part of the way back to Red Butte before nightfall. Once he reached the settlement, though, he wouldn't go to the stage station until later, after his mother and Gil had turned in. That was the way he liked it. To kill time until then, maybe he would hunt up Angus and Culley, he told himself. He hadn't been hanging around very much with them lately. He had come to realize that they were just small-time bullies, not real desperadoes like Judson's gang.

Like *him.*

The hand hadn't ended, though, by the time a commotion broke out at the mouth of the tunnel that led to the top of the butte. The yelling drew the attention of the poker players, who put their cards down and went to see what was going on. Still feeling the whiskey he had drunk, Dave stumbled a little as he got to his feet to follow them.

A couple of riders had emerged from the tunnel and were headed toward Judson's cabin. They were leading another pair of horses, and each of those mounts had a man tied facedown over the saddle. That sight brought some excited comments from the men with Dave.

"Damn, that's Hallett and Gomez ridin' in," one of the outlaws exclaimed. "They were out on patrol. Wonder if those are some of our boys ridin' facedown."

"More likely somebody who tried to sneak in here and see where we've been holed up," another man suggested.

A third man added, "You can bet those bodies came from the shots we heard earlier."

That made sense to Dave, too, and another possibility had sprung to his mind. The dead men might be Bo Creel and Scratch Morton. He wanted to see their faces, and he had to restrain himself to keep from running ahead of the others. That wouldn't look too good. He didn't want them to think that he was just an excitable kid.

By the time the group of outlaws reached Judson's cabin, the riders had already gotten there and dismounted. They were busy with the grisly task of cutting the ropes that held the corpses on the other two horses. As Dave and his companions came up, Dave thought that the two dead men didn't really look like Creel and Morton, from what he could see of them . . .

Then the last of the bindings parted under the sharp knives wielded by Hallett and Gomez, and the corpses slid off the horses to land with dull, heavy thuds on the ground, like sacks of grain. The way they fell, they came to rest on their backs, with their sightless eyes gazing up at the fading light in the sky.

And Dave Sutherland found himself staring in shocked horror at the bullet-riddled bodies and dead faces of his friends, Angus and Culley.

CHAPTER 27

The canvas bag containing the supplies Bo and Scratch brought with them had gotten a good soaking. The biscuits inside it were soggy, misshapen lumps that nobody would want to eat, short of being faced with death by starvation. Several strips of jerky were wrapped tightly in oilcloth, though, and they were still edible. And of course the canned peaches Ponderosa had put in were still fine. The Texans used their knives to open the air-tights and had a decent supper of peaches and jerky. They saved a couple of cans of peaches for the next day.

There were no trees around here, but Bo was able to scavenge enough dried branches from some scrubby mesquite bushes to make a tiny fire, which they hid from any unwanted watchers by building a little wall of rocks around it. The heat generated by the flames wasn't much, but it was welcome when the desert chill set in that night.

By morning both men were stiff from sleeping on the hard ground, but their clothes and guns were dry, they had food and water—although not much food and the water stunk—and their horses were well rested. Both men were ready to resume their search for the hideout being used by Rance Judson and his gang.

"I gotta tell you," Scratch said as they mounted up after splitting a can of peaches for breakfast, "I ain't lookin' forward to ridin' back through there again."

"There's been no sign of Angus and Culley," Bo said. "It's too far-fetched to think that they might follow us in there and ambush us again."

"Stranger things've happened," Scratch said with an ominous frown.

Bo supposed that was true, but the cleft in the earth formed by Hell Creek was the fastest way to get where they needed to go. Both men hitched their horses into motion and started along the narrow ledge again.

The shadowed air inside the cleft hadn't warmed up yet, so remnants of the night's chill still hung in it, and would until the sun was directly overhead at midday.

Bo and Scratch didn't mind. Both men had lost their hats during their dunking in the creek and weren't looking forward to riding out in the open again in the heat of the day, with nothing to shield their heads.

It took them about an hour to ride through the cleft. When they emerged at the far end, they immediately spotted the rusty brown splashes on the rocky ground. They reined in, and Scratch grunted, then said, "Somebody spilled a lot o' blood here."

"Two somebodies, from the looks of it," Bo commented as he studied the stains on the rocks.

"Angus and Culley?"

"Maybe. That's the most reasonable explanation. We know they were headed in this direction, and we heard those shots not long after that."

"Who do you reckon they ran into? Judson's men?"

Bo thought it over and then nodded. "That makes sense. We never ran across anything to indicate that those two were part of the gang. They seemed to be just layabouts and bullies."

"And they weren't with Dave when he rode out here before," Scratch said.

"That's right." Bo rubbed his chin as he pondered the situation. "Maybe they knew that Dave was tied in with the gang and wanted to be part of it themselves. But you saw what happened when we tried to follow Dave through that canyon southeast of here. Judson's sentries opened up on us without any warning."

"So Angus and Culley bumped into some of the outlaws and got themselves ventilated for their trouble, before they could explain what they were doin' out here. That sound right to you?"

Bo nodded again. "Sounds right to me. But short of seeing their bodies, I don't know how we could prove it."

"And it ain't like we care overmuch if they got themselves shot up either. They did their doggonedest to kill us after all."

"That they did," Bo agreed. He saw a trail of rusty brown spots leading off to the east and pointed it out to Scratch. "They slung the bodies over some horses and took them back to the hideout. You can see where the blood dripped."

Scratch grinned. "That's as good as an arrow pointin' the way. Nice o' the varmints to be so helpful."

Bo heeled his horse into motion. "Let's see if the trail goes toward that butte we saw the other day."

The drops of blood played out after a while, which wasn't surprising. The blood had gotten sluggish in the veins of the corpses and stopped flowing. But the general direction the killers were going was well established by then, and sure enough, it led toward the low, squatty butte that had come into sight by then.

"There's no doubt in my mind now," Bo said. "That's Judson's stronghold."

"Do we need to head back to Red Butte to fetch help?" Scratch asked.

Bo shook his head. "I want to get closer first, get the

lay of the land a little better so we'll know what we're facing."

"Sounds good to me."

The sun was high enough now to be uncomfortable as it beat down on their uncovered heads. There was nothing they could do but put up with it, though. Not surprisingly, the butte was farther away than it looked to be. Appearances were usually deceptive out here, and it always took longer to get somewhere than you thought it should. Also, the terrain was more rugged coming at the butte from this direction, and the trail twisted and turned quite a bit, making the ride that much longer.

"There must be some shortcut we missed," Scratch muttered.

"Don't worry, we'll get there," Bo assured him. "As long as we can see the butte, we won't get lost."

"Better hope we don't run into the same bunch that got Angus and Culley, if that's what happened."

"Keep your eyes and ears open."

"That's just what I'm plannin' to do," Scratch said, "but you could damn near hide an army in this place if you were of a mind to."

Bo knew that was true. And right about now, as he and Scratch approached the butte that had to be the outlaws' hideout, he wouldn't have minded having an army on his side . . .

Dave had spent the night at the gang's camp on top of the butte, and it hadn't been a very pleasant time for him. His reaction on seeing the bodies of Angus and Culley had been unmistakable. Judson had pounced on him right away, grabbing him by the shirt collar, shaking him, and demanding, "You know these two, don't you?"

"I . . . I . . . They're friends of mine from town," Dave had stammered.

"You told them how to get out here?"

"Hell, no!" Dave had summoned up enough daring to sound indignant. "I'd never do that, Rance. You know that. Fact of the matter is, I haven't even been spending that much time with them lately."

"Then what in blazes are they doin' out here? Did you let them follow you? That's almost as bad as tellin' 'em our secret!" Judson had drawn his gun then and prodded the barrel against Dave's chest. Dave had never been so scared in his life. "I ain't forgot how Creel and Morton followed you that other time," Judson went on, and his tone made it clear that he was seriously considering pulling that trigger.

"I swear, Rance, they didn't follow me," Dave had replied with a gulp. "I don't know what they're doing out here."

Judson had looked at Hallett and Gomez and demanded, "Where'd you run into them?"

"At the north end of that big cleft where Hell Creek runs," Hallett explained. "They rode out of there bold as brass just as we happened to come along. You said you wanted us to get rid of anybody who saw us on patrol, Rance, so we did."

Judson jerked his head in a nod. "Yeah, that's good."

"That's not the way I came up here, Rance," Dave had said then, wanting desperately to convince Judson to point that gun somewhere else besides at him. "You see, they couldn't have followed me."

"What were they doin' out here in the badlands then?"

All Dave could do was shake his head in ignorance and answer honestly, "I have no idea."

"They were alone?" Judson asked of Hallett and Gomez.

Both of the outlaws had shrugged in response to the question. "We saw no one else, Señor," Gomez said.

Judson had started to calm down then. He let go of Dave's collar and holstered his gun, giving Dave reason to breathe a little easier. But then Judson had pointed a finger at him, and to Dave it looked almost like the barrel of a gun. It represented potential death, that's for sure.

"You're stayin' here," Judson had decreed. "This is almost over, and I don't want to risk you foulin' anything up."

Dave hadn't come out here prepared to stay, but he was willing to go along with Judson's decision. He knew his absence would worry his mother, and deep down that still bothered him some. Of course, Gil wouldn't give a damn whether he ever came back to Red Butte, so that made it easier for Dave to cooperate with the outlaw leader.

"Sure, Rance," he'd said. "That's fine with me."

"But I'll be keepin' an eye on you," Judson had growled.

"I won't let you down," Dave promised.

So he had spent the night in one of the cabins, knowing that the outlaws were suspicious of him. That shaky probation, with swift, violent death the reward if Judson decided that he had violated it, didn't make for a very restful sleep. Dave was weary and gritty-eyed when he got up the next morning.

He was hunkered next to one of the open campfires, drinking a cup of coffee, when he saw Judson ride out of the tunnel leading to the ground. Dave grunted in surprise and said, "Where's he coming back from, this early in the morning?"

One of the outlaws at the fire with him said, "Rance rode out durin' the night. He does that pretty often. He don't say where he's goin' and we don't ask." The owlhoot gave Dave a hard look. "Probably be smart for you not to start askin' a bunch of questions either, boy."

Dave nodded. "I understand." He was already in Judson's bad graces to a certain extent. Poking into things that were none of his business would just make matters worse.

Judson seemed agitated about something as he dismounted, turned his horse over to one of the men, and went into his cabin. Dave wondered what was going on.

He didn't have to wait long to find out. Judson came back out of the cabin a short time later and called all the men together. Approximately twenty-five outlaws gathered in front of the adobe shack that served as Judson's headquarters.

"Listen to me, men," he said, raising his voice a little so that he could be heard clearly. "Tomorrow we'll be pullin' our last job."

That announcement brought mutters of surprise from the outlaws. Some of them sounded angry as well. Judson motioned them to silence and went on.

"Our last job," he repeated, "but our biggest one. This is the big casino, fellas. The stagecoach left Red Butte today, a day earlier than usual, bound for Cottonwood."

That came as a shock to Dave. He hadn't heard anything about the next run being made a day early.

"What they're tryin' to do is throw us off," Judson continued, "because when the stage comes back tomorrow, it's gonna be carryin' the payroll for the last six months for the Pitchfork Mine!"

Dave caught his breath. This was news to him, too. In the past, the mining syndicate had always sent in the payroll on one of its own wagons. He knew because Judson's gang had held up one of them, as one of its first jobs in the territory, in fact.

As if Judson had read Dave's mind, the boss outlaw said, "Ever since we hit that payroll wagon when we first drifted over here, the minin' syndicate's been holdin' back the wages from the workers, tryin' to figure out a safer way of gettin' them to the mine. They decided to bring the money in by stagecoach, and they're in a hurry about it because the miners are threatenin' to go on strike if they don't get paid. Six months of wages for a crew that big adds up to a heap of *dinero*. When we've got our hands on it, we'll split up and go our separate ways. We've had a good run, boys, but it's time to call it quits."

There were still a few dissatisfied rumblings at the thought of breaking up the gang, but most of the men were excited about the amount of loot they stood to gain from this final job.

Dave felt an uneasy stirring, though, for a different reason. He had gone along with it before when Judson wanted to hold up the stage, even though he hadn't taken part in those robberies himself. But that had been a matter of looting the mail and holding up a few passengers. Just something to kill time and keep the men occupied as much as anything else.

But losing that mine payroll would be a major blow to the Sutherland Stage Line. The owners of the mining syndicate would probably hold Dave's mother responsible for the loss. That would be the final straw. The stage line would collapse.

And just how did Judson know the payroll was coming in by stage? How did he know that the stage had left a day early? Dave hadn't given him that information, because Dave hadn't known it himself.

He remembered the way Judson had gone somewhere during the night and ridden back into the hideout just shortly before this unexpected announcement. Dave's thoughts ran ahead to their logical conclusion . . .

Judson had a partner that no one knew about, someone in Red Butte who was tipping him off. Judson had met with whoever it was the night before, and had learned about the payroll shipment. Someone from the mine? That had to be the answer, Dave thought. The superintendent maybe, or one of the engineers.

A harsh voice cut into Dave's wildly racing thoughts. "Sutherland, come with me," Judson ordered. "I got to talk to you."

The crowd of outlaws was breaking up now. Judson would go over the details of the job with them later, when it was closer to the time for them to strike. For now, his attention was focused on Dave again, who swallowed and managed to say, "Sure, Rance. What do you need?"

"Come in and have a drink," Judson said with a jerk of his head as he started back into the cabin.

Dave followed him. He wasn't the least bit thirsty, and it was mighty early in the day for a drink anyway. But he wasn't going to argue with Judson, so he took the cup of whiskey that the boss outlaw poured for him. Judson splashed some of the rotgut into a glass for himself and sipped it. He sighed in satisfaction and then said, "I was up most of the night, so I'm gonna get some sleep. Before I do, though, I figured I'd best get things straight between you and me."

"Whatever you say goes with me, Rance, you know that."

"Even though it's your ma's stagecoach we'll be holdin' up tomorrow?"

Again, Dave felt that sharp pang of uncertainty. He had thought all along that it was all right with him if the stage line went under. He hated working on it and knew he would never get along with his brother. But now, faced with the actual, imminent fact, it was harder to swallow than he'd thought it would be.

"I'm a member of the gang," he forced himself to say. "I just hope you understand that I can't ride with you—"

"This time you can," Judson cut in. "This time you're gonna."

"But, Rance—"

Judson tossed off the rest of his drink. "I'm not arguin' with you, Sutherland, I'm givin' you an order. I want you where I can keep an eye on you."

"Blast it, Rance, you know I'd never betray you!"

Judson gave him a hard look. "Even though your ma's gonna be on that stage when we stop it at Hell Creek?"

Dave's breath seemed to freeze in his throat. For a second he couldn't even talk. Then he said, "Wha . . . what are you talking about? Ma doesn't go along on the runs."

"She went this time. Creel and Morton have disappeared. That means your brother and that old man had to take the stagecoach to Cottonwood and pick up the

288

payroll. Since Pine's not over that shoulder wound yet, your ma insisted on going along, too, just in case they needed some help."

Dave closed his eyes and rubbed a hand wearily over his face. That sounded just like something his mother would do, all right. He wondered briefly what had happened to Creel and Morton, but that didn't really matter. What was important was that his mother was going to be in danger, along with Gil and Ponderosa.

He steeled himself, knowing that he had no other option than to go along with what Judson said. "I made my choice a long time ago," he said. "I'll ride with you. I'll do whatever I have to."

Judson grinned. "That's what I was hopin' you'd say, kid. Now get out of here so I can get some sleep."

Dave drank the rest of the whiskey in his cup, barely tasting the fiery stuff as it burned down his throat. He gave Judson a nod and left the cabin, glad for the bracing effect of the liquor because he was shaken to his very core. He knew what he had to do, all right . . .

Because he had lied to Judson. Somehow he was going to get out of here and warn his mother what was going to happen tomorrow at Hell Creek.

CHAPTER 28

All morning long, Dave watched for an opportunity to get away from the outlaw camp, but it seemed like every time he drifted toward the corral, one or more of Judson's men started staring at him. He wondered if

Judson had somehow spread the word for the rest of the gang to keep an eye on him.

Anyway, he realized, even if he got his horse, he would still have to ride down that tunnel in order to leave the hideout—and there were guards at the bottom of it who might well have orders to stop him if he tried to escape. There had to be some other way . . .

During the early afternoon, as the sun beat down on the top of the butte and the heat became more stifling, most of the outlaws except for the ones who were on guard duty at the tunnel dozed off in their daily siesta. Dave found himself a shady spot next to one of the cabins, sat down and leaned back against the adobe wall, stretched his legs out in front of him, and tipped his hat down over his eyes. Soon he gave every appearance of being sound asleep.

But in reality he was wide awake, peering out through slitted eyes under the pulled-down brim of his hat. As the camp grew quieter and more somnolent, Dave bided his time. Only when he was confident that most of the outlaws were asleep did he move again, standing up and moving as silently as possible toward the edge of the butte.

Judson had chosen the gang's hideout well. At first glance, the natural tunnel through the interior of the butte appeared to be the only way to reach the top. As long as the gang could defend the tunnel entrance down below, no posse of lawmen could approach them. And even if enemies did make it into the tunnel, they could be cut down easily as they emerged from it.

Nor could anyone climb up the sides of the butte, Dave discovered as he began making a circuit of the edge. The walls were too steep, too sheer. With the proper climbing equipment, a man might be able to make it up in a place or two, but not a big enough group to make a difference.

No, Dave concluded fairly quickly, a posse couldn't climb the walls of the butte . . .

But one man *might* be able to climb down.

It was a crazy idea, Dave thought, and he felt a tingle of fear go through him as he peered down the rugged cliff toward the ground so far below. It wasn't really all that far in relative terms, he told himself, but it wasn't easy to think in relative terms when you were talking about falling that far. Plummeting to the ground from this height would mean broken bones for sure, and probably a broken neck.

But if he could make it to the ground, he could sneak around the butte, surprise the guards at the tunnel mouth, get the drop on them, disarm them, and tie them up. They kept their horses concealed in an area just inside the tunnel, in case they need to mount up and ride in a hurry. He could take one of the animals and be halfway back to Red Butte before any of the other outlaws discovered what had happened.

As soon as that plan had laid itself out in his head, he knew it wouldn't let go of him until he tried it. He would be risking his life, sure, but if he waited and did nothing, his mother's stage line would be ruined at the very least. Considering how ruthless Judson and his men were, her life would be in danger during the holdup, too. Dave knew he would never be able to live with himself if anything happened to his mother because he stood by and didn't even try to warn her.

He didn't want her forgiveness for everything he had done so far. He had made his decisions and would live with whatever happened to him, good or bad. His only concern now was her safety.

He glanced at the cabins and saw that none of the outlaws were moving around them. Then he took a deep breath and slipped over the edge of the butte at a place where it looked like he might be able to climb down.

The going was relatively easy at first. A fissure in the rock formed a narrow chimney. By bracing his feet against one side and his back against the other, he was able to work his way down the chimney. His boots weren't really made for such work and he had to guard against them slipping, but he made fairly good progress for a while, stopping every so often to listen intently for shouts of alarm coming from the top of the butte. So far, he hadn't heard any. No one knew he was gone.

It was too much to hope for that the fissure would take him all the way to the ground, and sure enough, after a few minutes of work that had him drenched in sweat, the opening narrowed down to nothing. Dave braced himself at the bottom of it and leaned out to see where he could go next. If he couldn't find a promising route, he would have to climb back up and start over. He didn't want to do that, because it would only increase the risk of discovery that much more.

After a moment, he decided that there was a suitable foothold in reach if he dangled full-length from the bottom of the fissure. He would have to support his weight on his hands while he found the place with his foot. He took his hat off, sleeved sweat from his forehead, and gathered his courage. He jammed the hat back on his head, then let himself slide out the bottom of the fissure, twisting as he slid so that he could catch himself with his hands.

His fingers clamped themselves to the rock. Just as he'd planned, he wound up dangling from their precarious grip as he searched with the toe of his left boot for the tiny projection he had seen a moment earlier. After what seemed like an eternity he found it and was able to take some of the weight off his fingers, which had begun to cry out from the strain of holding him up. He pressed himself hard against the rocky wall and paused to catch his breath again.

While he was doing that his right foot sought another toehold. He didn't find one, but he did spot another small, jutting rock to his left that he could grab hold of if he stretched for it. He had no choice—he had definitely come too far to turn back now—so he let go with his left hand and reached for the new hold.

Once he had it, he was able to swing his body to the left. His right foot replaced the left one on the original toehold, and he found another with the left. That was the way it went again and again as he slowly lowered himself down the face of the butte. He measured his progress in inches now, not feet, and he sometimes had to move a considerable distance to one side or the other before he could gain anything downward.

It felt like every muscle in his body was on fire. From time to time he began to tremble, and he had to stop right where he was and wait for the shaking to pass before he dared to resume the descent. He was sweating so much, he imagined it was sluicing off him like a waterfall. More than once, his grip almost slipped because his fingers were so slick. He had to be careful of that, too.

When he reached down with his right foot and it found what felt like a nice wide ledge, he almost sobbed with relief. Carefully, he lowered his left foot to the ledge, too, and then leaned against the wall again to rest, heaving great ragged breaths as his pulse thundered inside his skull and his heart felt as if it were trying to leap out of his chest. The shakes hit him again and didn't stop for several minutes.

Finally, the trembling ceased, though, and his pulse slowed down a little. He thought he was in good enough shape now to look around and see just how far he still had to go to reach the ground.

He was utterly shocked to see that he was standing *on* the ground at the base of the cliff. It wasn't a ledge under his feet after all.

He had made it.

Dave slumped all the way to the ground then as if all

the muscles in his body had suddenly turned to jelly. Tears ran from his eyes and mixed with the beads of sweat covering his face. He was down. He had escaped.

Well, not quite, a small voice in the back of his brain warned. He still had to get his hands on a horse and make it back to Red Butte.

As he lay there recovering from the ordeal of the descent, he continued listening for shouts of alarm from above. The outlaw camp was still quiet, though. Luck had been with him so far. Dave believed in luck, and he started to think he was going to get away. He didn't deserve to have fortune smile on him, that was for sure, but his mother did. She had never done anything except work hard and try to make something worthwhile for her family.

When he thought he had rested enough, and when he didn't want to risk waiting any longer, Dave pushed himself to his feet. He checked his gun, even slipped a cartridge into the sixth chamber, the one that was usually carried empty under the hammer. Then he began making his way along the base of the cliff, circling the butte toward the tunnel entrance.

The guards who were posted there stayed out of sight in a clump of rocks just beside the tunnel mouth. Those boulders were jagged pieces of rimrock that had fallen off the butte in ages past. When Dave saw them, he knew he was getting close to his goal. He wiped his gun hand against his trousers and then drew his gun from its holster.

The two guards were sitting on smaller rocks, smoking and talking in low tones. With every bit of stealth he could muster, Dave slipped closer and closer to them. Their backs were turned toward him, and as he listened to their casual conversation, he knew they had no idea that anything was wrong. There had been no alarm concerning him being missing from the camp.

He was about to tell them to throw down their guns and put their hands in the air when one of his feet bumped a rock and sent it rolling against another one. Even that tiny sound was enough to warn the outlaws. They leaped to their feet and started to whirl around, clutching rifles.

Dave struck first, slashing a blow toward the head of the man closest to him. The barrel of his Colt thudded against the man's head with stunning force. The guard's knees unhinged, dropping him to the ground. His rifle slipped out of his fingers and clattered on the rocks.

In a continuation of the same move, Dave swung his gun toward the other man, earing back the hammer as he did so. The guard found himself staring into the barrel of the Colt at short range, with Dave's thumb on the hammer being the only thing that held back fiery death.

"Don't," Dave grated. "Put the rifle down."

The outlaw hesitated. "You can't shoot me," he said after a tense heartbeat of silence. "They'd hear the shot up yonder if you did."

"I've come this far. I'd risk it."

And that was the truth, Dave thought. He would blow this man's head off if he had to, grab a horse, and make a run for it. He knew the badlands at least as well as Judson's men did. He thought he could give them the slip, or at least stay ahead of them long enough to reach Red Butte.

The man must have read the dangerous determination in Dave's eyes, because he sighed, then bent slightly and let the rifle slide from his fingers onto the ground.

"Now unbuckle your gunbelt and sling it away," Dave ordered.

"You're a damned fool, Sutherland," the guard said as he slowly did as he was told. Dave knew he was stalling but didn't call him on it. Freedom was so close now he could almost touch it.

"Turn around."

Fear leaped into the guard's eyes. "You're gonna kill me anyway? Damn you—"

"I didn't say I was gonna kill you," Dave broke in, "but I will if you don't do what I tell you."

Grudgingly, the man swung around, keeping his hands elevated. He glanced back over his shoulder and tried to jerk out of the way as he caught a glimpse of Dave leaping toward him, but he was too late. The barrel of Dave's gun slammed into his head and knocked him sprawling unconscious to the ground, too, just like his companion.

Dave studied them for a second. He'd planned to tie

them up, but he decided he didn't want to take the time to do that. They were both out cold. He ran into the tunnel instead and found the horses.

He was a stranger to the animals, so they were a little skittish around him. Despite that, he managed to get one of them untied and led it outside. He glanced at the guards again, saw that they still weren't moving, and swung up into the saddle.

He had barely gotten the horse moving when a sudden clatter from behind warned him. Twisting around in the saddle, Dave saw that the first man he had knocked out must have been shamming when he came out of the tunnel. The man was awake and moving now, crawling and lunging toward the rifle he had dropped earlier. Dave had holstered his gun while he was getting the horse. He grabbed for it now.

The outlaw snatched up the rifle and tipped the barrel toward Dave just as Dave's Colt cleared leather. Both weapons roared at the same time. Dave's shot was more accurate. The guard's head jerked back as the bullet bored into his brain and exploded out the back of his skull.

Dave didn't escape unscathed, though. What felt like a giant fist slammed into his side, and he had to grab the saddle horn to keep from toppling off the horse, which was more spooked than ever now by the gunfire. Dave dropped his gun and hung on for dear life as he tried to bring the plunging horse under control. He had to ignore the fiery pain emanating from his side and filling his body. The shots would bring the rest of the gang from on top of the butte. He had to get away from here—*now!*

Finally getting a good grip on the reins and clamping his knees against the horse's sides, he jabbed his boot heels into its flanks and said, "Hyaaahhh!" The horse leaped forward in a gallop.

With his vision blurred by the pain, Dave was sure where he was going. But he was getting away from here as fast as he could, that was the important thing. He had a lead on any pursuit, and that would have to be enough.

Because he had to get back to Red Butte and get help. He knew he was badly wounded, but he didn't care about that. Whatever happened to him, he deserved it. He would accept his fate, as long as he could save his mother.

And in the back of his mind, he couldn't help but wonder . . .

What had happened to those two saddle-tramp Texans?

The two shots made Bo and Scratch rein in and look at each other. The shots had come very close together, so close that they almost blended into one sound. But during the long years since leaving Texas, the drifters had heard enough guns go off that they were able to separate the reports.

"A rifle and a handgun," Bo said.

Scratch nodded. "That the way I got 'em pegged, too. Maybe a mile off?"

"Yeah," Bo agreed. "And they came from the direction of that butte."

They were closing in on the imposing physical feature that they suspected of being the outlaws' hideout. It was their plan to get close enough to scout out the place, maybe get lucky enough to spot some of Judson's men coming or going so they would know for sure this was the gang's stronghold and perhaps discover the way in and out as well.

But whatever had caused that swift exchange of shots might interfere with their plans. They were more alert than ever as they continued making their way through the rugged landscape toward the butte.

Suddenly, they heard the drumming of hoofbeats somewhere ahead of them. Bo pulled his horse to the left, behind a boulder that was twice as tall as a man.

"Come on," he told Scratch. "We'd better get out of sight until we see who's coming."

Scratch nodded and sent the bay behind the boulder as well. Both men dismounted and drew their guns. When they edged their heads around the big rock, they could see for about two hundred yards along the draw they had been following.

The horse they had heard came into view, moving at a steady run. The man in the saddle was slumped forward over his mount's neck. He swayed a little from side to side, and he appeared to be clutching the saddle horn with both hands to keep himself from falling off.

Those things told Bo and Scratch that the rider was hurt. Maybe hurt bad. He looked like he was ready to topple out of his saddle at any second.

Then the horse gave a little lunging leap to clear a pile of small rocks, and that caused the rider to straighten momentarily instead of slumping forward. Both of the Texans caught enough of a glimpse of his face to recognize him.

"Good Lord!" Scratch burst out in surprise. "That's Dave Sutherland!"

"Looks like he's wounded, too." Bo had seen a dark, ragged stain on Dave's shirt. Now Dave was leaning forward again, clearly struggling not only to stay mounted, but also to stay conscious.

"We'd better grab that horse and give Dave a hand." Scratch started out from behind the boulder where they were concealed.

"Hold on a minute." Bo's voice was sharp. "If Dave's out here, he can't be up to any good. He's probably been at the hideout."

"We're here," Scratch pointed out. "Anyway, I don't care where he's been or what he's been doin'. Abigail wouldn't like it if we let him die."

That was certainly true enough. Bo nodded and said, "Let's try not to spook the horse. It wouldn't take much for Dave to get thrown."

They moved farther out into the draw, getting in the path of the horse and holding up their hands. The animal spotted them and slowed. Both Texans hoped that it wouldn't turn around and bolt back the way it came from. Then they would have to get their own mounts and give chase.

Instead, Dave's horse came to a gradual halt and then stood there, watching them curiously as its nostrils flared and it gave a small shake of its head. Bo and Scratch approached the animal with caution, holding out their hands. Scratch talked quietly in a low, soothing tone. He was better with horses than Bo and always had been. Broncs just responded well to him for some reason.

Dave's head was still down. He didn't seem aware of the Texans' approach or even that the horse had stopped. But he groaned and started to topple to his right as Bo and Scratch reached the animal.

Scratch grabbed the reins while Bo leaped forward to catch Dave. He staggered a little under the weight of the injured young man, but managed to stay on his feet.

"Yeah, he's been shot, all right," Bo said. "I can see the bullet holes in his shirt."

"In and out, eh?" Scratch asked.

"That's right. The wound's in his side. Doesn't look too deep. Probably hurts like hell, though, and he's lost a lot of blood. That's why he passed out."

Dave's head hung limply from his neck now. He was out cold.

"We'll have to patch him up and get him back to town—" Scratch began.

He stopped when he and Bo both heard the same thing.

More hoofbeats, this time from a lot of horses. That meant a lot of riders, and they were coming fast.

"I don't like the sound o' that," Scratch said.

"Neither do I," Bo agreed. "Could be that whoever shot Dave is looking for him to finish the job. We'd better get him out of sight."

"Yeah, but where?"

Bo looked around. Beyond the boulders where he and Scratch had been hidden earlier, the edge of the draw rose in a fairly steep slope for about forty feet. Bo spotted a narrow slit in the rock, halfway up the slope.

"Up there," he said as he pointed. "That could be the mouth of a cave. If it is, it might be big enough for us and the horses."

"And if it ain't, we'll be stuck up there in plain sight. Sittin' ducks, in other words."

The swift rataplan of hoofbeats continued to draw nearer. "We don't have time to do anything else," Bo said. He bent a little at the knees so that he could sling Dave's senseless form over his shoulder. As he straightened, he went on. "Send Dave's horse on down the draw and grab ours. Let's move!"

CHAPTER 29

Scratch grabbed the reins of his and Bo's horses, then slapped Dave's mount on the rump and yelled at it. The horse leaped forward and galloped off down the draw as Bo and Scratch began climbing toward what they hoped was a cave.

If it wasn't, they were probably in a lot of trouble, as Scratch had said.

Bo went first, toting Dave's unconscious form. Scratch followed, leading the dun and the bay. The horses picked their way up the slope, as sure-footed as the humans, or more so. Little rocks rolled down behind them in miniature avalanches. All the Texans could do was hope that those rocks would stop sliding before the other riders came along; otherwise some sharp-eyed pursuer might spot them and know where the quarry had gone.

Assuming, of course, that the slit in the rock above them really was the mouth of a cave . . .

It was. Bo reached the opening a moment later and staggered through it with Dave on his shoulder. The passage bent just inside, which made it even harder to see from the ground. If Dave's horse kept going it would serve as a distraction, making the pursuers think that Dave was still ahead of them, and with luck they would ride right on past this spot without even glancing up at the rocky slope.

"You're gonna have to give me a hand with these horses," Scratch called from behind Bo. "It's too narrow to bring both of 'em through at the same time."

Bo stumbled deeper into the cave, which was not more than five feet wide. The cut extended perhaps twenty feet into the hillside, and a tiny shaft of light at the rear of it was evidence that another passage led to the surface, although it was too small to let anything through it except the sun and some air.

But that kept the narrow chamber from being too dark or stifling. Bo lowered Dave to the ground and then turned back to take the reins of his dun from Scratch. He pulled the horse deeper into the cave, out of sight from down below. Scratch followed with the bay. Neither horse liked the cramped quarters, but they couldn't do anything except switch their tails back and forth angrily.

"I'll stay back here to keep the horses from stepping on Dave," Bo said, his voice little more than a whisper. That was enough in here. "Keep an eye on the draw to make sure those other men go on by."

Scratch nodded and slid along the wall toward the entrance, barely able to get by his horse. He drew his gun again as he moved up to the cave mouth. He could still hear the hoofbeats and knew that the riders were very close now. He and Bo had gotten out of sight with Dave and the horses just in time.

Edging just one eye out far enough to see, Scratch watched as more than a dozen men went past, riding hard. Their horses were kicking up quite a bit of dust, and that, along with the fast pace they were setting, made it highly unlikely that any of them would notice the narrow entrance up the slope. They thought they were still hot on Dave's trail.

Scratch saw enough hard-planed, beard-stubbled faces to know he was looking at a bunch of owlhoots. The grim looks on their faces told him that they were on a killing mission, too. He waited until they had all ridden past and were well out of earshot before he moved back from the cave mouth and called to Bo, "They're gone. Never even looked in this direction, as far as I could tell."

"Did you recognize any of them?" Bo asked.

"Not for certain, but they damned sure looked like hardcases to me."

"Judson's men," Bo muttered.

"If that's the case, how come they were after Dave? We had him figured for one of them, didn't we?"

"Yeah, but maybe there are things going on that we don't know about." Bo knelt beside Dave. "I'll see what I can do for him."

A quick examination of the wound showed that Bo's original estimation had been correct—a bullet had ripped through Dave's side, entering and exiting cleanly and taking a chunk of meat with it, as well as causing the young man to lose quite a bit of blood. Bo thought Dave would be all right, though, if they could get some real medical attention for him without too much of a delay.

Bo cleaned the wound with water from one of the canteens, then tore up one of his extra shirts for bandages. Dave groaned again and shifted around some while Bo was working on him, but he didn't regain consciousness.

"Do we load him up on one o' the horses and make a run for Red Butte?" Scratch asked.

Bo studied the way the shaft of sunlight was slanting through the little opening in the roof of the cave. "We'd never make it to town before nightfall, especially with one of the horses carrying double," he said after a moment's thought. "And we'd run a big risk of running into those varmints who were chasing him, too. Might be better to wait until morning. Likely Judson's men will have given up and gone back to the hideout by then."

"Or else they'll be combin' these badlands for him even more than they already are."

Bo shrugged. "We'll have to take that chance. As weak as Dave is right now, he doesn't need to be riding. And we sure couldn't outrun those hardcases with him."

"Yeah, you're right. Gonna be a long night in here, though, what with three of us and two horses." Scratch rubbed his jaw. "Don't look like we're ever gonna get to that hideout, does it? Trouble keeps gettin' in our way."

"It's got a habit of doing that, all right," Bo said with a nod.

It was cooler in the cave than outside; that was one small advantage that it had in the heat of mid-to-late afternoon. Scratch kept watch near the door while Bo sat with Dave, wondering when—or if—the young man was going to regain consciousness. Bo didn't think that Dave had lost enough blood for the injury to prove fatal, but despite his experience at patching up bullet wounds, he still wasn't a doctor.

As the light of day was fading from the cave, Dave finally roused from his stupor. He groaned as he had done from time to time all afternoon, but then he lifted his head and rasped, "Wh . . . where am I?"

Bo leaned over him, resting a hand on the young man's shoulder to keep him from trying to get up. "Take it easy, Dave," he said. "You're all right. You're safe now."

"Wh . . . who . . . ?"

"It's Bo Creel. Scratch is here with me."

Dave shifted a little, and then winced as pain must have shot through him.

"Don't try to move," Bo went on. "You've been shot. Can you tell me who did it?"

The scuff of boot leather on the stony floor of the cave made Bo glance over his shoulder. Scratch had heard the talking and come back here to see if Dave was awake.

"How's he doin'?" Scratch asked.

Bo shook his head. "Don't know yet." He leaned closer to the wounded man again. Dave had opened his eyes for a moment, but they were closed again now. "Dave, can you hear me? Who shot you?"

"J-Judson . . ." Dave whispered without opening his eyes.

"Rance Judson is the one who shot you?"

Dave's head moved from side to side, just an inch or so. "Not . . . Judson . . . One of his . . . men."

"It was his gang that was chasing you earlier?"

"Y-yeah." Dave's eyelids flickered for a couple of seconds. Then his eyes opened again and he started to grow more agitated. "Gotta . . . gotta tell . . . my ma . . ."

"I'm sorry, Dave, your mother's not here," Bo told him. "You can tell her whatever you want to tell her once we get back to Red Butte."

"No! Can't!" Bo had to hold him down now to keep him from thrashing and probably starting those wounds to bleeding again. "Gotta save . . . Ma!"

"Your ma's fine, boy," Scratch said. "She's back in Red Butte, safe and sound."

Dave's eyes were wide and almost bulging out of his head. He opened his mouth to say something else, but before he could get the words out, his eyes rolled up in their sockets and his muscles went limp again. He sagged back down onto the floor of the cave.

"Is he dead?" Scratch asked.

Bo shook his head. "No, he's still breathing. He just passed out again. He's too weak to get himself all worked up that way. That's why I don't think it's going to be safe for him to travel until tomorrow."

"Well, I reckon we'll just try to keep him comfortable until then. You want me to open another can o' them peaches? We got two left."

"Sure, go ahead," Bo said. "We need to keep our strength up, and we haven't eaten since this morning. We'll save some of the juice for Dave, though, for when he wakes up again."

"Yeah, that might perk him up a mite," Scratch said as he dug one of the remaining airtights out of the bag tied to his saddle. "Be dark soon, and I don't reckon Judson's men will start lookin' for him again until mornin'."

"Yeah. At least we know now for sure who shot him."

"But not why," Scratch pointed out.

"But not why," Bo agreed.

He had a hunch they were going to need to find out the answer to that question just as soon as they could.

Dave didn't regain consciousness again during the night. Bo and Scratch took turns standing guard and snatching what sleep they could on the hard, rocky floor of the cave. The horses were restless, but they didn't give too much trouble other than relieving themselves, and of course they couldn't be blamed for that.

Once again, Bo and Scratch had been out here in the badlands longer than they had intended, and even though the peaches had kept them from starving, both men were pretty hungry by the time the gray light of dawn began to seep into the cave.

"The stage is gonna be startin' for Cottonwood after a while," Scratch commented, "and we ain't there to handle the run."

"No, I guess Gil and Ponderosa will have to take it," Bo said. "Unless Abigail was able to hire somebody else, which doesn't seem likely."

"I feel like we're lettin' her down." Scratch nodded toward Dave's still form. "But I reckon savin' her boy's life ought to count for somethin'."

"Yeah." Bo rasped his thumb over the beard stubble on his chin. "I'd still like to know why Judson's men shot him."

"Because I was . . . tryin' to get away . . . and warn Ma," a weak voice said from the back of the cave.

Bo and Scratch glanced at each other and then moved swiftly to Dave's side. The young man's eyes were open again, and while his face was still haggard and washed-out, he seemed a little stronger and more coherent. The Texans hunkered on either side of him, and Bo asked, "What do you mean, you were trying to warn your mother, Dave?"

"Judson's gonna . . . hold up the stagecoach . . . when it gets to Hell Creek."

"On the way to Cottonwood, you mean?" asked Scratch.

Dave managed to shake his head. "No. On the way . . . back."

"Well, then, you don't have to worry," Bo told him. "The coach won't be coming back until tomorrow. That gives us plenty of time to get back to Red Butte and then ride out tomorrow to make sure Judson gets an unpleasant surprise when he tries to spring that holdup."

Dave lifted a hand and clutched at Bo's sleeve. "No!" he gasped out. "You . . . you don't understand . . ."

"Don't get so worked up, son," Scratch said. "You lost a lot of blood, and you need to rest—"

"Don't understand!" Dave cried. "The stage is coming back . . . *today!*"

Bo frowned. "You must be confused, Dave—"

"No! Stage left . . . a day earlier . . . nobody knew about it . . . bringing back big payroll for . . . Pitchfork Mine."

Bo stiffened and said, "Good Lord! That's why those miners haven't been coming into town lately. They haven't been paid in lately!"

Dave managed to nod as his grip of Bo's sleeve loosened. "Yeah," he whispered. "No payroll since . . . Judson stole the first one . . . six months ago."

Scratch let out a low whistle. "If those wages've been pilin' up for that long, there must be a heap of 'em!"

"That's right," Bo agreed, grim-faced. "A big payoff."

"Last job," Dave muttered. "Big casino, Judson called it."

"How do you know about this, Dave?"

"Because I was . . . a member of the gang until . . . until I found out . . . what Judson's planning. Tried to get away . . . to warn Ma . . . she's in . . . danger."

"Seems to me like it's your brother and Ponderosa who are in danger," Scratch said.

Again Dave clutched at Bo's sleeve. "Ma went . . . with them . . . to Cottonwood! She'll be on the stage . . . when it gets back to . . . Hell Creek!"

That news rocked both of the Texans. "We got to stop Judson somehow," Scratch said. "If his whole gang jumps the stage, Abigail and Gil and Ponderosa won't stand a chance!"

"Maybe he'll call the job off since Dave got away."

Dave shook his head. "Not Judson. He knows . . . he won't have a shot at this much loot again . . . any time soon."

"He's right, Bo. That varmint'll go through with it." Scratch nodded toward the wounded young man. "Anyway, Judson probably figures that Dave didn't make it, bleedin' as bad as he was. If he hadn't run into us, he would've fallen off his horse pretty soon and died out in that hellhole."

"Yeah," Bo said, "Judson will be there at Hell Creek, waiting for the stage. But so will we." He straightened from where he knelt at Dave's side and went on. "Sorry, son, but we've got to get back to Red Butte and get help as quickly as we can. The ride's not going to be very pleasant for you."

Again, Dave shook his head. "No. You two . . . leave me here."

"We can't do that!" Scratch said. "You're hurt."

"I'll be . . . all right. Leave me a gun . . . some water. Send somebody out here . . . when you get to Red Butte. But get there as fast as you can . . . help my ma . . ."

What the young man was suggesting made sense. Bo and Scratch could make much better time getting back to the settlement if they didn't have to take Dave with them. Forcing one of the horses to carry double would slow down both of them, unless one of the Texans went on ahead and left the other to bring Dave.

But that would mean whoever was left behind would miss out on the fight, and neither of them wanted that.

"All right, Dave," Bo said, reaching a decision. "We'll do what you say. With any luck, somebody from town will be out here to fetch you in and get some medical attention for you before the day's over."

"Go ahead," Dave urged them. "Don't . . . worry about me." His mouth twisted bitterly. "Whatever happens to me . . . I deserve it."

Bo and Scratch couldn't argue with that. Dave had admitted that he was part of the outlaw gang, after all, just as they had suspected.

Still, though, if he died that would hurt Abigail, and they didn't want that either.

"One more thing," Dave said as the Texans began making their preparations to depart. "Judson has got . . . a partner in Red Butte."

"Besides you, you mean?" Bo asked.

"Y-yeah. I don't know who it is . . . but there's somebody . . . working with him . . . and feeding him information."

"Rutledge," Scratch said. "Got to be."

"That's bound to come out when we bust up Judson's gang," Bo said. He had an extra Colt in his saddlebags. He took it out, loaded it, and placed it on the cave floor next to Dave, within easy reach. Scratch set one of the canteens on the floor on Dave's other side, along with the can containing a fair amount of peach juice.

"Prop me up," Dave requested. They did so, helping him sit up so that his back leaned against the wall of the cave. "Thanks. This way I can see . . . if anyone's comin'."

"Someone will be coming, all right," Bo promised

him. "Somebody who will take you back to Red Butte."

"Just . . . stop Judson."

Scratch nodded. "You got our word on it."

They said so long to Dave, then checked to make sure none of the outlaws were around before they left the cave, led the horses down the rock-littered slope, and mounted up when they reached the bottom of the draw.

"You know," Scratch said, "if anything happens to both of us into town, nobody'll know that boy's up yonder in that cave. He'll starve to death, or die o' thirst . . . unless he uses that six-gun on his own self."

Bo shook his head. "Dave's life isn't the only one riding on what we do today. So are Gil's and Ponderosa's, not to mention that payroll for the Pitchfork." A grim smile tugged at his lips. "I'm afraid dying's not an option for us right now. It'll have to wait until later."

CHAPTER 30

Bo and Scratch knew that the fastest way back to Red Butte was to retrace the trail they had followed to this point. There might have been shorter routes, but if they struck out blindly in this wild, rugged country, they might waste time following paths that turned out to be dead ends.

So they headed back to Hell Creek and followed the

stream south, past the spot where somebody's blood had been spilled a couple of days earlier, through the cleft where the narrow ledge ran alongside the fast-flowing creek, past the waterfall and the pool where they had camped after the ambush by Angus and Culley, and on down through the arid wasteland where the thirsty ground swallowed much of the creek, shrinking it in size. The Texans pushed their mounts as fast as they dared, but they had to be careful, too. If one of the horses came up lame, or even worse, stepped in a hole and broke a leg, that would be disastrous.

The sun rose higher, reached its zenith, and started down the western sky before they reached the bridge where the stage road crossed Hell Creek. The long hours it had taken to get here chafed at Bo and Scratch, because they knew that if everything had gone according to plan, the stagecoach with Abigail, Gil, and Ponderosa on it, along with that mine payroll, would have already left Chino Valley and now would be rolling in this direction. They reined in when they reached the bridge and looked around, halfway expecting to see some of Rance Judson's outlaws coming after them.

The area appeared to be quiet and deserted. "Judson's not here yet," Scratch said.

"But he can't be far off," Bo replied. "We can get to Red Butte and get back out here with some help before the stage gets this far."

Now that they had reached the road, they could

finally put their horses into a gallop on the relatively smooth, level surface. The bay and the dun already had a lot of hard miles behind them, but as usual the horses responded gallantly. They stretched out and ran at a ground-eating pace as the Texans headed toward Red Butte.

The towering butte itself soon came into sight, and that encouraged Bo and Scratch. They pressed on, keeping the horses moving as fast as possible, and at last they came to the settlement.

If what Dave had told them was correct, no one was at the stage line headquarters, so they rode on past and headed for the marshal's office instead. Bo and Scratch were both so tired from the action of the past few days that they stumbled a little as they dismounted and looped their reins around the hitch rack in front of Tom Harding's office. They went to the door and opened it without knocking.

Harding looked up in surprise from his desk. "Howdy, fellas," he greeted them. "I thought you boys had decided to move on after all."

"Who told you that?" Bo asked.

"Why . . . Gil Sutherland. He said you weren't around yesterday, and nobody knew where you'd gone, so he and Ponderosa were going to have to take a special run to Cottonwood."

"Ponderosa knew where we set out for, but he didn't know when we were going to get back. I guess he thought something must have happened to us."

"Where have you been?" Harding leaned back in his

chair. "No offense, but you look like you've been through a wringer."

"Just about," Scratch said. "But there's no time for explanations now, Marshal. We got to get a posse together and head back out to Hell Creek as fast as we can."

That made the lawman sit up straight. "A posse! What for?"

Bo hesitated, remembering what Dave had said about Judson having a secret partner here in Red Butte. It seemed unlikely that Tom Harding could be that partner—Harding had been the marshal here for quite a while and had made a life for himself in the settlement—but Bo felt a twinge of suspicion anyway.

They had to trust somebody, though. Bo said, "That stagecoach is carrying the past six months' wages for all the miners at the Pitchfork, and Judson knows about it."

Harding's mouth fell open as he stared at the Texans. Neither of them thought he was a good enough actor to be faking his reaction. He hadn't known anything about the payroll coming in on the stage until this moment.

After a second, Harding got over his shock and shot to his feet. "Damn it!" he burst out. "Flynn should've warned me about this! Who else knows about it?"

Bo shook his head. "I'm not sure, but what's important now is that *Judson* knows about the payroll and intends to hold up the stage. If Gil and Ponderosa try to put up a fight, the outlaws are liable to kill every-body on it."

"And Abigail Sutherland went with 'em!" Harding muttered with a look of horror on his face, further convincing Bo and Scratch that he wasn't Judson's partner. He grabbed for his hat and said, "Come on."

"Where are we going?" Bo asked as the three men left the office.

"Over to Rutledge's freight yard. Those men who work for him are the most gun-handy hombres in town. If we're goin' up against Judson's bunch, we'll need help. I'll deputize 'em—"

"Hold on," Bo said, stopping Harding with a hand on his arm. "I'm not sure we can trust Rutledge. Even if we can, why would he help us? He's been trying to run Abigail out of business for months now."

The marshal grimaced. "Yeah, you're right about that. But who else are we gonna get?" He waved a hand at the buildings along the street. "The folks who live here in Red Butte are good people, but they're not gunfighters. I can get a dozen men who'll be willing to go with us, and they'll do their best, but I don't know if they'll be any match for Judson and his band of cutthroats!"

Harding was right, and as Bo and Scratch glanced at each other, they knew it.

"Let's see what Rutledge has to say," Bo suggested. If nothing else, the freight line owner's reaction to the news might tell them whether or not he was tied in with the outlaws. Bo and Scratch checked their guns, easing them in their holsters, as they approached the big freight barn with Harding. If Rutledge was Judson's secret partner, they might be facing a gunfight before they ever got back out to Hell Creek.

To their surprise, though, the barn was empty, and so were the corral and the wagon yard. When Harding called out, a wizened old man hobbled out from the rear of the barn.

"That's Tomás," Harding said. "He works for Rutledge, mending harness and such." To the old Mexican, Harding asked, "Tomás, where's Señor Rutledge and the rest of his men?"

"Gone," Tomás answered. "The señor and all the others, they ride out yesterday. I have not seen them since."

Harding was flabbergasted. "But . . . but where could they have gone?"

"To join up with Judson maybe," Bo said.

The marshal swung toward him. "Are you sayin' that *Rutledge* is workin' with the outlaws?"

"It's startin' to look like it," Scratch said.

"But Rutledge's wagons and his stagecoach have been held up, too."

"What better way of diverting suspicion from himself?" Bo said. "Rutledge accused Mrs. Sutherland of the same thing."

"It makes sense," Harding admitted. "What are we gonna do now?"

"Are you still willing to put a posse together and go

out to Hell Creek even though it's out of your jurisdiction?"

Without hesitation, Harding nodded. "Damn right I am."

"Do that then. Find the best men you can, and explain the situation to them so that they'll know what they're getting into. Then get there as fast as you can."

"What are you two gonna do?"

"We're heading back out there now," Bo said.

Harding stared at them. "But . . . if you do that it's liable to be just the two of you against Judson's whole gang!"

Scratch grinned despite his weariness. "Then there'll be plenty o' the varmints to go around, just the way we like it!"

Ponderosa Pine's wounded shoulder ached considerably from the jarring it received from the swaying, bouncing stagecoach, but he was a tough old bird. The bullet holes had healed up enough already that the trip hadn't started them bleeding again. Ponderosa could put up with the pain. It wasn't much worse than the rheumatism he'd been putting up with for years anyway.

He would be glad to see Red Butte again, though. A part of him wished that those two saddle tramps, Creel and Morton, had gotten back in time to handle this run.

Another part was glad, though, that he'd been forced to ride shotgun for Gil. It wasn't every day that a fella got to guard a small fortune. If there was any excitement, Ponderosa would be in the thick of it, and he wouldn't mind a chance to prove that he was still a good man in a fight, no matter how old he was.

If only Miz Abigail hadn't insisted on coming along . . .

Ponderosa didn't know what he was more worried about—Abigail's presence on the coach, where she might be in danger, or the possibility that Rance Judson and his gang might try to steal the mine payroll.

In a way, that seemed unlikely to Ponderosa, though. Nobody had known ahead of time that the payroll was going to be on this special run except Flynn, the mine superintendent, and Abigail. The news had come as a surprise to both Gil and Ponderosa when Abigail told them about it. Evidently, she and Flynn had been working on the deal for quite a while. That wasn't really a shock to Ponderosa; he knew that Abigail was a canny businesswoman. She had learned a lot from working with her late husband.

But just because she had set all this up didn't mean she had to come along. She was riding inside the coach, and Ponderosa knew that she had a pistol in her bag. If any outlaws tried to stop them, she'd said before they left Red Butte, she would give them a warm welcome.

So far, there had been no sign of trouble on the trip. The stage had reached Cottonwood without any unusual incidents. Thatcher Carson, his wounded arm still in a sling, had met with them there and the local bank president, who had been keeping the payroll in his vault, had turned the money over to Gil and Ponderosa early that morning. It was in a sturdy chest with metal straps holding the lid closed. The chest was too big for the boot at the back of the coach. It would have to ride inside with Abigail. Carson was still upset that he wouldn't be there at the Pitchfork to take charge of the money and see that everyone's wages were doled out properly, but Flynn would just have to take care of that himself.

Now most of the return trip was behind them. The coach had made its stop at the final relay station between Chino Valley and Red Butte. A few more miles and they would be home.

Ponderosa spotted the line of mottled green that marked the course of Hell Creek. "Almost home, boy," he said to Gil, who sat beside him handling the reins. "Maybe we finally put one over on ol' Judson. He don't know nothin' about that payroll we're carryin'."

"Maybe," Gil said, but he didn't sound convinced. The boy was a natural-born worrier, Ponderosa thought.

The coach rolled on until the bridge over Hell Creek was only a couple of hundred yards away. Gil lifted the whip and popped it over the backs of the team, obviously anxious to get home. The sharp crack filled the air.

Then, less than a second later, another sound

erupted. The ground shook, and the middle of the Hell Creek bridge lifted into the air as flame and smoke blossomed upward through the shattered planks.

Somebody had just used dynamite to blow the bridge to kindling.

Gil hauled back hard on the reins. Beside him, Ponderosa yelled, "What're you doin'?"

"The bridge is gone! We can't go on!"

"Gil! Ponderosa!" Abigail cried from inside the coach. "What's happening out there? What was that explosion?"

Neither of them had time to answer her, for at that moment horsemen came boiling up out of the creek bed and galloped toward the slowing stagecoach. Even at this distance, the masks over their faces were visible.

Rance Judson had waited until the stage was almost back to Red Butte to strike the finishing blow.

"Turn the stage around!" Ponderosa shouted. "We'll make a run for it!"

Gil shook his head stubbornly. "It's no use! You know we can't outrun them."

"We can damn sure try!" Ponderosa lunged for the reins with his good hand. If Gil wouldn't try to get them out of this, then Ponderosa would just have to do it himself.

Gil shoved him back. "Forget it! It's too late, Ponderosa. They've got us."

Ponderosa stared hard at him, eyes narrowing in sudden suspicion. "What's wrong with you, boy?" he demanded. "You're actin' almost like you're in on it with those varmints."

Gil's eyes turned flinty and cold, and suddenly Ponderosa felt like he had been punched in the gut. He didn't want to believe the thoughts that were going through his head, but Gil wasn't giving him much choice.

"Gil!" Abigail said from inside the coach. "Gil, for God's sake, what's wrong?"

Gil reached for his gun.

But before he could touch it, gunshots roared. Muzzle flame spurted from the revolvers in the hands of the charging outlaws. Bullets whined around the stagecoach.

Gil's eyes widened in shock. "What the hell!" he exclaimed.

"Looks like a double cross," Ponderosa grated. "They're gonna wipe us all out."

As if to punctuate his words, a bullet snatched Gil's hat from his head. He cursed and grabbed the reins again, hauling the team around with one hand while he popped the whip with the other. The horses lunged against their harness, but despite their efforts, the coach couldn't move very fast. The outlaws were almost on top of it before the team began galloping back the other way.

Ponderosa twisted around on the seat and used both hands to swing the scattergun into line. That hurt his wounded shoulder, but it was too late to worry about anything like that. He fired both barrels and was rewarded by the sight of an outlaw being driven out of the saddle by buckshot. Beside him, Gil yelled and whipped the horses for all he was worth.

But it was too late, the outlaws were too close, and even though Ponderosa intended to go down fighting— he was already stuffing more shells into the Greener's barrels—he knew that he and Gil and Abigail were all doomed.

CHAPTER 31

Bo and Scratch heard the explosion and knew it couldn't be anything good. They had taken the time back in Red Butte to haul their saddles off their played-out mounts and slap them on fresh horses that Marshal Tom Harding told the livery stable owner to let them use. On those animals, they had ridden hard out the stage road from town, heading for Hell Creek. They came in sight of the stream just a few seconds after the blast, in time to see some of the debris from the shattered bridge still falling to the ground.

They saw the outlaws on horseback streaming out of the mostly dry creek bed, too, and charging toward the stage.

"Gil's stoppin!" Scratch shouted in alarm. "Why don't he turn around and make a run for it?"

Seeing what was happening, Bo's brain suddenly made some connections that it hadn't before. He muttered, "Good Lord!" as a theory suggested itself to him.

"What is it?" Scratch asked.

"No time to explain now. Let's go!"

They urged their mounts on to even greater speed. As they approached the creek, they heard the outlaws open fire. *Double cross,* Bo said to himself. It was all making sense now. Judson's secret partner was none other than Gil Sutherland. In the two attempted stage holdups Bo and Scratch had witnessed when Gil was on the driver's box, the young man had tried to give up. Of course he would, because he was in on the whole thing with Judson and wanted to protect his secret while at the same time preserving his own neck. Gil could have found out about the payroll, too, if Abigail hadn't just told him about it.

Now, though, it appeared that Judson was hell-bent on betraying his partner, wiping out everyone on the stage, and keeping all the payroll for him and his men. Gil was trying to get away, and the booming of the shotgun told Bo and Scratch that Ponderosa was putting up a fight, wounded shoulder and all, but it wasn't going to be enough.

Unless a couple of drifters from Texas could somehow change the odds . . .

They had to slow down when they reached the creek, let their mounts pick their way down the bank, across the stream bed, and up the other side, but once that was behind them, Bo and Scratch fogged it after the outlaws again. They drew their Winchesters from the saddle boots and opened fire, picking off a couple of the owlhoots from behind.

At the same moment, more riders suddenly appeared at the crest of a small rise ahead of the stage. Bo's heart sank as he thought that these newcomers were more members of Judson's gang, and now the stagecoach would be pinned between two hostile forces.

But when the strangers opened fire, their bullets were directed at the would-be thieves. It was the bandits who unexpectedly found themselves caught in a cross fire, with Bo and Scratch closing in on them from behind and half a dozen riders coming at them from the front with guns blazing.

"Who're those hombres?" Scratch shouted over the pounding of hoofs and the crackle of guns.

"Don't know, but I'm glad they showed up when they did! We might have a chance now!"

The outlaws still outnumbered their opponents, but Bo and Scratch and their mysterious allies had the element of surprise on their side. Seven or eight of the outlaws went down in the first minute of the fight. Dust and powder smoke filled the air. A few members of the gang gave up and tried to make a run for it, only to be shot out of their saddles.

Several of the outlaws were still right behind the stagecoach, though. One of them leaped from his horse and landed on the rear boot. He began clambering on top of the roof while Ponderosa tried frantically to get his shotgun reloaded in time. The old-timer snapped the weapon closed and lifted the barrels, touching off both of them just as the outlaw coming toward him fired a pistol. The double load of buckshot practically blew the outlaw in half and flung him backward off the stage, but Ponderosa was hit, too. Bo and Scratch saw him knocked to the floorboard by the bullet.

Puffs of gun smoke came from the coach's window. Abigail was in there, and she was putting up a fight.

Bo saw Gil jerk abruptly to the side and figured the young man was hit, too. The reins must have slipped from his hand, because the team veered off the road, clearly out of control and running blindly, driven half-mad by the shooting. The horses began to make a wide curve . . .

That was more than the careening coach could stand. As Bo and Scratch watched in horror as they closed in, the stagecoach began to tip. The singletree snapped like a matchstick as the coach went over and began tumbling. Wheels splintered and axles shattered as the coach slammed into the ground again and again.

When the overturned vehicle finally came to a stop, the cloud of dust around it was so thick that it could barely be seen. Bo and Scratch rammed their rifles back in the sheaths and galloped toward the wreck as fast as they could.

Because some of the outlaws were headed for the coach, too, and they were going to get there first . . .

The bullet had only creased Ponderosa on the arm, but even that glancing blow packed enough punch to knock him off the seat. Before he could pull himself back up, Gil was hit next. Ponderosa saw the blood spurt from his side. The young man lurched and dropped the reins. Ponderosa made a grab for them but missed, and the terrified horses left the road and started across open country.

The next thing Ponderosa knew, he was flying through the air and the sound of a grinding crash filled his ears. He slammed into something—probably the ground—with bone-jarring force and rolled over and over. Each time he rolled, pain stabbed into his body. The world was red and hazy and dust choked him, and he was on the verge of passing out when he finally came to a stop.

But the sound of hoofbeats close by forced him to lift his head. He saw that he was lying on the ground, all right, and Gil was sprawled a few yards away, covered in blood. Beyond Gil was the coach, battered and broken but still roughly intact. It was upside down, and both doors had been sprung open during the crash. Ponderosa felt a surge of relief as he saw Abigail Sutherland crawling out through one of the doors. She might be hurt, but she was still able to move anyway.

Ponderosa's relief was short-lived, because a tall, burly figure strode through the dust, reached down, grabbed Abigail's arm, and hauled her roughly to her feet.

The old-timer recognized the man's ugly, craggy face from wanted posters he had seen in Tom Harding's office.

Rance Judson.

Judson grinned as he held onto Abigail with one

hand and reached into the wrecked coach with the other. He brought out a stack of bills banded together and stuffed it into his shirt, then grabbed another and another. Judson was trying to get as much of the payroll as he could. At the same time, he had Abigail to use as a hostage if he needed to, and she was too stunned by everything that had happened to put up a fight.

"Judson!"

That hoarse cry came from Gil, who was forcing himself to his feet. His left arm hung limp at his side, probably broken in the crash. His shirt was sodden with blood from the wound in his side, and crimson sheeted his face from a large gash opened up in his forehead. He looked like he was on the verge of collapsing again, but he forced himself forward, trying to pull his gun as he did so.

"Let her go, you double-crossing bastard!" Gil shouted.

Judson swung around to face him, pulling Abigail with him. The boss outlaw grinned. "You should'a known I wouldn't give any of this loot once I didn't need you anymore, boy. You thought you was so smart, throwin' in with me, but you were always a fool."

With that he reached for his gun, his draw blindingly swift compared to the badly injured Gil's. Judson cleared leather first with ease, and the gun in his hand roared as smoke and flame belched from its muzzle. Gil was so close the tongue of flame from Judson's gun almost touched his chest as the bullet drove into him and threw him backward. Gil's gun fell from his hand, unfired.

Judson holstered his Colt again, and started to turn back to the wrecked coach to grab some more of the money that had spilled from the payroll chest. But then he changed his mind and headed for his horse instead, jerking Abigail along with him.

"Come on, woman," he said. "You're goin' with me."

Ponderosa tried to get up and stop him, but he couldn't move because of the stabbing pains in his chest. All he could do was groan in despair as Judson flung Abigail onto the back of his horse and climbed up behind her. Then the boss outlaw wheeled his mount to ride away from there with a hostage and at least part of the loot.

Judson stopped short, though, as a vagrant breeze blew away some of the dust and gun smoke and revealed three tall figures sitting there on horseback, blocking his escape.

The Texans . . . Creel and Morton . . .

And Jared Rutledge.

As the battle continued, Bo and Scratch saw one of the riders who had unexpectedly joined their cause break off from the others and race toward the overturned coach, too. Scratch recognized him and exclaimed in surprise, "It's Rutledge! How come him and his men are fightin' Judson's gang? I thought—"

"It's too long a story," Bo broke in. "I think Rutledge is on our side, or at least on Abigail's. Come on!"

Judson and a couple of his men had reached the coach, but the dust kept the Texans from seeing exactly what was going on. Bo and Scratch heard a shot, though, and as they came out of the choking, eye-stinging cloud, they saw Judson flinging Abigail up onto his horse while his men stood guard. Rutledge emerged from the dust, too, arriving at the same time as Bo and Scratch. "Where's Abigail?" he asked in a voice thick with emotion.

"Over yonder," Scratch said, pointing at the wrecked coach and the outlaws. The three men moved closer as Judson mounted up and turned his horse. He was flanked by his two men, who were just about the only members of the gang left. The others were dead, wounded, or fleeing as Rutledge's men gave chase.

Judson reined in sharply as he saw Bo, Scratch, and Rutledge confronting him. His face contorted with hatred as he called, "Outta my way, you sons o' bitches!"

"You're not taking Mrs. Sutherland anywhere," Rutledge said. "Let her go."

Judson shook his head. "Not hardly, mister. She's my ticket outta here. I didn't get but a little of that payroll, but I'll be damned if I'm gonna hang." Without taking his eyes off the three men in front of him, he growled an order to his men. "Blast 'em outta the way!"

Until now, Abigail had looked stunned, only half-conscious. But she suddenly came to life in Judson's grip, twisting around and clawing at his face with her fingers. He yelled a curse and struggled to control her, but she tore herself loose and fell to the side, tumbling off the horse.

With Abigail out of the line of fire, Bo and Scratch didn't have to hesitate anymore. The outlaws opened fire first, as Judson thrust his gun out and screamed incoherently as he triggered it, but just as they had done more than forty years earlier on a sunny spring day at San Jacinto, the Texans ignored the bullets whistling around their heads and returned the fire calmly and swiftly.

For one, two, three heartbeats the deafening roar of guns filled the air, along with the acrid smell of powder smoke. When the weapons finally fell silent, both of Judson's men were on the ground, driven from their saddles by the deadly accurate shots of Bo, Scratch, and Rutledge. Judson had stayed mounted somehow, but the gun in his hand sagged as he looked down at himself. Blood welled from at least four wounds in his body. He opened his mouth to speak, but more blood choked him as it came up his throat and spilled from his lips. He dropped the gun and bent forward, lying almost double over his horse's neck. His arms hung limply in death. His horse, spooked by the shots and the coppery smell of blood, danced around skittishly. Rutledge flung himself out of his saddle and raced forward to pick up Abigail, who still lay on the ground. The fall had knocked the breath out of her. As Rutledge lifted her, he said, "Abigail! Are you all right?"

She stared at him in confusion, but managed to nod and say, "I . . . I think so."

She didn't say anything else because after that Rutledge was kissing her, pressing his mouth to hers urgently.

"What the hell!" Scratch said.

"Looks like we had a lot of things wrong, right from the start," Bo said as he thumbed fresh cartridges into his Colt. He was aware of the silence that now lay over the flats just east of Hell Creek.

The battle was over.

And judging from the way Jared Rutledge was kissing Abigail Sutherland, so was the war.

CHAPTER 32

The posse from Red Butte arrived shortly after that, but they weren't needed any longer. Most of Judson's gang had been wiped out. The few outlaws who had gotten away would probably drift right on out of this part of the territory as fast as they could.

Dr. Chambers followed the posse in his buggy, thinking that his services might be needed, and sure enough, he found himself with plenty to do. He examined Gil Sutherland first, then looked up at Abigail, who stood nearby looking on with a grimly worried expression on her face. Rutledge stood with her, one arm around her shoulders for support. The doctor shook his head and said, "He's still alive, Abigail, but there's nothing I can do for him."

She managed to nod. "See to Ponderosa, then," she said. "He's hurt, too."

Abigail came and knelt beside her oldest son. "Gil," she said, her voice shaking. "Gil, why?"

His eyes flickered open. "M-Ma . . ." he whispered. "I never meant . . . never meant for you . . . to get hurt . . . just didn't want to . . . be stuck here . . . rest of my life . . . trying to . . . trying to . . ."

He lifted a trembling hand. Abigail took it in both of hers. He squeezed her fingers with all the strength left in his body and said in a clear voice, "I'm sorry."

Then he was gone.

Bo and Scratch shook their heads as they watched the tragic scene. Abigail's shoulders slumped and she began to sob as she continued holding Gil's lifeless hand. Rutledge knelt beside her and put his arm around her again, and she leaned against him as she cried.

The Texans turned away and went over to the spot where Dr. Chambers was taking a look at Ponderosa. "How's the old pelican doin'?" Scratch asked.

"Old pelican, is it?" Ponderosa demanded in an indignant tone. "I told you before, I ain't that much older'n you!"

"Sounds like he hasn't lost all of his strength," Bo said with a smile.

Chambers nodded. "He's got a bullet wound on his arm and some cracked ribs, at the very least. Riding back to town, even in a buckboard, is going to be pretty painful for him. But I think he'll be all right."

"Darn right I will be," Ponderosa said. "Miz Abigail's gonna need plenty o' help after this."

Bo glanced over his shoulder at Abigail and Rutledge and said, "I hate to break this to you, Ponderosa, but I'm not sure the Sutherland Stage Line is going to be in existence much longer."

"What'n blazes are you talkin' about?"

"I think it may merge with Rutledge's line."

"Have you gone loco? Doc, prop my head up so's I can see what that crazy Texan's talkin' about."

"I'm not sure that's a good idea," Chambers said. "You should lie as still as possible."

"Dadgummit, somebody lift me up!"

Bo and Scratch moved in on either side of Ponderosa to help the old-timer sit up enough to see how Abigail had stood up and was wrapped in Rutledge's embrace now, her face pressed against his chest as she cried tears of grief for her son.

"Good Lord!" Ponderosa said. "Whatta revoltin' development *that* is!"

By the time a week had passed, things were pretty well back to normal in Red Butte, although the settlement had been buzzing for several days about everything that had happened. All the money for the miners' payroll at the Pitchfork had been recovered, although some of the bills were stained with Rance Judson's blood. The miners didn't seem to care.

Dave Sutherland had been brought in from the cave where Bo and Scratch had left him and was recuperating at Dr. Chambers's house along with Ponderosa Pine. He was going to recover from his wound. He fully expected to face a trip to Prescott after that, and a trial for his part in some of the robberies carried out by Judson's gang, but when Bo, Scratch, Marshal Harding, and Jared Rutledge got together to talk about that, they reached a different conclusion.

"Abigail's already lost one son," Harding said. "I know it goes against the oath I swore, but I don't want to see her lose another to prison."

Rutledge nodded. "I agree. Several of those outlaws got away as it is. I don't see that one more will make a difference. Anyway, Dave won't ever be doing anything like that again. He'll be too busy helping his mother run that stage line."

The four men were gathered in Harding's office. Behind the desk, the marshal leaned back in his chair and frowned at Rutledge. "We're not gonna go back to having trouble between the two of you again, are we?"

Rutledge laughed and shook his head. "No, I'm out of the stagecoach business, Marshal. In fact, I'm going to give my coach to Abigail to replace the one that got wrecked."

"Does she know that yet?" Bo asked.

"No, I haven't told her."

"She's liable to argue about taking it. She's got a proud streak, and a stubborn one, too."

"I know," Rutledge said. "When I offered to buy her out, I made the mistake of telling her that the only reason I wanted her to sell to me was so that she could marry me then, the way I wanted her to."

"Everybody in town figured that you two hated each other," Harding said.

"I was attracted to Abigail the first time I saw her," Rutledge admitted. "But she was married to Will Sutherland then, so of course I never said anything. But I figured that since Will had her, he didn't need to have a stage line, too. By the time he passed on, the rivalry was so well established that I . . . I was just a damned fool, that's all."

Harding grunted. "Yeah, I'd say hirin' a bunch o' hardcases wasn't the best move you could've made. You liked to stirred up a real war here in town, Jared."

"That was never my intention," Rutledge insisted. "I'll admit that my men were pretty proddy at times . . . but they didn't cause any real trouble beyond a few brawls. And they won't be doing that from now on. I've made that clear to them. Anyway, I was glad to have them around when it came time to settle things with Judson's bunch."

Scratch said, "I still ain't sure how come you were out there followin' the coach. We had you figured for Judson's partner, instead o' Gil."

"And I had really come to believe that maybe there was a connection between Abigail and Judson. It's hard to believe now that I could spout such foolishness, but frustration can do some strange things to a man's mind. Makes it hard to think straight sometimes."

"That ain't frustration," Scratch said with a grin. "That's love."

"Anyway," Rutledge went on, "when the stage left for Cottonwood a day earlier, I figured something unusual was going on. That's why I decided to follow it there and back with my men. If there really was a connection between Abigail and Judson, I wanted to know about it. And if there wasn't, I was worried that Judson's gang might jump the stage and then Abigail would be in danger. That's how it turned out, of course."

"What I want to know," Harding said, "is how Gil found out about that payroll. Abigail claims that nobody except her and Flynn out at the Pitchfork knew about it."

Bo said, "We'll probably never know for sure since Gil's dead, but my guess is that he overheard Abigail and Flynn talking about it a long time ago. Flynn admitted that they'd been working on the deal for months. Abigail never knew that Gil found out, though, until it was too late."

Harding nodded. "Gil resented havin' to pull so much of the weight after his pa passed on. I guess that's why he decided to team up with Judson, rake in a big payoff, and rattle his hocks outta here. He didn't stop to think that Judson would probably double-cross him."

"And Dave fell in with the gang because he thought it would be exciting to be an outlaw, and because he didn't want to work," Bo said. "He sees now what a fool he was, or at least he claims he does."

"Well, he's gonna get the chance to prove it, if we stick to the deal we just made here and don't turn him over to the sheriff in Prescott," Harding said. He looked around at the other men. "I reckon we're still all in agreement?"

Bo, Scratch, and Rutledge all nodded. "Dave can do more good for society here, learning how to be a decent, hardworking young man," Bo said, "than he can breaking rocks in Yuma Prison."

"That's right," Scratch said. "Some hombres just naturally belong behind bars, but I don't reckon Dave is one of 'em."

Harding laced his fingers together over his belly and looked at Bo and Scratch. "That leaves you fellas," he said. "What do you plan to do?"

Scratch said, "Miz Abigail will still need some help for a while, until Dave and Ponderosa get back on their feet."

"I'll give her all the help she needs," Rutledge insisted.

"Are you sure that's a good idea?" Bo asked. "If you really want to bring her around to your way of thinking, Rutledge, you need to realize that she's a woman who wants to stand on her own two feet before she does anything else."

Rutledge rubbed his jaw and grimaced. "Yeah, you're probably right about that, Creel. You sure that you and Morton don't mind sticking around for a while?"

"I reckon we can stand it," Scratch said with a grin.

A short time later, though, after the Texans had left Harding's office and were strolling back down the street toward the stage line headquarters, Scratch said, "It ain't gonna be easy, watchin' that Rutledge fella courtin' Miz Abigail. Hell, you can already see that she likes him. He's gonna win in the end, ain't he?"

"Depends on how you look at it," Bo said. "He's going to still be here working while we're riding on down the trail, seeing what's past the next hill or on the other side of the next river."

Scratch laughed. "Yeah, there's that to consider," he said. "I reckon there's more than one way o' winnin'!"

Center Point Publishing
600 Brooks Road • PO Box 1
Thorndike ME 04986-0001 USA

(207) 568-3717

US & Canada:
1 800 929-9108
www.centerpointlargeprint.com